Letting Frogs Go

by

Liz Ferro

Letting Frogs Go

Contact Information: info@thewildrosepress.com

Cover Art by *Lea Schizas*

The Wild Rose Press, Inc.
PO Box 708
Adams Basin, NY 14410-0708
Visit us at www.thewildrosepress.com

Publishing History
First Edition, 2024
Trade Paperback ISBN 978-1-5092-5587-0
Digital ISBN 978-1-5092-5588-7

Published in the United States of America

Dedication

Dedicated to all my soul friends. You ladies know who you are, and I couldn't do life without you.

Chapter 1

January 2023

Emma stepped out of her front door onto the ornate wrap-around porch of her beautiful white colonial. It was the Baroque-style home she had always longed for—back when things like that seemed important. Cold darkness was settling in like a nasty mother-in-law coming for the weekend—unwanted and unavoidable. Taking over without a thought for how uncomfortable others might feel. She pulled her cashmere wrap tighter around her athletic body and tried to fend off the biting cold without spilling her Malbec.

The air felt cruel against the exposed skin of her face and hands. In her head, she could hear her esthetician chastising her for not putting a protective serum on before literally facing the elements. But hell, this is South Carolina, and although the calendar showed January, meteorologists haven't made mention of snowflakes as long as she could recall. The hanging paper lanterns and giant, green ferns that have always given the porch a warm, inviting Southern vibe seemed almost comical in this weather. Intense shivers suddenly raked her spine and made the hairs on the back of her neck stand at attention, and she knew she couldn't solely blame the unexpected low temps and downy flakes floating gingerly in the dusky air. It was the way the wind got caught in her eyes and made them water. Sudden gusts like that still transported her directly back to that sickening day on Lake Michigan.

She took a deep breath through her nose, pushed back the strands of brown hair that had come loose from her ponytail, and then let the air out of her mouth slowly—her yoga instructor would be proud, but it wasn't quite enough to push the haunted memory from her mind. She gazed on the whitewashed, time-worn wooden steps that led up to her homey front porch. How many times had she bounded up those steps two at a time on a particularly beautiful day, or sat on the top step in pure contentment with a cup of coffee or glass of wine? It's incredible how many memories and milestones a simple set of stairs can hold. Images of Caroline in her various Halloween costumes over the years. A black cat or a princess doing her best to stay still for a picture among the carved pumpkins and decorative cornstalks. She even dressed as a nurse a couple of years in a row, which made her smile inside, since her daughter, now in her mid-twenties, was a traveling nurse in Germany.

Emma's eyes remained laser-focused on a particularly ornery-looking splinter while she reminisced, and the heartwarming memories of this old porch in its younger days danced through her brain. Caroline's first day of school pics—year after year. Fourth of July gatherings of friends and family with crickets chirping in the boxwood and fireworks lighting up the night like a meteor shower. The smell of Evening Primrose that mingled with the celebratory bubbles of champagne when Bobby made tenure at Furman. The sweet smell of magnolias while they read the newspaper and drank too much coffee together on a lazy Sunday afternoon. As the splinter came into focus, she reprimanded herself for not taking the time to repaint what seemed to be the stairway to her entire life. The fluffy flakes swirled on the wind with a fragile beauty that held her attention longer than most anything could these days.

She couldn't wait to tell the girls that Greenville was getting snow for the first time since they were in high school together thirty-five years ago. Emma began a slow, exaggerated descent down each fluff-covered stair, and enjoyed watching each footfall send poofs of sleepy, silver snow fairies flying in sparkles as the flakes caught the porchlight. Although she wasn't generally a fan of cold and snow, she had to admit that it felt whimsical. Magical even. When she reached the bottom of the stairs and walked onto the crunchy frost-covered lawn, she stopped and tilted her face toward the sky. Feeling an almost brave defiance, she closed her eyes; and let the flakes land on her unprotected face. She wondered if it were true that no two snowflakes were the same. It didn't seem possible, but then, so many things seemed impossible before tonight.

As she walked back up to her favorite seat, she wished that this crazy invasion of downy snow drifting from the indigo sky was the strangest thing going on in her life. However, Southern town or not, it wasn't the most shocking, and didn't even come close to the worst thing to happen to her today. Only a few hours earlier, as she watched the moving truck pull out of the circular driveway, she received the news that rocked her world harder than any divorce ever could.

I need to group text RaRa, YoYo, Sleazin and

Zipper, she thought. *Or maybe just YoYo at first. I don't know if I can handle everyone right now. I'm never sure about anything anymore.*

Emma and her crew were each christened with nicknames that they accepted graciously, the way a Southerner accepts a glass of sweet tea and enjoys it with a smile. There was no other way to take it. If you made a fuss it would only earn you a worse name and a reputation as a total wimp.

Susan had become Sleazin by the end of Sophomore year due to the rhyme (they thought they were so clever) and her long line of "boyfriends." She wasn't exactly shy with the opposite sex, or with anyone for that matter, and was a standout as the lead in every school musical. She became sort of famous around town for her amazing singing voice, as well as the "talent" she displayed at the cast parties.

Heather had been Zipper since she was a tween. She had a long, straight figure with legs that went on forever. When she got a little older, rumors were that she could undo a guy's zipper with her mouth, but that is yet to be proven in a public setting.

Yolanda–YoYo–was never without her toy yo-yo. She got it when she was in eighth grade from her favorite grandpa and learned how to do tricks with it like Walk the Dog and Skin the Cat. By complete coincidence, her last name was Duncan, although there was no relation to the owners of the yo-yo company. She always had Bubble Yum gum and her Duncan–even when she did modeling gigs at the mall. She became known as the bubble-blowing beauty who could do tricks with her yo-yo even better than all the boys.

Rachel had the good fortune of earning not one but two nicknames. She was Rapunzel because she had the most gorgeous, long, thick, auburn hair that made every girl in Greenville green with envy. And she was also RaRa because she was a fun and bubbly cheerleader for the football team.

Nicknames were indeed serious business in the 1980s.

It was such a different time then, and in her opinion, the 80s seemed to be the age of the nickname. Most kids sported their monikers like a badge of honor, because truly, if someone took the time to think of one for you, and it stuck, you felt like your people really got you and you had made it in life. Names were carefully chosen for you back then, and a person couldn't help but feel a sense of accomplishment for earning one—even if it wasn't the most complimentary.

Many nicknames were based in some way on the way a person looked. Everything seems to be based on looks in high school, but then again, most people never really grow out of that, do they? Some of the best names were the perfect combination of a jab at the person's looks and their birth name. Only a true friend could make fun of your looks, your personality, or your name and get away with it.

Emma let her mind wander to some of the crazy nicknames given to kids she grew up with–a welcome diversion from the drama of the day. One guy in her high school, who stood a lanky six feet two inches tall and played goalie for the hockey team, came to her mind and she smiled. How he walked and the way he could bend and defend the goal, earned him the nickname of Gumby. He resembled Shaggy from

"Scooby Doo" and was stoned just as often, but Shaggy never stuck, because when he donned the huge, square-shaped pads on his arms and legs, and the skates that added another two inches to his height, you couldn't help but see Gumby skating out onto the ice at the start of a hockey game. He was called Gumby by literally *everyone*, including the school principal and even his own mother. In fact, Emma never knew his actual name.

On the opposite end of the spectrum from Gumby, there was a kid nicknamed Sponge, who was all of five feet five inches in high school and shopped for jeans in the "husky" department at Sears.

Sponge's real name was Sam, but he had yellow hair and looked squishy, especially when he smiled, which was all the time. Sponge was also quite hilarious. SpongeBob Squarepants wouldn't exist for another thirty years, but the Sponge Emma knew back then could have been the inspiration for the good-humored cartoon character. However, if it had been completely necessary to specify the shape of Sponge's pants, they wouldn't have been square. They would have been round, or maybe oval. She giggled out loud as a clear memory from 4th grade materialized in her mind–something she hadn't thought of for decades. She remembered how the students were broken up into reading groups, with their desks moved out of rows and arranged in squares and rectangles. Everyone was busy reading with their assigned group while the teacher stopped at each cluster to listen to kids read. When the teacher had her back turned, Sponge and Susan started throwing a pen back and forth at each other until Zipper intercepted it and whipped it so hard, it spun through the air and stuck straight into the side of Sponge's head. He sat there for a minute in slight shock with a blue Bic pen jutting straight out of his head near his temple. When he pulled it out, the contrast of red blood in his blonde hair was both alarming and disturbing. When he ran out of the room, Heather quickly followed him.

The teacher was unaware of these shenanigans, and Sponge ended up being okay.

Apparently, his head absorbed things like a sponge and his nickname stuck hard just like that pen.

Emma earned the nickname of Ma in part because it's short for Emma, but mostly because she was considered the mother hen of their group. In high school, Emma was the designated driver most nights—even if it was by default. It seemed that no one except her thought about the drive home until the end of the night when everyone was already hammered. Ma strived to stay ahead of what could *possibly* happen with boys, adults, and anything else that served as a potential threat to their precious world of fun and friendship. The other girls didn't always like it or appreciate it at the time, but she watched out for each of them with the eyes of an old soul. Everyone's parents considered her to be the responsible one because she was the one who got their assess home for curfews, and the one who made everyone call her immediately after dates or nights out without her. That's why she knew the proposition she had been holding in the back of her mind for months might lead to the others revoking the "ma" aspect of her moniker when she let it loose on them.

She shook her head to bring her thoughts back to the present. *Freakin' menopause. My mind wanders off these days more than a little kid at a carnival. That's it. I'm ready to take Doctor Wallace up on his offer. I hope everyone else will be as into the idea as I am. Maybe I should start small and only call one of the girls—maybe YoYo or Rachel—and they can rally the rest of them for me.*

The news she was planning to share with her best friends was piling up faster than the snowflakes. She had been wrestling with herself about sharing such a daring proposition, because she was still unsure about it herself. But at this point in the game, there were absolutely zero reasons for her to keep it to herself any longer. It was time to take everything out of her proverbial back pocket and let them see it already. And, really, to hold anything back from them at this point would be quite comical in her mind since the bond they all share is deeper and stronger than the roots of the Medusa Tree that crowns the Swamp Rabbit Trail. So, what was the worst that could happen? Worse than what already had happened? She told herself that if they didn't want to participate, she would do it herself, and that would be okay.

Another gust of wind whipped her ponytail up and around like the tail of a winning racehorse, and just like that, her thoughts sped back to that day. Even though it was so long ago, she could still see, feel, and even smell it as if it were happening now. Her anxiety had been worse than ever lately, and second-guessing everything had officially become her new favorite pastime. She knew it had to do with the divorce, but she began to think it was partly due to her grand entrance into the "change of life," and of course, the new cancer diagnosis.

Almost involuntarily, she closed her eyes and clasped her wineglass to her chest with both hands like some sort of chalice, and second-guessed herself for the millionth time about that Labor Day on Lake Michigan with her friends.

Chapter 2

Emma's mom and dad were avid divers and the founding members of the How the Wet Was Fun Scuba Club in Greenville, South Carolina. The club members came in all shapes and sizes, with a variety of backgrounds and age groups as well. While trying to come up with a name for the club, her father, Michael, thought it would be funny to name it Get Fit or Dive Tryin', but her mother, Lillian, ever the pragmatic one, thought it might make people feel like they had to be in Jane Fonda shape to be a member (or that they might die diving) so they went with a name that would hopefully appeal to everyone who loved scuba diving as much as they did.

Membership grew faster than they had expected, and meetings were held on the last Wednesday of every month at a local dive shop called Under Pressure, or at a coffee shop if the owners of Under Pressure were out on a diving excursion. Bucket list dives were often the topic of the meetings, and Lillian and Michael had a map of both the United States and the world that they unfurled proudly at the beginning of each meeting. The maps were laid out neatly on a table, or sometimes tacked to the wall so everyone could see. Tiny red dots were made with felt-tip markers in every place a club member had dived. Filling the maps with dots brought a special thrill—as well as bragging rights. Of course, it appealed to most of the club to dive in warm, turquoise waters among neon fish and exquisite coral. Places like the Cayman Islands, Thailand, and the Great Barrier Reef were among the most popular travel destinations for adventurous and alluring dives, but there was a small subgroup among the members who enjoyed exploring shipwrecks, no matter where they were located.

Michael and Lillian found themselves becoming more and more intrigued by a fellow member named Rick, who was well-known among the community for being an underwater archeologist of sorts. He lived for wreck diving and had been trying to talk Michael and Lillian into joining him on a dive over Labor Day Weekend to check out the Milwaukee wreck in Lake Michigan. For Rick, sharing his passion for shipwrecks with others was half the fun, but not everyone enjoyed the cold, dark lake water as much as he did. The way he talked about the experiences he encountered while discovering and exploring sunken ships, sparked an interest in Lillian and Michael that neither of them had considered before forming the club, but the desire to learn the history behind the wrecks, combined with Rick's contagious enthusiasm, lured them in hook, line, and sinker.

Rick explained that the Milwaukee Car Ferry launched from Cleveland in 1903, moving rail cars and their large goods around the Great Lakes through the Roaring Twenties until October 1929, when it succumbed to a violent October storm on its way across Lake Michigan. Since the ship didn't have a radio, no one knew what happened until a Milwaukee wreck diver discovered it in 1972 about three miles off

Whitefish Bay, just north of the city of Milwaukee. Apparently, the waves rocked the boat so badly that the railcars the Milwaukee was transporting broke free and bent the Seagate, letting in the stormy water and sinking the massive vessel. All 52 crew members perished with the boat. Murky, dark lake water dives were nothing new to Rick, but for Lillian and Michael, this would serve as their first.

"You guys gotta join me. She's humongous. And when she sank, one of the railcars escaped and got pinned beneath the ship. And the wheelhouse came off, so you've got to follow a line one hundred feet to get to it. Better history than any museum." Rick coaxed.

"Yeah," Michael said. "Like *20,000 Leagues Under The Sea*. And we all know how that ended."

"Michael! You're too much. Don't be silly," quipped Lillian as she playfully slapped his shoulder.

Rick interjected "I know you're both up for the challenge. Deep water and poor visibility aren't enough to scare you two off, is it?"

"Hell no, it isn't," Lillian retorted a little too quickly. "I love the idea."

Michael saw his wife's expressive eyes that rivaled the royal blue of the Caribbean sky and sparkled like its waters on a sun-soaked day, light up and shine brighter than ever, telling Michael that a plan had basically already been hatched.

He loved the strong and determined stance her petite frame took on as a wickedly beautiful smile stretched across her delicately featured face, and he could already see the wheels turning in Lillian's headstrong and willful mind. The excitement seemed to make her freckles do a happy dance across her sweet face, and he knew he was about to take a trip to Milwaukee. He just hoped they weren't going to die trying.

She pulled her deep auburn hair up into a ponytail, indicating that things just got real, and said, "Oh. I know. We can bring Emma and make it an end-of-summer trip before she goes back to school. Plus, she can drive the boat for us while we dive. This will be perfect."

"If we can tear her away from her friends, that is. Now that she's eighteen, she won't be too psyched to hang with her 'rents during her last precious days of summer vacation," Michael said, half-jokingly.

With an answer for everything, Rick chimed in. "Hell, she can bring her friends with her. I have a big old lake house that has been in our family for years, and a good-sized boat waiting for us on the docks to boot. I mean, having a boat, and a house on Lake Michigan that I can use whenever I want, are really the only good things about my midwestern relatives," he said while laughing so hard he had to use the tail of his Hawaiian shirt to wipe the sweat from his upper lip.

A few weeks later, Michael borrowed a cream-colored Fleetwood Bounder RV trimmed with rust and goldenrod stripes, that could fit Lillian and him, all five teenagers, the scuba gear, and way too many oversized bags filled with whatever the girls considered to be the bare necessities for a weekend on the lake. The drive from South Carolina to Milwaukee was long, but the girls made it go a little faster by entertaining themselves with games and listening to each other's tapes on their Walkmans. The smell of bug spray and Coppertone mixed with stale cigarettes inside the RV, but Heather assured everyone it was better than road-tripping with her brothers and their stinky feet.

Emma adjusted the bright orange foam headphones over her ears so she could enjoy the full sound of Madonna singing “Papa Don’t Preach” directly into her ears. She leaned her head back on the vinyl bench and let out a contented sigh as she gazed around the camper, taking in the happy vibes from her awesome friends, and even her mom and dad perched up in the front. *This weekend’s gonna be bitchin’*, she said to herself with a smile.

****

In true Michael and Lillian form, they arrived at the address that Rick provided a bit early. The AAA Trip-Tik got them there in great time, with a campground stop partway, and they went straight to the dock to prep for the big dive that had been scheduled for right after lunch. The peanut butter and jelly sandwiches Lillian had made the night before, and carefully wrapped in wax paper, were doled out to Emma and her friends so they wouldn’t be hungry before boarding the boat.

Blustery end-of-summer wind pushed strong wafts of fuel tanks and dingy boat cabins around the docks, but it was no match for the layers of hairspray and Dippity-Do that each of the giggly girls sported in their oversized hairstyles. The chipped wooden planks beneath their flip-flop-clad feet gave off enough heat that told them summer wasn’t dying quite yet and would hold on by the skin of its teeth for as long as it possibly could.

“Girls, put your life jackets on. Y’all can’t board until you do,” Michael said while checking and rechecking his scuba equipment. He was always the careful one. It was in his nature.

The beat-up old life jackets were already lined up on the dock, presumably to air them out a bit after being sweat-soaked and put away wet all summer long.

"Daaaaad. Gnarly!" Emma squealed much more dramatically than usual, for the benefit of the other four girls.

"Safety first, Emma," he retorted without looking up from the gauges of his air tank.

"But they're gonna cover our mint new swimsuits," Emma argued.

"Emma, do what your father says. You know the rules on the water, and we talked about this when we asked you and your friends to help us on this dive," her mom said matter-of-factly. "This is the only thing we are asking you to do for us while you're here. We appreciate your driving the boat for us, and when we're done, you girls have the rest of the weekend to do whatever you want," she said with a smile and a wink. "We won't cramp your style."

All five girls just stood there staring at the life jackets lying flat on the splintery faded gray dock, hoping they'd disappear if they gave them the stink eye long enough.

Their noses wrinkled in disgust because they smelled dingy and old, like a grandma's gross basement, but they pulled the faded orange life jackets over their heads as delicately as possible, with careful consideration of their big hair. Heather had a Flock of Seagulls hairdo that seemed to attract the gulls of Lake Michigan. They swooped in and hovered like kites over her head until she swatted at them, shooing them off.

She hoped it wasn't going to be like that boring old horror movie with all the birds her dad watched every time it came on late-night TV. Jeez, that was like a relic from before the Civil War or something.

The sweat was already trickling down Emma's back, and she cringed as it created a little pool among the ruffles of her neon pink bikini bottoms. "It totally feels like I'm wearing a straight jacket in a sauna," she whined.

"Like, totally. These things pretty much sucked all the fresh air out of the entire universe," Susan agreed. "I can't wait to get this thing off so I can meet a hottie and get *him* off."

Rachel and Yolanda cracked up uncontrollably, and Emma mockingly reprimanded Susan by using her well-established nickname. "Chill, Sleazin. My dad's right over there."

Heather pulled each of the belts on her lifejacket as tight as it would go on her lanky, lean frame and asked, "Did any of you guys bring baby oil? I want to catch rays today, for sure. After this, we should see if we can get wine coolers somewhere. Do y'all think they have Mad Dog 20/20 in Michigan?"

"I have Johnson's Baby Oil and Hawaiian Tropic," Ra Ra said, holding them out for Zipper to see. "I don't see why they wouldn't. If they don't, I bet they have Sun Country Wine Coolers or at least some Boone's Farm. I saw a couple stores on the way here. Maybe we can hang outside one of them and give someone money to go in and buy for us."

Heather considered the options in Rachel's hands and attempted to make the life altering decision of which one to pick for optimal tanning results. She pointed to the dark brown bottle of Hawaiian Tropic, which Rachel promptly threw to her, and said, "Awesome plan. Savage tan here I come."

"It's gonna take at least two bottles of that stuff to cover those long ass legs of yours, Zipper." Yolanda teased.

"No duh." Emma said with a huge grin.

"Yeah, yeah. I like being straight and long like a zipper. You can call me fly. Get it? She burst into a fit of laughter that ended in a snort, which made the rest of the girls crack up as well.

"Don't have a cow, Zip." YoYo quipped between gut busters. "We get it, already! Hey, gimme some of that stuff when you're done with it. I don't need a tan, but I like the way it smells."

"You're like so lucky to have such beautiful dark skin, YoYo, Emma said.

"Thanks."

"For sure, black is beautiful and so are you. You're gonna be a famous model. Even more famous than Christie Brinkley," Emma responded.

"Gag me with a spoon," Sleazin chimed in. "Why don't you guys go make out or something. Enough with the lovefest."

"Um, that actually doesn't sound too grody," YoYo joked, and once again they all doubled over in fits of hilarity. They all knew-even then that Yolanda liked girls, and that her only interest in guys was purely because she found the hydraulics intriguing. Like their dicks defied gravity, which she had to admit was a pretty cool trick, even if they didn't make the magic happen for her.

"Am I interrupting something, girls?" Rick said,

unintentionally scaring the crap out of all five of them.

Petrified that he heard what they were saying, the girls stood frozen in stunned silence, which Yolanda quickly broke with the loud POP of a giant Bubble Yum bubble.

Rick chuckled. "Be sure you don't swallow that gum. It'll stay in your stomach forever, ya know."

Before anyone could answer, Michael and Lillian were upon them and greeting Rick with big toothy smiles and bear hugs.

"Emma, girls, this is Mr. Nagy," Lillian said

"Oh, please. Mr. Nagy is my dad. I know I'm getting up there, but they can call me Rick. It's great to meet you girls. Sorry if I snuck up on you there. I said hello, but you were all howling so hard you didn't hear me."

The girls did their best "talking-to-grown-ups-voices" as they all said, "Nice to meet you, Rick" in sing-songy unison.

Emma noticed that Rick was a little taller than her dad, much tanner, and more muscular than him as well. He looked old to her, but then again, everyone over twenty-five looked old in her eyes. She figured he was about her dad's age, maybe a little younger, but you could tell he was always in the sun. His skin was a deep mahogany and he had tons of freckles. Reddish brown wisps of hair stuck out from beneath a red and black western styled bandana that he fashioned into a doo rag. She couldn't see his eyes because of his neon wrap-around mirrored glasses, and she thought he dressed more like a college kid than an old dude. He had a laid-back way about him, and as she listened to the banter between Rick and her dad, she decided she liked how he teased her parents and got away with it. He was pretty funny. He cracked some cheesy water-themed dad jokes, like, "I could use some kelp with these air tanks," and "We could take a ride after the dive just for the Halibut," so he was probably more Pee Wee Herman funny than Eddie Murphy funny, but at least it would be a fun boat ride.

"Emma, your mom and dad told me you're quite the captain. Thanks so much for driving us today." He made sure to include all the girls with a nod and a smile as he said, "And thank *you all* for being here. This is a crazy weekend out on the lake, so it'll be helpful to have y'all on board to make sure other boaters don't miss the scuba flags or do anything stupid that would put us in danger when we resurface."

"You're welcome," Emma responded politely, plastering on a polite smile.

"Well, should we get on board and head out to the site?" Rick asked.

"Let's do it," Michael said with such earnest enthusiasm that Emma thought it was funny and unusual for him. He always seemed to be in dad or ex-military mode.

"Um, Mr. Nagy?" Heather asked timidly.

"Rick."

"Like, sorry. Rick?"

"Yepper."

"Would it be okay if I brought my boombox on the boat so we can, like, listen to tunes while y'all do your dive? Or maybe just on the way out to the site and back?"

Rick slid his glasses down the bridge of his nose and smiled. "She isn't called Sweet Emotion for nothing. Tuneage is always welcome."

"Thank you." Heather was so happy, she bounced up and down a couple times—little mini jumps of excitement. If it were Sleazin' who asked, Emma would have thought she was flirting with the guy, and chances are she would have been right.

"Let's rock-n-roll." he said, and everyone made their way onto the boat.

While Rick, Michael, and Lillian helped each other suit up, Emma drove the small boat three miles over the dark blue water and tiny crests of white to the dive site. She had been over the plan with her parents several times and always worried about something unexpected happening.

So, she'd even found a map of Lake Michigan at the library and studied it before they left for the trip.

RaRa, YoYo, Sleazin', and Zipper crowded in the back of the boat to stay out of the way, and put on a Cyndi Lauper cassette tape while fussing with their sunglasses and suit bottoms. Once they reached the site, Emma slowed the boat to a stop and joined the adults.

"My parents told me you are a master diver just like they are," she said to Rick, since her parents seemed to be engaged deep in conversation with each other.

"Guilty as charged."

"It looks like my mom and dad have their usual scuba gear, but they also have smaller tanks I don't think I've seen before."

"Oh, those are called pony tanks. This is a very deep dive, more than one hundred feet down, so the pony tanks are used as a reserve or in case there are any problems with the regular tanks."

Emma's parents joined their conversation just as Emma asked Rick how long it would take to get to the surface if you ran out of air one hundred feet down.

"The rest of your life," Michael chimed in as they all put on their diving hoods and snickered at the joke.

"Guys, that's not funny," Lillian said, chortling. "But seriously, let's do one more gear check on each other. Rick, are you sure you want to wear that hood? It's kind of thin for this dive, don't ya think? I have an extra one if you want to use it."

"Aww, Mom. Do I have to? The other kids will make fun of me. I'm just joshin' ya. Thanks anyway," Rick said as he pulled his fins on. "We'll cross a thermocline or two, but this hood should be good enough for forty degrees."

Lillian waved him off with a flick of her hand and then beckoned for the girls to huddle up and join the conversation before they jumped in the water.

"Okay, girls, we're about to get in and do a couple of personal safety checks on our masks and stuff, but I want y'all to remember the dive should take us a total of thirty to thirty-five minutes at the most. This is important. The actual dive time will be about twenty minutes, but we'll need five or so minutes on the way down to allow our bodies to pressurize once we reach certain depths, and the same thing on the way back up so that we can adjust safely before we reach the surface. Also, don't forget to watch for other boaters. They're supposed to stay a minimum of one hundred yards away from us once we raise the diver-down flag, but there are probably a lot of drunk people out on the water today, so keep a sharp eye out for us."

"Who volunteers to keep an eye on the minute

hand?" Michael asked the girls.

"We're all experienced, but it's nice to know someone will notice if we're taking a little too long," Lillian reassured them.

"I have a Swatch Watch I got for my birthday," RaRa said enthusiastically as she waved her wrist in the air.

"That's great, Rachel. Thank you. Emma has her watch as well. Thank you so much to all of you. Wish us luck down in the murky depths," she said with a bright smile and wiggling fingers to add what she thought was an expression of creepiness. The divers all checked their dive lights. It was a bright afternoon, but soon enough visibility would be all but impossible if their lights failed. Michael even had a back-up.

Emma did a couple of fast and small head shakes at RaRa and told her mom she had it under control. She watched her friend, who was studying her colorful plastic watch, pleased she was taking the dive seriously. The three adults, resembling sea lions or maybe seals dressed as condoms for Halloween, plunged into the water, doing their personal checks, then gave the "OK" sign to each other and to the girls on the boat, signaling the start of their descent.

"Why are they making rings above their heads with their arms?" Heather asked Emma while cranking up the volume on the boombox. "They look like they are doing the YMCA dance but got the letters wrong."

Emma ignored her friend and yelled, "Be careful!" to the trio as they began to disappear under the dark blue water, and then they were gone. She turned to Heather and said a bit too forcefully, "Turn down that music until they come back up, would ya?"

"Geez, Ma, don't have a cow."

"Sorry, Zip, I just wanna be sure we can hear and see what's going on around the dive site until they are back on the boat. Then we can crank it up and have some fun."

"I know. You're right," she said, and turned the music off. This is, like, a pretty serious dive since they have those extra tanks and have to wear those bogus hoods and everything. I'm sorry."

"It's cool," Emma said without taking her eyes off the water.

"What should we do for a whole half an hour, y'all?" RaRa chirped. "Too bad I didn't bring my Ouija board. That would have been totally awesome to do on a boat."

"I've never heard of anyone doing a Ouija board or séance on a boat, and definitely not in broad daylight," Susan said with a sly smile. "But I love to try new things."

YoYo said, "I have an idea." Her sudden burst of enthusiasm caused a violent coughing fit.

"What the hell? Are you okay?" Rachel ran to Yolanda's side–ready to whack her on the back.

"Yeah. Swallowed my gum," she answered, tears streaming from her eyes.

"Oh, thank God," said RaRa, "because I can't remember the Heimlich or CPR from the class I had to take last summer so I could lifeguard at McCarter. Don't scare me like that." She thought back to the long hot days in the high lifeguard chair where she sat in fear of anything happening on her watch. Who knew if she would remember what to do? That job wasn't as much fun as she pictured it in her head. It was half boredom and half yelling at stupid boys to stop running. At least no one had died.

"I could show y'all some new tricks I learned on my yo-yo," Yolanda said between a few additional coughs and a quick throat-clearing.

From behind, Sleazin' wrapped her arms around her friend between her bikini bottoms and the lifejacket and lifted her off the ground. "You need to get a better handle on swallowing." she said with a hearty snort. "Get it?"

"We can't all be as talented as you in that department, girl. And that gross shit doesn't really apply to me," YoYo retorted without hesitation and a silly wink, and her tongue stuck out of the side of her mouth.

Sleazin' put her down with a thump that echoed through the water below their feet. "We could play truth or dare."

"Nah. Not on a boat and we only have thirty minutes," Heather chimed in.

Rachel took her life jacket off and rearranged her boobs in her bikini top. "I'm gonna tan until it's time to go." She tilted her face skyward.

The girls all agreed this would be the best way to pass the time and still be able to keep a good eye on the site. Everyone arranged themselves in an area where they could see the water but sit with their legs stretched out in front of them for the best ray-catching potential.

As the boat swayed in the warm sun, they drifted off into a peaceful daze. Fifteen minutes went by, and so did a few boatloads of hot, rowdy guys. They couldn't wait to get back to shore to investigate the local (and visiting) talent. Amidst a serious conversation regarding the order for shower taking when they got back to the house, their discussion was abuptly halted by an unsettling sound. They sat perfectly still and exchanged wary glances, wondering if they all heard the same thing. They were surrounded by opposing sounds of frolicking boaters and the lull of soothing, rhythmic waves hitting the side of the boat. But the "fwissshhhh" they heard followed by a loud, flopping splash broke through all the other noise and sent shock waves over the surface of the water and into their core. They not only heard it but also felt it. It was like the sound a whale makes when it surfaces and then dives back down.

"What the hell? Did you hear that? It sounded like a whale. This is a lake. There shouldn't be whales here," Susan exclaimed as all the girls jumped to their feet and turned in different directions, looking for the freshwater whale.

"Emma, it hasn't even been twenty minutes, so it can't be them yet, right?" RaRa asked while proudly checking her Swatch Watch.

Emma scanned the water near the flags and could make out a diver but couldn't tell who it was. "Yeah, I don't know. Maybe there's another dive team down there and they came up in the wrong place. That happens sometimes." There was another boat a couple of hundred yards away, and though she couldn't see a diver-down flag on the other vessel, she wasn't really concerned yet.

They all watched the diver very carefully, and silently, for a minute, and Emma wondered if she should have someone look for binoculars. Then she chastised herself for not bringing a pair.

"That looks like a guy," Heather said. "And he's swimming toward us."

"He's kind of swimming," said Rachel. She wiped the sweat off her forehead and zeroed in for another close look by squinting her eyes, making a bunny nose, and cupping her hand above her eyebrows. "It looks more like he's wading forward slowly with one arm than actually swimming."

As he neared the boat, Emma could tell that it was Rick, because she recognized the different-looking, thinner hood he was wearing and remembered that her mom was concerned about it. "Oh, that's Rick. He's probably just messing with us."

"I don't know, Emma. He kind of doesn't seem right," YoYo said, in a nervous voice.

When he reached the boat, he was floating face down and bobbing in the water like a dead fish.

The air seemed to go completely still, and Emma couldn't hear anything but a frightening whoosh of blood to her ears. She went from half-joking to full-on serious mode.

"What the hell, Ma?" Tell him to stop. That's not funny," Rachel squealed.

Emma leaned over the edge and reached down into the water to give Rick a nudge. "Rick, are you okay?"

A cold silence greeted them, causing a wave of panic to wash over the girls. Emma's heart thundered, adrenaline rushing into her bloodstream in a way she thought was reserved for skydiving or rollercoasters.

YoYo grabbed Heather's hand and squeezed it hard while repeating, "No, no, no, no," in a low and guttural voice.

Emma yelled, "C'mon. Help me turn him over."

Susan lunged to help, but leaning so far over the side, they couldn't flip him over on his back. They only managed to turn his head to the side so that his mouth and nose were above the water. His mask was missing and there was a bloody cut on his forehead.

RaRa let out a scream that startled them all and burst into tears as she backed away from the boat's edge and made her way to the back corner, where she curled up in a tight ball and rocked.

"Jesus Christ, Ma, is he dead? What do we do?" Susan screamed.

Emma leaned in as close as she could to his face, while Susan helped to hold his head up. He wasn't responding or talking, but there was a gurgling sound like he was choking. His eyes suddenly flew open like a window shade rolling up too quickly, but she could tell they weren't focused on anything. A white film clouded over his blue sky-colored irises. With big, round, vacant eyes, he began gasping for air.

Heather and Yolanda let go of each other's hands and raised them to their mouths in terrified disbelief. "Oh my God." "OH MY GOD!" was all Emma could hear them yelling from behind her as she took hold of the strap on his gear that held the tank and tried to pull it up with as much strength as she had ever used in her life. Susan jumped to her feet and screamed. Yolanda was now crying.

Emma reached down and around to the front of his wetsuit, where the equipment was clipped in and tried to hold him up from there. She had climbed over the railing of the pontoon, floating about two feet above the surface, and she was already struggling with the weight of it all while holding onto the boat with her left hand.

The last thing she needed to do was end up in the water with him.

Sweat ran down her forehead and tears of panic pricked the back of her eyes. Fatigue was settling in. Tears spilled over and she searched the surface for her parents. *Where the hell are they? Are they hurt too? I don't know what to do.*

"Guys, help me hold him up." she screeched at her friends.

Yolanda, Susan, and Heather snapped into action like they had been jump-started or shocked with electrodes. They all tried to bend over the boat and take hold, but there were too many of them, and not enough places on Rick's slippery suit that they could grab.

"Is there a rope?" Heather yelled. "Maybe we could tie him to it and pull him out."

Emma's strained voice cracked as she said, "I wish I knew how to get this fucking equipment off. Maybe if we had a knife, we could cut him out of it. Susan, stay here and help me keep him up. Heather, go get RaRa and YoYo and tell them that they *gotta* help us. We're all going to scream for help, but y'all are going to wave your hands over your heads while we hold him. We need to get someone's attention NOW."

Heather promptly let go of Rick and joined the other two girls, who were now both on the floor of the boat. Both girls' life jackets were off now, and RaRa's head was resting on YoYo's shoulder, her face pale. She wasn't crying anymore, but huge hiccups erupted periodically from her chest. YoYo had both her arms wrapped around her in a tight bear hug, snot running down from her nose. Heather squatted down in front of RaRa's face and took on a voice no one had ever heard come out of her mouth before. It sounded like a calm, caring kindergarten teacher trying to get a crying child to let go of its mother's leg at drop-off. Gently, she took hold of Rachel's hands.

"RaRa," she said, "listen to me, girl. We are all scared. That's okay. But we *all* gotta do our part, or this man is not going to make it. You are brave and strong, and I know you can do this shit. Now, you both need to stand up and help us wave down a boat right now."

YoYo had already let go of Rachel and watched her sit up slowly. She saw her breathing begin to slow down and her eyes get a little bigger in recognition of what Heather was saying and what needed to be done. RaRa looked imploringly from one friend to the other, as both she and YoYo wiped the snot and left-over tears from their cheeks and upper lip.

"That's right. You got this. You're the best cheerleader in three motherfucking counties. Let's hear that voice and see some arm action, bitch." Heather said with an enthusiastic smile as she helped Rachel to her feet.

"I got this." Rachel ran to the side of the boat, screaming for help. They each took a spot and did the same, mentally willing someone to cross over the hundred-yard border they had been protecting up until now. The girls put every ounce of energy into jumping, screaming, and waving—but to no avail. If it hadn't been Labor Day weekend, and if Lake Michigan wasn't so big, maybe someone would have noticed them, but everyone seemed to be hollering and jumping about, albeit for much different reasons.

Emma was thinking about trying the radio but didn't want to let go of Rick. She looked down at her aching fingers and noticed something twisted underneath Rick's left shoulder strap. "Hold him tight and don't drop his head." she said frantically.

She let go with one hand and searched underneath his body once again. This time, she felt something long and stretchy and followed it up with a closed fist, like petting a cat's tail. At the end of it was something small and hard. It felt like…Was it? Oh God, yes. It was a whistle. She pulled the stretch cord up as far as it would go and tried to lean in a bit closer as she took in a deep breath and blew. The first attempt was weak, sounding more like the initial squeaks of a tea kettle before its full-blown squeals. Of course, it was full of water. She gave herself a quick mental pep talk, shook the whistle vigorously, and saw tiny droplets of lake water catch the sun as they scattered every which way, took another deep breath and let it rip. This time, she got a long, loud whistle. She repeated it again and again until she began to shake from trying to push so much air out of her lungs. In her mind, it felt like forever, but within minutes, she caught the attention of a family passing by.

The man—Emma assumed it was the dad—noticed the girls' dire need for help and immediately drove over, parked next to the Sweet Emotion, and jumped aboard. The mom ran to their radio and began yelling into it, but Emma wasn't sure who she was trying to call. She was busy explaining the situation and that her mom and dad were probably going to come up any minute, but had to make stops along the way, or they would get decompression sickness. She was anxious for her dad to surface because, as a paramedic and a retired Army Ranger, he would know what to do.

While the words spilled over her lips faster than an auctioneer's, the dad from the other boat grabbed RaRa's life jacket from the boat's floor, jumped in the water, and placed it around Rick's neck to help keep him afloat while turning him onto his back. He was in the middle of telling his son to get in the water and help him pull Rick on board the Sweet Emotion when Emma saw her mom swimming toward the boat, and her dad trailing right behind her. From the commotion, it was clear there was an emergency.

Michael swam faster than anyone knew he could, and when he reached Rick, he pressed the release valve on his equipment so that it would be easier to do a rescue carry from the side of the boat to the back where the ladder was.

With no time for introductions—only for instructions—Michael told Lillian and the other dad to get on board, and that he would push Rick up from the water, while everyone on board would need to do a log lift to get him on the boat. Even with all hands on deck, the dead weight was excruciating, but they finally managed. Michael immediately started CPR and asked Lillian to grab his knife from the console so he could cut open Rick's neoprene suit. The girls, still reeling from all that had already happened, stepped back and watched Michael work on Rick. Emma shuddered and realized that the dreadful thing she had been imagining hadn't come true.

"We're gonna need to get him to shore and call 911," Michael said. "Maybe we can radio ahead that we have an emergency and paramedics can meet us there."

"I already called the Coast Guard," the mom from the other boat yelled. "They said to start heading toward shore, and they'll intercept us and take him from there. They're radioing for an ambulance to meet them at shore."

Before they had gotten their pontoon going, the Coast Guard was coming up fast. When they pulled up alongside, one officer jumped aboard while another led them back to shore.

Emma watched the other family get smaller and smaller and briefly wondered how they would be able to go on with the rest of their day after what had just happened.

On shore, Rick's body was placed on a stretcher and the EMS crew moved him into the ambulance after instructing everyone else to wait on the boat for the police to come and get statements.

As a sharp contrast to the sorrowful situation, Cyndi Lauper's happy and quirky crooning of "The Goonies 'R' Good Enough" played in her brain like a relentless earworm. She wanted it to stop, but visions of a beetle on its back with arms and legs frantically moving about as it grasped at the last moments of life took over her thoughts. Dying bugs and pop songs. She felt like she was going nuts and that she might throw up.

Lillian brought the girls in for a group hug and asked them if they were okay. No one responded with words, but remained in the hug huddle until the police arrived to ask their questions. When they got there, they told everyone that Rick had died in the ambulance on the way to the hospital. They still wanted to take statements because they were unclear what had happened. Emma and her friends sat and stared, unable to speak right away.

The EMS crew had left a couple of people behind to make sure no one else had any injuries. Even though it was a hot Labor Day, the girls were very cold, and they all had a hard time breathing, so the paramedics gave them water and oxygen. A female paramedic asked Emma what happened to them, but she couldn't get any words out. Only tears.

The Labor Day Incident—as it is now referred to—happened on a Saturday. On the following Tuesday, Michael and Lillian were informed that Rick had had an air embolism and there was nothing they could have done to save him.

It took a long time for the girls to even talk about the incident, but they all felt bonded together permanently by what happened. Emma couldn't speak for the rest of them, but even after years of therapy, she still felt overcome by survivor's guilt. It didn't matter that her therapist and even her friends would say there was nothing she could have done to help him. She still wondered, *what if I had known more about the gear? What if I had been stronger and got him out of the water sooner? What if we all worked harder to get help faster?*

It didn't matter how many therapy sessions she went to, residual guilt continued to hit her heart in the catastrophic waves of a tsunami.

"What do you mean it's snowing?" YoYo sounded incredulous and out of breath.

Emma pushed her front door closed against the cold and made her way to the warmth of her kitchen. "I mean big, fat fluffy cold white stuff is falling from the sky. Why are you breathing so hard? Did I catch you at a bad or *good* time?" Emma rinsed her wineglass in the white Farmhouse sink and took a new one from the built-in glass cabinet. She studied the glass for a minute before pouring a fresh glass of Malbec.

YoYo said, "Girl, I wish. No, I'm on the Peloton. I gotta keep this booty tight, ya know? With all that snow, everything must be shut down. I guess you're gonna have to postpone that orgy you've been planning."

Emma let out a loud cackle that she didn't even recognize as her own.

"Are you sure the white flakey stuff isn't your boozy neighbor's coke stash blowing away in the wind?" She giggled so hard at her joke that she started to cough.

With YoYo's reference to Boozy Becca, Emma poured only half a glass, but laughed right along with her friend. "I only call her Boozy Becca because it just flows, plus she does tend to get tipsy pretty often. I'm really not one to judge. I have a nice sized glass of wine in my hand as we speak."

"Yeah, I hear ya. I just love your stories about her. They crack me up. Isn't her dog's name Shiraz or some shit?"

"It's actually Chablis."

"Of course it is."

Emma took a seat at the kitchen island. She was still laughing, but quickly changed topics before she changed her mind altogether regarding the real reasons she called her friend.

"He left today," she said.

"Girl, what are you talking about?" It was obvious that YoYo stopped pedaling and Emma could picture her friend wiping sweat with a small towel from her serious, but beautiful face. She always envied YoYo's gorgeous dark skin. When she got serious, her deep brown, almond eyes took on a fierceness that could rival Samuel L Jackson's.

"He left four months ago and was technically long gone way before that."

"I know," Emma said, reminding herself silently that her friend was getting heated because she had her back. "That's not what I meant. He sent the U-Haul and some movers today to get all his precious antiques out. You know that just makes everything more real. Once his precious shit is moved into the new place, it's the final nail in the coffin."

"That man sure loves his old shit. And I guess he loves the shiny new stuff too."

Emma had met Bobby Fisk when they were both freshmen at Furman University. It was a typical college love affair that included two major breakups or timeouts, but they ended up back together both times and got married the summer after graduation. The Fisk family was well known in Greenville for their import/export furniture business, as well as an extremely large and profitable antique store in town. People came from all over South Carolina to shop at Fisk Antiques and Curiosities.

Emma started working there during college breaks and had a knack for design and merchandising that made folks literally gasp when they stepped inside the charming store. Because of Emma's keen eye and magical merchandising skills, it was packed to the gills with one-of-kind finds, and the inventory and design plan changed almost every two weeks. She even concocted a special scent for reed diffusers that made people swoon. They became a big part of the store's allure, and the profits as well. Emma combined an earthy and sexy blend of palo santo, white lavender, eucalyptus, redwood, and a hint of sea salt that she obtained through the Fisk import-export business and taught herself how to create the diffusers. The packaging of the sumptuous sticks was so beautiful, it could have been a box full of dog shit and people would have still fought over the last one on the shelf.

By the time she graduated college, people saw Emma as a best-kept secret and would pay her enormous amounts of money for interior design, using the store's inventory and her amazing way of combining quirky, homespun style and elegant high-end European pieces with a healthy helping of upscale, Southern charm. She poured all of herself into her family and the family business first, but truly thrived on the creative outlet and the pulse of her 'side projects'.

Since Bobby's siblings ran the business side of things, and his parents still had a hand in helping Emma run the day-to-day of the antique shop, he was free to pursue a position as a Professor of Art History at Furman University. It was there that he met the shiny new thing that YoYo was referring to. She was a Studio Art major, and the rest was history. As was their marriage.

Emma didn't respond in words, but with a bit of silent sadness, followed by a loud exhale into the receiver.

"Ma, I'm not trying to be cruel. Love is a battlefield. You took care of everything, and he only took care of himself. Hey, at least now all that dusty old crap is out of the house, and you can do your magic in there the way YOU want to."

"Did you just throw some Pat Benatar lyrics at me?"

"You caught that, huh?" YoYo said with a knowing, deep chuckle, and her sudden huff and puff said she was pedaling again.

"Talking to y'all is like a power wash for the soul. I knew I called you first for a reason."

"Yeah, yeah. Girl, something else is weighing on you besides heavy flakes of snow and solid oak sideboards. Spill it."

Emma shifted her weight nervously on the island stool and cleared her throat. This was why she went to YoYo first. She knew she could be silly with her and get serious too. YoYo would understand the importance of getting everyone together without having Emma spell it out for her first. The mere fact that Emma reached out would be enough. Among other things, the Labor Day incident gave them this ability to read each other and accurately weigh the gravity of each other's descriptions of various situations, problems, or rants.

"I know this is kind of last minute, but I want to get everyone together. Preferably here."

"In Greenville?"

"At my house. I need y'all here, all in one place. I have news."

There was a heartbeat of silence on YoYo's end, and Emma thought she could almost hear the powerful beat of her friend's heart. She got lost in the rhythmic beat of what was more likely to be the music coming from her bike while Yolanda absorbed and processed Emma's words.

She broke into Emma's tiny trance. "Have you ever

heard of a kiki?"

"Huh?"

"A kiki," YoYo repeated. "It's a special kind of party. Most people connect a kiki with the LBGTQ community, but anyone can have one. It's just a gathering of good friends where they listen to music, drink, gossip, share stories, and let it *all* out. There's no holding back at a kiki. It's supposed to calm your nerves, reduce anxiety and fight against despair, ya know?"

"This is an actual thing?" Emma asked, the wine leaving a dry residue in her mouth. She wondered if she had those purple "Joker smiles" in the corners of her lips.

"Girl. Yes." YoYo retorted loudly. Emma could picture her beautiful friend's megawatt smile, and imagined how it could have blinded her right through the phone.

"Wait. Didn't that band Scissor Sisters do a song about this back in, like, 2012?"

"Okay, I know I threw some Pat Benatar at a bitch but are you seriously saying the words scissor sisters to a lesbian?"

They both roared so hard that tears came to their eyes, and Emma snorted.

"I got you, girl. I'll call the others and we'll have ourselves a kiki. Oh, and by the way, if you have to start shoveling snow, be sure to bend at the knees to save your back. Or just move further south. I would love to have you here in Florida."

"Now that your mom is gone, you can always move back here, ya know."

She chuckleded again, but in a melancholy way

this time. “I know.”

“Let me know what everyone says, and hopefully when y’all can be here, K?”

“I got you. G’night, girl. Love you.”

“Love you too. Talk soon.”

Emma set the phone down on the cold marble. Tears filled her eyes, and she felt something deep within her, which she hoped was relief.

Chapter 3

February 14th was never a date that Emma put much stock in or held in high regard. Not even when she and Bobby were together and happy. In her opinion, a regulated day to be romantic kind of took the romance right out of it. It all seemed so fake, phony and contrived, designed to sell cards and flowers and boost restaurant bookings at the end of winter when no one in their right mind wanted to go out. But this year she wished she had accepted YoYo's offer to come up for the weekend. Instead, she said she would wait until everyone could gather at once. So, Emma spent Valentine's Day planning the menu for their visit, shopping for special wines, ensuring that she had on hand a case of each one's favorite in addition to the perfect pairings for main courses.

She kept herself busy finding new towels and sheets for the guest rooms and putting together little gift baskets with inside jokes and unique treats. In the decades since they had all graduated college, there had only been two years they had not gone away for a weekend together. But this year was special because they were all coming to her house, and now, with Bobby's things out and her new things in, it was truly hers–hers to share with her favorite people and no walking-on-eggshells around Bobby. Even though they couldn't all clear their schedules for February, at least coming in mid-March meant that a gorgeous Carolina spring would be in full bloom.

They would all arrive Thursday evening for a long weekend together, so Emma woke up early that March morning to put the finishing touches on the house before they came. She grabbed a pair of scissors and went outside to cut some peonies from the lush bush on the side of her house. She had always loved her peonies, and a smile came to her face as she fondly recalled Caroline pronouncing the name of the beautiful flowers as paninis instead of peonies when she was six years old. The colorful beauty they brought to her yard with their round, poofy blooms made her feel happy and lucky, as did a good panini when she had a craving, she supposed. But cutting and bringing them indoors to create simple and romantic arrangements made her heart even happier, especially when she was entertaining people she loved. Some early season bees seemed to share her sentiment. A couple fuzzy, chubby bumblebees bumped into one another around her hands as she clipped the last bit of greenery, humming their favorite pollination tunes.

While Emma had been preparing for a month for this special weekend with her friends, she didn't feel like she needed to impress them. Their friendship was much deeper than that. She just wanted everything to be special to show her gratitude for their visit, and because of the important things she was about to share with them.

And who was she kidding? Shopping and preparing for her best friends to come over was like Christmas and her birthday all rolled into one. She relished it like cold lemonade on a hot, humid day, and there would be plenty of those to come in the long hot Carolina summer. After cutting flowers from her garden, she went to each guest room, placing welcome baskets on the dressers, the brand-new towels on the foot of their beds, and a fresh flower arrangement on each nightstand.

She arranged a bottle of everyone's favorite wine on the counter, with some Prosecco for good measure, as well as a variety of tapas that included little bowls of olives, chocolates, and cashews. She had baked a couple of different types of quiches and went to the specialty cheese shop to get the best variety, along with some yummy crostini. The beautiful serving platter that RaRa sent her for her 50th birthday was perfect for veggies and hummus. While placing the puffy pink peonies in a green, vintage, milk-glass vase, she wondered exactly what YoYo had said to everyone to get them here. It's not an easy feat for her friends to have both the time and ability to get away simultaneously. She thanked the universe for conspiring in their favor.

Heather lived in Atlanta, working as VP of Communications for a huge healthcare system downtown. She liked to joke that she still uses her mouth to do amazing things. She never had kids and takes pride in the fact that she has a happy, open marriage, and that she is now officially considered a cougar. Well, she considers herself to be one, anyway.

Susan was on her way to a successful songwriting and singing career when she met her husband in a club in NYC. They had a son, who was now an officer in the Marines and lived in Italy. She got divorced five years ago after seventeen years of marriage and currently lived in New Jersey. She told her friends that she was just happier not being married. From what they all understood, there were no hard feelings at all with her ex. They were just better off as friends and co-parents to their son. Emma thought she still performs when and where she can, but her career as a commercial real estate broker took up most of her time—as does having drinks and creating shenanigans with the other, younger brokers.

Rachel had built her life in Scottsdale and owned a very successful yoga and reiki wellness studio. She started cheating on her husband with one of the male yoga instructors many years ago and has been divorced for what seems like forever. She didn't have kids but had always wanted them. It just never worked out for them, which she sees as meant to be. "If the universe wanted me to be a mom, she would have made me one," she often says.

Yolanda moved down to Florida to take care of her elderly parents. They moved into a gated community in Miami when they left Greenville after her dad's retirement. Back in the day, YoYo was flying in and out of Miami for modeling gigs all the time, so spending time there more permanently was easy at first. She had a very serious girlfriend for a few years. They had their ups and downs but were considering starting a family with the help of a sperm donor. The relationship ended before they started the process, and Emma has always felt that YoYo regretted it.

As her parents gradually lost their independence and relied more heavily on her, Yoyo's modeling career took a backseat to her role as their caregiver. They adopted her when she was three years old, and she couldn't imagine not being there for them after all they did to give her a great life. After all these years, there was always someone who didn't get how she fit into the family, because she wasn't white. She had learned to not let it bother her too much, and it only rankled her when people assumed she was the nurse or caretaker instead of a concerned and dedicated daughter. Once her parents had both passed away, Emma longed for her friend to move back to Greenville. But she knew YoYo loved the nightlife and the women in Miami, and that she also hoped she could model again someday—even if it was for "Metamucil commercials" or "old lady clothes" she would say in self-deprecating jest.

Whatever YoYo had said to them all to get them here must have been quite the conversation, but one she didn't bother asking. All that mattered was they would all be here for the kiki party in a few hours.

****

Emma floated around her kitchen, simply giddy that her friends were all here, talking over each other and cackling louder and louder with each sip of wine. She had opened the front door because she felt it gave a more welcoming ambiance, and because she loved to hear the crickets as the sun went down, but the sound of those suckers had been drowned out for more than an hour now.

She took one last-minute quiche out of the oven, buzzing from the intoxicating scents of warm, fluffy eggs and perfectly browned crust that playfully intertwined with RaRa's signature sandalwood oil and the wisteria that invited itself to the party through the open window.

She stepped back and fanned herself while taking

in the beauty and energy of her friends. She was optimistic that she could make it through tonight—even with the heavy things she planned to lay on them during their visit.

Like always, everyone congregated in the kitchen at first and conversations had a certain polite nature to start with. They began with complimenting outfits, hair, and even fingernails, and gradually grew into polite questions about jobs, kids, and hobbies. As close as they were, they still needed that time to ease into being together and in person again. High school was a long time ago.

Emma's new décor—without Bobby's crap cluttering everything—looked so light and fresh, and everyone made sure to comment—and compliment—heavily on that. Emma ate it up like it was the one and only filet mignon at a tofu dinner party.

"Girls. Let's go into the living room and get this kiki started. Grab some food and more bottles."

"I got the nuts," Susan exclaimed.

"Of course you do," teased YoYo.

RaRa curled up on the floor because she preferred it, while everyone else circled the table on the light gray sofa and puffy club chairs. Heather propped herself up with comfy throw pillows and gently placed her wineglass on the large, custom-cut wine barrel coffee table Emma had shipped from Napa Valley.

"If anyone spills on Emma's new shit, she'll probably kill you," Heather said only half kidding.

"Oh my gosh. It's fine. Seriously, don't even worry about it, y'all."

"I won't worry about it," YoYo said. "But I pity the fool who does it."

"Stop. I don't care. That's not what this is about. We're here to get real. I mean-REALLY REAL."

"Are y'all ready to do this kiki thing?"

"Hell yeah, we are. But, c'mon. I've been thinking about this. What could we possibly tell each other about ourselves that we all don't already know?" Susan quipped.

"I know for a fact that I have some big things to tell you that y'all don't know yet, but I would rather have a few of you share some icebreakers first. I've never done a kiki before and want to dip my toe first," Emma said, trying not to get emotional, while fat tears threatened to push their way out of her hazel eyes.

YoYo piped up after chewing and swallowing a chunk of smoked gouda. "Girl, there's no wrong way to do it. We can just start sharing stories, dishing about things that bother us or that we're going through. But someone else besides the host can get things rolling."

Heather jumped to her feet in excitement. "I'll start." she exclaimed. She turned her attention to Rachel and, barely able to contain herself, said, "RaRa, tell that story about the orgasm that made you poop."

"Whaaaaaaat?" They all exclaimed in unison. YoYo and Susan fell into each other with laughter, bumping shoulders on the cozy couch.

"Oh my God, Zip. How is that even close to *you* going first?"

"You heard YoYo. I'm getting the ball rolling on this bad Johnny."

"Mmm hmm. I'm really starting to regret ever telling you that story, Heather. If I hadn't had too many Moscow Mules that night, I probably would've been able to take this to the grave."

Susan was tipping her wineglass precariously in one hand as she erupted with amusement that shook her whole body. It was dangerously close to spilling when she pointed her free hand at RaRa and said, "That certainly gives new meaning to the word cum shot."

They all fell over in fits of hilarity again, this time including RaRa.

Once she caught her breath, she exclaimed half-defensively, "Stop. Let me explain…if I must." She shot a squinty-eyed, sideways glance at Heather for opening the *zipper* on her lips that she promised to keep closed.

"So, I was at home—alone for once—and had a kink in my neck. The kids had given me one of those big ol' Wizard Wand personal massager things for Mother's Day, so I decided to take it out and use it on my neck and shoulders. I don't know what came over me, but all the vibration made me move the wand lower and lower over my body, and before I knew it, my yoga pants were kicked off on the floor, and I was in a squatting position, using the wand to, you know, pleasure myself."

"You had a kink all right." Susan said with a wink.

"Do you want to hear the story or not?"

"Sorry, oh great and powerful *wizard*."

"Well, yes. Exactly! Those things are so damn powerful, even on a low setting. I was in my bedroom and felt like I had to bend over in order to take the intense vibration. I was holding myself up by leaning one hand on my dresser while the wand did its magic in the other hand and, BAM. I came so hard; it shot out of my butt like a bullet from a gun. There. Satisfied? Y'all know my secret now."

"Was it a Super Soaker gun, or more like a T-shirt cannon at a ballgame?" Susan asked in between hoots and hollers.

"No. It was just one little rabbit turd," RaRa answered sheepishly.

"I'm sorry, I couldn't hear all of that over all the laughter. Can you tell it again?" YoYo joked.

"That's hilarious, RaRa. And only *you* could make pooping during an orgasm even remotely cute," Emma said. "I'd say this kiki is off to a great start."

"I'd say. Open another bottle—or three." Heather added.

Chapter 4

"I'll go next," blurted Susan. "Since Zipper made RaRa spill the beans about her little bean-sized turd, I'll come clean about a couple things that I've been keeping to myself. I mean, I'm always the first to say that we all know *everything* about each other. So, let me start with the silly stuff first. About a year ago, I got a tattoo on my ass that says, Scratch and Sniff."

"Shut the front door—or in this case—back door, I guess." Heather howled. "We need to see this."

"It's true." Susan snickered. "I probably would've kept it to myself but felt like I should fess up after RaRa got thrown under the fuckin' bus."

She stood up, turned around, and yanked her black leggings down with one hand so everyone could see the round, apple-sized tattoo on her pear-shaped ass. It was artistically drawn to look like the stickers that covered all the kids' notebooks and folders at school in the seventies and eighties. There was a thick, dark border around it, and smack in the middle it said 'Scratch-N-Sniff' in big, purple letters that oddly resembled the font from The Partridge Family logo.

"There you have it," Susan said with a hearty laugh. She pulled her pants back up, and over her butt, reclaimed her spot on the couch, and added, "Do I have any takers?"

While she waited for the howling to subside a little

more, she swirled the deep red wine in her glass and admired its legs. "This wine has legs for days, just like you, Zip," she said. "Okay, that takes care of the silly side. Now for the more serious bit.

"I haven't told y'all this–or anyone, for that matter, mostly out of fear of being judged. Or maybe fear that no one would find me funny. I don't know. But I have been so frustrated and bored from not really performing anymore, so I decided to start taking a beginning improv class. I wanted to challenge myself in new ways but still be seen on stage. I liked it so much that I took a couple of storytelling and stand-up workshops as well. I hate feeling invisible, which seems to be almost inevitable for women as we age."

"That's the truth," Heather chimed in while the rest of them nodded in agreement and continued to recover from the gut-busting laughs they just shared.

She added, "Growing old is depressing. Women really do become invisible at a certain age, while it seems that all of society deems men more interesting as they get older."

"I don't want to become invisible and ignored just because people don't want to see my sunspots and wrinkles or listen to my boring stories about what I had for lunch or my latest doctor's appointment," Emma interjected with a chuckle.

"*Anyway*," Susan continued, "there are some small clubs near me where I started performing standup and singing about once or twice a month. I noticed that I began to feel less emotionally disconnected and hopeless, ya know?" She put her hand up to her lips, as if she could taste the microphone and feel the energy from an adoring crowd.

"It was just what I needed to help heal my heart and feel less invisible. I not only felt seen, sometimes I even felt wanted, which, of course, I loved."

"I read an article in the *New York Times* that said comedy is the new sexy," Emma interjected.

Heather added, "That's true." I bet you get hit on all the time. And not even because you're attractive."

"Thanks a lot," Susan said with a grin, knowing exactly what her friend meant by the statement.

"It just feels amazing to make people laugh. Oh my God, that reminds me of this one guy. He wasn't hitting on me I don't think, and he was probably in his mid-sixties, but after a show I did once at a VFW, I was getting a drink at the bar, and this dude from the audience came up to me and said I was so funny, he laughed his dick off."

Rachel said, "Well, that's a unique, um, compliment. It kind of reminds me of that song by King Missile called 'Detachable Penis.'"

"Ewww. Or maybe a strap-on." said YoYo with a smile.

"Oh my God." Emma sniggered while giving Yolanda and Rachel a faux look of reprimand. "What did you even say to that?"

I said, "Well, I hope the cleaning people find it, and turn it into the front desk. You're probably gonna want that thing back, I imagine. And then *he* said that I was funny offstage too, 'But this is a VFW, honey. There ain't no cleaning people on the payroll.' To which I responded, 'Well, eventually someone will sweep up the place and find it with popcorn and pistachio shells stuck to it.' He hooted loudly, thanked me for the visual, and bought me a drink"

"Now, I'm laughing *my* dick off," Yolanda said with a cackle.

"I love that you're doing that, Sleazin." Good for you for really putting yourself out there." Rachel said. "To be honest, as much as I love teaching yoga and even being desired by some of the students at times, I've been having trouble with my confidence lately."

"Girl, I don't believe that for a second," Yolanda said. She got up to put a few more snacks on her plate before snuggling back into her seat. "You without confidence is like a tropical bird in a cage. It's just shocking and weird and just plain wrong."

"I appreciate that, but it just started happening."

"How can that be? You're surrounded by thirty-year-olds who are dying to get into your hot yoga class and probably your hot yoga pants too."

"That's part of the problem. This is hard to explain." She leaned over to set her wineglass on the table and stayed seated on the floor but straightened her posture, indicating she was getting serious.

"I don't want anyone to know this, because it isn't very "yogi" of me, and it goes against every shred of my beliefs regarding Reiki, crystals, and the ancient practice of yoga into the late stages of life, but I don't want to get old. The style of yoga I do, and some of my other athletic interests are extremely physically demanding, which is why it attracts a younger group of students. I don't ever want to tone down my practice because my body won't let me do what it used to when I was younger."

"I hear that." Susan said.

"You two are talking about completely different reasons for fearing the loss of your abilities and body contortions during sweat sessions," Heather said, holding a dark chocolate bonbon up to her lips, her lipstick still perfect like it was tattooed on.

"Hey! I want to keep my sex life physically demanding too. It's just that I do some hardcore retreats that include hiking, climbing, and hot yoga, and I want to *keep* doing them because they make me happy. I suppose they have been my identity for most of my adult life. I'm at a weird stage where I feel sensual, empowered, and kickass but also insecure at the same time because I'm always the oldest one in the room—and I'm not just taking the class, I'm *teaching* it. I'm less concerned about how getting older will affect my looks, although I have my share of vanity, but losing my physical ability scares the living shit out of me. I feel like I have a shelf life, like I want to do as much as I can *while* I still can."

"Well, you still can, baby." YoYo said earnestly.

The energy in the room palpably shifted from teasing and joking with each other to getting real and deeply empathizing. Emma loved the direction the conversation was heading so naturally.

A door was opened and RaRa decided to walk through it. "I feel like we have been through everything together that a group of friends possibly could—and more. I mean, Labor Day solidified us forever. Don't y'all agree?"

"We share everything, as evidenced by my turd-blasting story. So, why is it that we never, *ever* talk about the big M?"

"Mount Rushmore?" Yolanda teased.

"Mercury In Retrograde Rising?" Heather joined in.

"No," Rachel answered with a wink and a smile.

"Mammograms?" said Emma, wanting to join the fun.

"Yes, to mammograms. But still no." Rachel shook her head with deliberateness emphasized by a pursed-lip smile. Her face lit up and took on the determined look it did in high school whenever the football team was behind, and it was her mission to get everyone to rally as she waved her pom-poms.

"No, girls. *Menopause*. For some odd reason, it's a taboo subject. Yet we all go through it. We're all going through it right now, I'm assuming. And I, personally, feel like I'm going out of my skull. I feel like I can't talk about it with anyone. Obviously, I can't talk to my students. The practitioners I work with are mostly younger and wouldn't understand, and I can't admit to anyone that I'm not only losing sleep but also my hair and my confidence right along with it. I used to love my hair. Now, I wear it up even when I don't need to because I don't want to notice how sad and limp it is."

"Rapunzel, I'm sure you're exaggerating. Your hair was the envy of our whole class. Boys included," Emma said.

"That's why you were voted 'Best and Biggest Hair' in the yearbook senior year, honey," said Susan.

"But I guess that's the point, isn't it? At least partly. So many of these beauty standards wormed their way into us in high school," said Rachel. "And we internalize them without even thinking."

"Yeah," said Heather. "And then we just feel bad about ourselves and don't even know why."

Like an exclamation point on the new topic, a sudden gust of wind burst through the open window, the curtains billowing like sails on a boat. With that, the universe granted them permission, the floodgates opened, and they started spilling all that had been trapped behind the dams in their minds. Each of them eager to speak about what they had been keeping bottled up, what had seemed unspeakable until that moment. The excitement to share their thoughts and feelings about menopause was electric and created an energizing, connective current in the room that was palpable.

They were pinging like cell towers, talking over each other about what they were going through. The night's stillness wafted in, and it seemed they all needed to take a breath at once. As they paused to inhale, they all heard Susan saying, "I think all the hair RaRa lost from her head somehow found its way to take up residence in my butt crack."

The roar of laughter was so loud it could have woken up Boozy Becca next door—even after a bender.

"Stop. I'm serious," Susan said. "I've never had hair in my butt before. What the fuck? I mean, where does that shit come from? And, seriously, I totally get what you mean, Ra, about losing confidence. It's crossing over into other areas of my life, too. I'm starting to doubt myself about everything, and at work, I sometimes feel like I can't do my job. I even had to run into the bathroom and cry. That's not me at all."

RaRa picked up an empty wine bottle and thought about clearing up some of the mess but decided against it. The conversation was getting too good. She didn't want to risk breaking the spell. "Do you just feel overwhelmed or confused for no reason?" she asked Susan.

"Hell yes." I would never admit this to anyone, but I often have bouts of anger, or panic and anxiety that I never had in my life until now."

YoYo jumped in, "I hear ya. I haven't been feeling quite like myself since I turned fifty-three. The brain fog is all too real. And, you know, since my mom had Alzheimer's before she died, I was legit worried I might be losing it. And then there's the hot flashes."

"Oh my God, the hot flashes." Emma said. "The heat comes over you like a flare or a furnace."

"Right? There's no warning. Simply a whoosh and your internal thermostat is set at Heat Miser status. Especially when I'm trying to sleep."

"Fuck. The night sweats. I wake up and my skin looks slick and shiny like a glazed donut. And then I can't sleep, and I'm craving glazed donuts," Susan quipped.

"How about the back fat I never had before?" Heather said. "Back fuckin' fat! Or the fluffy weight gain in my stomach that I like to call my "running buddy." My little running buddy goes everywhere with me these days. The extra weight is like I'm hauling around a toddler, and I gotta pee all the damn time," she said with explosive chuckle.

"Sometimes my pee smells like roast beef," Susan said. "Should I be worried?"

"Jesus, girl," Yolanda bust in as she held her hand up to heaven and closed her eyes. "Gravy included?" A loud hoot escaped, and she opened her eyes, directing a look in Susan's direction of mock serious curiosity.

"I'm pretty sure that has nothing to do with menopause, but I could be wrong, and it's kind of hilarious," said Heather.

"It might," said Rachel. "My pits smell like fish sticks most of the time, and they didn't used to when I was younger, but I'm not worried. Maybe yours is from too much sex."

"I wish." exclaimed Susan. "I haven't been having it as much as I would like. I'm too dry. It feels like it did when I lost my virginity. I don't know why the hell Madonna was so into feeling like a virgin, because there's nothing fun about having it feel like the first time *every* time. That shit hurts."

"That sucks," Rachel said, "I'm actually more like the Bon Jovi Album, *Slippery And Wet.* All the damn time."

Susan gave her a sideways look and said, "That's *Slippery* When *Wet,* ya goofball, and thanks for rubbing it in. With the Sahara Desert I have going on down there, I'm far from wet these days, let alone slippery."

"I wish I wasn't, sometimes," answered Rachel. "That has been part of my problem. You may think I'm rubbing it in, but I always need to rub one out, if ya know what I mean. I'm worried that now that I'm fifty-three, my brain and my body aren't playing on the same team. They have become serious rivals, and I preach bliss and harmony for a living. My brain's not exactly a peaceful place to be."

"Seriously. It's like all the symptoms are battling for center stage," said Emma. "I'm hot and cold, and my body feels like I'm dragging it through mud most of the day. And you know what? I had always thought I would be so happy not to get my period anymore. But no one tells you that menopause is worse."

"True," Susan said with a wink. "It took me years to learn how to ride the dragon and now we have to start over with a whole new one to contend with."

"Only this new dragon has the technology. It's a Terminator dragon," Heather shouted over her shoulder on the way to the bathroom.

Emma set down her wineglass on the brass side table and wrinkled her brow. "They say this is all caused by hormone surges, but I feel like it's a hormonal revolution. There's a battle being fought and all we can do is suffer while the war wages until no one is left."

"I can picture the little buggers scurrying about with tiny cannons, guns, grenades and air bombs," YoYo said as she topped off everyone's wine, finishing the three open bottles. "Do the hormones run amuck at the end like they know they're on the way out? A final panicked hurrah as they retreat into the abyss, never to be seen again?"

Heather came back from the bathroom and jumped right back into the conversation as if she never left. "Yeah, and all this is happening while we're trying to function daily. You know, trying to appear normal in the grocery store, or a big work presentation when you really want to hide in a corner and cry, or tear someone's head off for looking at you funny."

"You aren't kidding," Susan said. "Testosterone is running the show now."

Emma nodded. "And with the withdrawal—or retreat—of things like estrogen and progesterone—something no one tells you—is that you can become less nurturing. I don't know about y'all, but I for one have been feeling that way. I'm so glad we're having this talk because I could never say these things out loud to *anyone* but the four of you.

"I have come to realize that I've lived most of my life solely to satisfy others and I've always put all my efforts into other people's feelings. Lately, I have felt so strongly about wanting to live a life that is satisfying *for* me, and that means something important *to* me. Think about all the women who just up and leave their homes without explanation to go find themselves. Or leave a twenty-year marriage after the kids move out. People judge those women harshly, but I have begun to understand it to a certain degree."

"Some get divorced and end up marrying a woman," YoYo said with a megawatt smile and another wink.

"Exactly." Emma said while tucking her hair behind her ears and moving to the edge of her seat. "When I first started going through the ups and downs of this craziness, at first it made me question what love even is."

"Isn't that a song by Foreigner?" Heather asked with a toothy smile and raised eyebrows.

"Zipper, I'm serious. I think about it all the time, especially because of the hormone changes. What is love and what's all of this about?"

A distant look that combined sadness and fondness flashed across Heather's face. She sprouted a little grin, took a sip of wine, and said, "When I was little, for Christmas one year I got one of those blow-up clowns that popped back up after you punched it. I had begged for that thing, circled it in the Sears Catalog, and left notes all over the house for my parents, "hinting" that I wanted one. My mom hated clowns, but they got it for me, anyway. She probably wanted to pretend it was my dad so she could punch it when no one else was around—after a few whiskey sours.

"Anyway, I loved that thing. It looked so shiny, fun, and jovial. You could punch it repeatedly, and it would still bounce back, smiling every time. Then I noticed a dried-up pine needle on the carpet that had fallen off the Christmas tree along with some stringy icicle tinsel. That shit got everywhere, but this pine needle caught my eye—a deep yellow and brown that clashed with our mauve carpeting. It was thick and sharp, like a big toenail clipping. You would have thought nothing in the world could have torn my attention away from the new, bouncy clown. But, for whatever reason, I picked up the pine needle and turned it over a few times on the palm of my hand before taking it to the clown's face and tracing the outline of its smile. Which promptly poked a hole in it. I shrunk back in dismay as I watched my new toy shrivel and die before my eyes.

"I think that's what love is. I think that's what aging is. I think that's what it feels like to grow old and lose love because out of nowhere you wither away, and nobody plays with you anymore."

"Damn, Zip, that's actually pretty deep. And kinda sad," YoYo said.

"Getting old is sad. Love is sad."

"It doesn't have to be. Or at least I try to tell myself that," RaRa interjected.

"I think love and aging are like letting frogs go," said Emma.

Susan tilted her head and said, "Oh, like you have to kiss a lot of frogs before you can find a prince?"

"No."

Emma shifted in her seat, paused for a deep breath,

and said, "Y'all remember how much I loved catching tadpoles and trying to get them to grow into frogs?" she asked rhetorically.

"Or when we would crouch next to the window wells of RaRa's basement and dig through the leaves and muck until we uncovered toads and frogs? I was always so happy and thrilled to have caught one, and I literally never wanted to let them go.

"Y'all would put them right back where you found them the second they peed on your hands, but I would take the frog home, find a special shoe box, poke holes in the lid, and fill it with sticks, leaves, grass, and whatever else I thought the frog would need so that I could keep him forever and he would be happy living out his days with me.

"When my parents saw the shoebox with the lid that looked like a maniac stabbed it to death with a fork—which she did—they always made me let it go. Each time I tried to keep a frog, quite convinced it would love being my new roommate, they went through the same laundry list of why it needed to live outside instead of in a shoebox in my room. 'Where would it get its food? It will miss its family. How will it go to the bathroom? It needs more space to jump and be free. It won't be happy. It must be let go or it will die', they always said.

"That's when *I* would respond by going through the same cycle of emotions every single time—denial, sadness, anger, and understanding.

"In my head, I answered them, *I will find it food. I will take it out of its box twice a day so it can go play and go potty and be free. I would never kill it*. In my mind I thought, *Who do my parents think they are, Dr.*

Fucking Dolittle? I'm keeping the frog.

"As I cupped him tightly in both hands, my tears welled up and then rained down on the amphibian's little head, causing him to blink both his eyes at once. If he peed on me, I wouldn't have known the difference between that and the flood from my eyes. It was like loving someone as an adult where no matter what you gave to that person, it wasn't enough to sustain the life of the relationship.

"To be left with just a shoebox with a bent up, perforated lid—and with painstaking attention to the detail of a frog's needs for survival—with green blades of grass torn up at the roots, crunchy fall leaves and rich dark soil but no frog was heart-wrenching. I can practically smell the rich, outdoorsy scent of the makeshift frog habitat just thinking about it. There is such hope, potential, and good-hearted intentions wrapped up in this childhood idea of what it takes to love and care for another living being. To me, this is the epitome of love and innocence.

"The attachment I felt to those frogs was inexplicably intense. In my head, I understood why I had to let them go, but it hurt my heart so much and so deeply. So I took my new friend outside to a nice, safe area around the bushes or the window wells, removed the lid of the box to hold him and say goodbye. I'd sit there, fat tears making salty streaks through the dirt on my cheeks. I hated the pain and vowed to never try to keep another frog ever again. Until the next time. Love is like letting frogs go, because what's right for you and makes you happy isn't what's right for them. It's like you feel deep emotion for something and you think you know what it needs to be healthy and happy. You think it should be enough to just love it, but when it belongs somewhere else, your love isn't enough to sustain its life and you gotta let it go. It hurts with a pain that sears your gut and shreds your heart. But the joy in finding a new frog starts the process all over again."

The friends were quiet, moved by the story and Emma's vulnerability.

"It's like menopause too," Emma continued, because aging isn't easy to understand. I think we want to hold onto our youth as tightly as we can. Like my little frog buddies. But to be truly happy, and accept life, we must let go."

"I think we're drunk," Yolanda joked.

Emma continued, "This is why I started to look at failed marriages and lost love and began to wonder, how many marriages have failed due to hormones? And how many couples would even consider that as a reason?"

"Most just think they grew apart. Weren't getting along. Lost connection," Heather said.

"Yeah," said Susan, "or that the woman is a bitch because she didn't want sex anymore."

Rachel added, "Ya know? It would be very interesting to know exactly how many of these scenarios could be attributed to menopausal symptoms."

"Like a study?" Emma asked.

"Well, yeah. That would make a pretty cool anthropological or sociological study, right? I always get those two confused," RaRa said as she took down and redid her high ponytail.

This is the perfect segue. Emma thought. *It's like I gave Rachel a script or something. It's now or never to ask them about it.*

"What if I told you *we* could all be part of a very important study that has to do with aging, and that could possibly take us out of menopause?" Emma said as she jumped to her feet in excitement.

"What kind of study?" they all asked in unison. It didn't take long for them to be back in sync. The decades and distance just faded away.

"Well, it's not really an official study, but it would be administered and monitored by a real M.D. who is also Board Certified in Anti-Aging and Regenerative Medicine by the American Board of Anti-Aging Medicine. I think he's licensed in six other states, aside from South Carolina," Emma said. She stood up straight, like she was giving her friends her best elevator pitch. She wasn't sure they would all go for this idea, but she had been hoping and praying they would.

"Oh, you're serious about this?" Heather asked.

"I'm curious," Susan added. "What exactly would be administered and monitored? That sounds like a whole other level. I'm intrigued."

"Me too!" Exclaimed Rachel with her usual boisterous enthusiasm. "But first, who the hell is this doctor, and where did you meet him?"

"So many questions." Emma said with a soft smile. "I'm relieved y'all at least want to hear me out. This is one of the two big reasons I wanted to have you here this weekend. I have some big news, as well as this huge, I guess we can call it, proposition."

Susan put her wineglass in the air and said, "Here's to getting propositioned." She brought the glass down, stuck her nose in as far as it would go, and inhaled deeply. With a level of enthusiasm that teetered between hilarious and perverse, she exclaimed, “Damn, this wine smells so good. I could fuck it.” And then she sneezed the wine out all over herself, and they all howled like lunatics, Susan included. It took them a while to calm down.

“So, who is this guy, what does he want, and how much is it going to cost?” Heather said with an arched, perfectly coiffed eyebrow once she had regained the power of speech-barely acknowledging her friend’s propensity to wine porn.

“His name is Walter. Well, Dr. Walter Wallace. He came into the shop a few times to buy accessories, mostly candles and stuff, and we got to talkin’. At first, I wasn’t sure about him, because, well, his handshake felt a little bit like a half-limp penis.” She giggled.

“Ma. As I live and breathe,” Heather said with feigned indignation as she clutched imaginary pearls with one hand and fanned herself with the other.

YoYo leaned into her, and belly laughed.

“Ha. Ha. Yes, Ma said ‘penis.’ Can I continue?” Emma offered a little wink. “He would stop in every week or so to browse and chat, and eventually he hired me to do some design work in his home. That’s when I really got to know him. He’s brilliant. Absolutely brilliant. He’s got more than twenty years of medical experience in a hospital setting but opened his own clinic here in Greenville about six years ago.”

“What kind of clinic is it? Like a med spa?” Rachel asked.

“Yeah, it’s like a med spa on steroids, and one that he takes on the road as well. He has specialty training in bio-identical hormone replacement therapy as well as aesthetic treatments with laser. And other science-based treatments. He is all about treating the inside and the outside of the body. He even studied in Saibaba Colony in India at one of the top Naturopathy and Medical Cosmetology Clinics."

"Have you been to his clinic yet?" asked Susan. "We will probably need to sign our lives away, promising not to sue him if anything terrible happens and we all turn into sex-crazed zombies."

"Nothing will go wrong," Emma answered. "It's a natural, herbal concoction. And, besides, y'all are already a bunch of sex-crazed maniacs or zombies."

"I want to try it," Heather said. "Maybe he knows something my arsenal of doctors doesn't know."

"Well, that's kinda what I'm getting at," Emma said with a bright smile. "I have gone to see him for Botox and a little filler. Oh, and micro needling."

"I noticed your youthful glow the minute we got here, girl." YoYo quipped. "I've never tried microneedling or filler."

"Well, we all aren't as lucky as you with your perfect skin, YoYo," Rachel said with a smile.

Heather leaned over Yolanda's lap and waved a manicured finger playfully in the air. "Oh, look who's talking, Rachel. You use wild, raw honey and kelp masks on your face, never had Botox, and you still look like Reese Witherspoon."

"Oh, I love Reese Witherspoon," Emma said, although she feared they were getting a bit off-topic. She didn't want to lose them before she had a chance to pop the question at hand.

YoYo chimed in, "Reese Witherspoon or Without Her Spoon—she can eat ice-cream off my body anytime." Hoots and hollers immediately erupted. Emma missed this so much. She sat and watched her friends crack up, and quickly pushed out of her mind the thought of having to tell them her second piece of news. She was just going to enjoy this moment. All of them together again in one place, enjoying each other with pure uninhibited joy. Yep, she would cherish it even if they said no to being Guinea Pigs for Dr. Wallace.

"So, other than Rachel, think about all the things we do to ourselves to preserve, prevent, protect and *patch.*" Emma said while trying to redirect the conversation in the right direction, although with this bunch, it might take GPS to do so. "You can only apply so many patches to an old pair of jeans before the original piece of clothing is gone and has been basically replaced by the patches."

"I don't know what you're talking about. Forget patches, girl. These days I'm using sandblasting and stucco," Heather joked.

Susan nodded enthusiastically and said, "Me too. And it's all so expensive. Every time I go in for one thing, whether it's a facial, Botox, filler, whatever, three or four *more* things are casually suggested to me that I should do, and that innocent suggestion becomes a worm that wiggles into my brain and takes up residence there until I make the next damn appointment. It all adds up, and it never ends."

"How 'bout that silk pillowcase you said you were gonna buy? It was supposed to decrease your sleep wrinkles or something?" Heather asked.

"Fuck that thing. It was called the Face First Forever Beauty Pillow. It had some special shape to cradle my face, cost almost three hundred dollars, and I couldn't fall asleep on it to save my life," Susan said, shaking her head.

"So much for beauty sleep, I guess." Rachel teased.

"It's crazy what we put ourselves through," Emma said. "That stuff is painful, time-consuming and costs more than my mortgage. They do say that beauty is pain, but remember that horrible MRSA infection I got from that laser procedure? It's not supposed to hurt that much."

"Ouch," Heather said. "I remember the pics you sent of that catastrophe. It made that burn I got from a peel look like nothing but a bit too much sun. I love my Botox, though. I wouldn't give that up for anything. Without it, the lines between my eyebrows would be as deep as coin slots. If I don't get rid of those things, someone would mistake my forehead for a fucking parking meter and try to jam quarters into it."

Susan added, "I'm with ya. There's no way I'm giving up my lash extensions, peels, and cleanses. I might cancel my mini lift for now, but I'm still doing the skintight procedures on my brow bone."

"And the ship has sailed on both of our boob jobs. We can't give that up either. Too late," Heather said with a little elbow nudge thrown in Susan's direction. "Besides, getting these Gummy Bears was money well spent." Heather pushed her boobs up and down. "I love them. And like Dolly Parton says, people always ask me if they're mine. Yes, they are—all bought and paid for."

"Wait, where did that idea come from? I never said anything about giving anything up. I haven't even asked y'all the big question I have yet." Emma's face flushed from the wine or the excitement, she wasn't sure which. Or hot flash. Probably all three.

"Let the woman speak, goofballs. We don't even know where she's going with all this build-up yet," YoYo said.

"You girls know I'm all for doing all the things a woman wants to do to themselves to feel good, beautiful, and vital. For me, these things are important and not anyone else, but I don't judge any woman for doing whatever she wants and for whatever reason. I think there is a certain power to be had in it, especially when it's just for you. I guess the point is, we all have our own reasons for wanting to look our best and remain youthful, and none of those reasons are wrong. Just like there's nothing wrong with embracing the aging process, if that's what you choose to do. Both choices are quite personal and should be empowering as well. What I wanted to know is, would y'all please join me in testing an experimental anti-aging drug that was specially designed and created by Dr. Wallace?"

"A drug? What kind of drug are we talking here?" Heather asked curiously.

"Well, it's not a drug, exactly. I don't have a better word for it, but it's a proprietary blend he has concocted and put into a capsule. He gave me a list of some of the ingredients, and they are all pretty much plant-based. Exotic stuff that I had to look up. I guess it's more of an elixir of sorts."

"What does he want us to do? Be lab rats for a vitamin pill?" Susan asked a bit snidely.

"Well, you won't believe this, but he heads up a luxury Scandinavian Wellness Cruise. And when he approached me, he wanted me to do it on the ship, in a contained environment with plenty of medical support and equipment in case something would go wrong." Emma gnawed on her bottom lip.

"Fuck no." Susan exclaimed.

"No cruises. I hope you told him that," said Heather.

"Girls, chill. Of *course,* absolutely *no* cruises. I explained the whole thing to him, and he understood. He said we could pick another location, but he wants us to stay there for a week to ten days, so he can monitor us for safety reasons."

"I want to see the ingredients list, even if it isn't the full list," Rachel says.

"I'll show you the list he sent me. I have it on my phone. It's an all-natural plant and herb concoction. I think the worst that could happen is that *nothing* will happen, other than a slight case of heartburn or something," Emma said with a wink.

Rachel tilted her head to the side and looked deep in thought before saying, "I don't know, y'all. I have my share of vanity like anyone else, but don't you think there's also great power and strength in not putting so much importance on outer beauty and feeling like we must fight against the natural way we age as women? You might think I'm nuts, but when I see an older woman with long hair, deep lines that show a map of the joys and sorrows of a well-lived life, and a warm smile that radiates her intelligence and experiences, I think there is nothing more beautiful. I respect and admire it. This is going to sound weird, but I have always loved the look of large, bony knuckles on an older woman. To me, they are the epitome of artistic creativity and the expression of what those hands have made and accomplished over the course of a lifetime. Like experience, sophistication, and art incarnate. I love big silver rings that speak a lifetime of creating that could only be expressed in overly pronounced bones under parchment skin. Creating life. Art. Creating experiences. It's like a beautiful old mahogany tree with large, gnarled roots and a profusion of burls that tell stories in a way that a delicate, young sapling could never convey."

"Woah. That's deep and beautiful," YoYo said after a moment of complete silence in the once buzzing room. "I'm so on board with this. Honestly, young women are gorgeous, of course, but I find older women incredibly sexy. There is something so appealing about life experience and I'm intrigued by the mental stimulation that I don't always get with women who are much younger than me. I find older people sexy. I've traced stretch marks with my finger and felt fuller hips ride on top of me as I pulled and pushed them away. Laugh lines are a turn on too. The act of biting into a shoulder while feeling the weight of soft breasts that have nurtured children against your own is incredibly hot to me."

YoYo's passion bubbled and spilled like celebratory champagne. She continued, "I feel like I can see both sides of the coin, as well as beauty in *all* women. As a model, I love and appreciate beautifully done makeup. But there's no match for the pure exquisiteness of a woman who steps out of the shower, sun-kissed and fresh-faced after a long, active day at the beach. She has a raw, ethereal glow that shines from inside, and carries it confidently while the perfect, smokey hues of twilight swirl around her like silk.

"Her beauty in that sweet spot of summer is as magical and intriguing as a lightning bug's warm, golden beauty-dancing upon a soft breeze that is scented with nature's perfume. I don't care how old a woman is. There is *nothing* more gorgeous than that."

"Yeah, yeah. That sounds lovely. Really beautiful. But it's also some happy horseshit. No offense," Heather said matter-of-factly. "Let's face it. Women can't win no matter what approach they take. If we do too much to ourselves, we're criticized; and if we do too little, we get shit for that too."

"I like the fact that what matters in life is love, experiences, travel, nature, art, and music. But I also like the idea of being pioneers in the advancement of women's empowerment on their own terms. If we want to look young and feel young too-for *ourselves*, that's pretty badass," Susan said.

Emma stood up and handed her phone to Rachel to see the list of ingredients and said, "I agree with you, Rachel. I really do. But Dr. Wallace said the drug wouldn't just make you *look* at least ten years younger—it would make you physically *feel* ten years younger, too."

Rachel took the phone and studied the ingredients.

Helichrysum or "Immortale" yellow blooming plant

Aguaje–a miracle fruit of the Amazon

Ashitaba–Japanese plant

Propolis Extract from bees in New Zealand

Eucalyptus Dives

Frankincense

Myrrh

Sandalwood

Olive Oil

Moringa Oil (From "The Miracle Tree")

Nicotinamide riboside (alternative form of vitamin B3)

Proprietary ingredients

Rachel passed the phone to Yolanda and said, "These look amazing. Although I do wonder what the "proprietary ingredients" are all about. I also can't deny that having the opportunity to *feel* like my younger self again would be so worth a try."

While studying the list, Yolanda responded, "I know that the ancient Greeks and Romans used rosemary as a medicinal herb. *Someone* had to be the first to try it back in 500 B.C.

"And what about the first person to try milk? That has always boggled my mind. Who the fuck was the very first person to go up to a cow, squeeze its tete, and drink the white stuff that came out of it? Someone had to be the first to do that shit too. Hell, someone had to be the first to do everything anyone's ever done, good or bad."

The phone got passed around as they feverishly conducted online searches.

Susan read out loud from her phone, "It says the Immortale plant is believed to hold the secret to eternal youth and that the flower never fades, even after it's picked. That's what I thought about losing my virginity," she said with a devilish grin. "But we all know how *that* turned out. Once I was deflowered, the bloom eventually wilted and faded. Wait, that's actually sad. Why am I laughing? Okay, girl. So, we only have to pick a place to test it for ten days and that's it?"

Emma explained they needed to take one capsule

every day for ten days under observation by Dr. Wallace in a place of their choice. If there are no adverse reactions during that time, they would continue taking the capsule every day for at least six months and commit to doing an email questionnaire once a week and Zoom meetings once a month to report changes in how they looked and felt. The energy in the room buzzed once more, and heat came over the women that, for once, wasn't due to hot flashes.

The strength of their bond, growing stronger by the minute, was palpable. "I need some adventure in my life, girls," Emma said. "I feel like I've been living for everyone else but only existing for myself. People do the same old boring shit every day and then they die. I refuse to be that person. We've done way crazier things than this and been through much worse together. So, please, do this with me. I want to feel like I sucked helium deep into my lungs and my heart screamed out, '"Follow the yellow brick road.'"

"Hell, my bucket list has become more of a fuck-it list these days. I'm in," Heather said.

"If we do it in a desert setting and the doctor monitors us closely there, I'm in too," Rachel said enthusiastically.

Yolanda clapped her hands in excitement. "I'm into the untamed wildness of the desert. The vast openness has a special appeal—unless that huge vortex and extra dry climate is gonna remind Susan too much of her kitty and piss her off." She teased as she got up and hugged Susan. "I'm in."

Susan hugged her back and said, "Fuck all, y'all. I'm in too."

It was agreed upon. They would take paid time off

and sick days, find an Airbnb in Taos, New Mexico, and test the magical elixir.

Heather looked at Emma and asked, "So, nothing has to change or be given up? My tits can stay intact?"

Emma was beside herself with happiness that her friends agreed to this incredible proposal. "Yes. Tits intact. In fact, since we don't have a name for it, why don't we call the experimental elixir TITS–which stands for Tits InTact Serum."

Susan said, "I like it. We're gonna be the guinea pigs that try it and see what happens—for the good of all women. Kinda like Tang was for the astronauts."

"Oh, my God. That crazy orange powder was so absurd, no one in their right mind would replace their fresh, real orange juice with it until the astronauts took it into space with them," Heather joked. "Next thing you knew, every mom was proudly serving Tang to their families, like each jar had been plucked straight from a grove of Tang trees."

"One small sip for woman, one giant gulp for womankind, "Yolanda chimed in. "So, this is like Tang In Training Serum, which is also TITS, by the way. Or how 'bout Twats In Training, since that's what most people would think we are, for being the test subject for some doctor we don't know."

Susan put her glass down on the coffee table and stood up, excited. "Tits, Twats, or Tang, we're testing it and this adventure is gonna be TITS."

Chapter 5

With the windows still open from the night before, the five of them woke, with minor headaches, to the sound of Boozy Becca yelling at Chablis, "Take a poop already."

As they passed the jam to smear on homemade scones and drank pots of coffee, they talked about the crazy decision they made the night before. "I still can't believe we're doing this, y'all," Rachel said. "You ladies know that normal rules don't apply in the desert, let alone when we're a bunch of test subjects for an experimental drug."

"*I* can't believe how loud Ma's neighbor is. Shit. And I'm always up for immersing myself in a place where normal rules don't apply. Plus, the desert is the exact opposite of being on a boat. That's all that matters to me," Susan said with her mouth full of blueberry scone.

"I searched Dr. Walter Wallace again last night before I crashed out, and I gotta say, even though he looks like the guy in Toy Story who stole Woody from the garage sale, his credentials are impeccable. I'm only slightly worried about the *proprietary* ingredients. But not enough to bail out. I mean, this *is* Operation TITS, right?"

"I'm not worried at all about the TITS testing or the ingredients. Not gonna lie, I'd drink my own pee if there was a guarantee it would turn back the clock," Heather said.

"I guess it can't be any worse than drinking wheatgrass juice," RaRa agreed. "That shit is horrible. I would rather gnaw on someone's actual lawn than drink and then belch up that stuff."

"Isn't that sacrilegious of you to say, Ms. Yogi Master?" joked Heather.

"Oh, who are we kidding? Forget about pee and wheatgrass—we'd all bathe in dog shit if it was scientifically proven to lift, smooth, and sculpt the skin. None of y'all better dare to deny it," Heather said while freshening up everyone's coffee. "And now that you mention the skeevy guy from that cartoon with the little goatee, that reminds me. Does it bother anyone else that the porn stache has come back into style, and why do all the young guys think it's cool to sport it these days? It wasn't cute the first time around, isn't cute now, and has become quite the pet peeve of mine."

Rachel put her hand over her cup, indicating she didn't need a refill while simultaneously giggling at Heather's observation.

"Girl, do you want some green tea or something instead of coffee?" Emma offered. "I should have asked you before. That's my bad. I'm still on a cloud from last night. Having y'all here and embarking on this TITS testing adventure has my head on a spin cycle or something."

"Oh, I would *love* some tea, Ma. Thank you." She looked at Heather and said, "I don't think I remember what the cartoon dude looks like, but I know exactly what you mean about the young guys and their stupid little seventies mustaches. I can't say I'm not nervous about this whole adventure, but *I am* in love with the TITS title for it."

Emma immediately buzzed around the kitchen. She practically floated to her pantry to dig out a variety of teas and some raw honey for Rachel before she put the kettle on the stove.

Rachel looked around at each of her friends with a palpable fondness. They all stopped talking and looked up as if they truly *felt* her need to say something.

"I am so excited about this, girls. I really am. I just can't help but feel a little guilty about it, though."

"Guilty? Of all the things I feel right now—like excited and nervous—guilt hasn't even made my radar," Heather said.

"I know, it might be weird," Rachel continued as she pulled her hair back from her face and wrapped it into a messy bun with a scrunchy from her wrist.

"Uh oh, putting her hair up. She means business," Susan said with a throaty voice.

"It's not that I'm against this thing, or that I don't want to do it. Because I do. It's just that I can't help but feel slightly guilty because it's like we're advocating for ageism against women, don't you think? I mean, it's not exactly feminist, is it?"

Heather cleared her throat with purpose. "I'm going to answer for everyone, because I'm Zipper, and that's what I do. I really don't think that's the case."

"I just worry that if we take part in this study, or experiment, or whatever, it's like we're judging or looking down on women who choose to age naturally and don't fight the process."

Emma took the squealing teakettle off the stove and arranged the teas, honey, and a tea towel with a matching cup and saucer on an ornate tray that most certainly would be acceptably served to the Queen of England. Then the silliest thought popped into her head—*Did Camilla drink chamomile tea on the Chamomile Lawn?*

She set the tray down gently in front of her friend and, with a warm smile and a nod in Heather's direction, said, "I can't speak for everyone, like Zip, but I don't feel that way at all about this. I don't judge *anyone* who chooses to do things to themselves that fight the signs of aging, and I *most definitely* don't judge anyone who chooses to take a more natural approach to it."

"I agree," Susan added. "And frankly, I'm glad we're not only getting real about this shit, but we're taking actual steps to make ourselves truly happy. It's like people are afraid to address the real thoughts, feelings, and motivations that women experience. RaRa. I get you. I know you want to take shit beyond skin deep, so to speak, which is admirable. But it's honestly not that deep for me. It's my life, my decision. No guilt."

"I woke up this morning second-guessing my decision to do this and wondering if I jumped into being a test subject just a little too quickly. I know I'm not quite as impetuous as y'all, but I love you. Thanks for getting me," Rachel said, somewhat despondently. "I don't think I could do this thing if I couldn't hash out all my feelings about it."

"One hundred percent, girl," Heather said as she got up and went over to hug Rachel. "It's understandable to have doubts. Hell, I'm sure we all have a little fear inside our hearts about this. For me, that's what makes it so enticing and exciting. But, if you change your mind, no one here will blame you or have hard feelings toward you about it. And I'm with Susan on this one. I don't look at this as a judgement of what anyone else does or doesn't do. For me, it's about having one life to live, and doing what's right for me, personally, to make it amazing before it's too late. I want my life to be the best and brightest before it's lights out, and that has nothing to do with what anyone else wants to do with their own lives. I don't want to change who I am or my entire look, necessarily. I just want to experience as much as I possibly can—and as many hot men as I can—while I'm here," she said with a wink.

"Speaking of men and experience," Rachel replied, "how much of this crap do you think they worry about? I don't think they experience *half* the pressure we do as women to stop the aging process—which is not only impossible—but also a natural occurrence for any and every living being."

"Right?" asked Yolanda, as a blob of fresh strawberry jam dripped from her lips.

Emma chuckled to herself as she reflected on the last few years with her ex-husband. To the group, she said, "I think it's crap. We get barraged with ads on our social media feeds, emails, TVs, and magazines for Botox, anti-aging serums, creams, and weight loss programs. I don't know if men get those same ads, but if they do, they probably scroll right past them with their confidence and self-worth completely unscathed."

She paused and took a deep breath. "Sorry, y'all. This is all too fresh for me, but I'm glad we're talking about it."

"I am too," Susan said, wrapping an arm around Emma's neck. "I'm going to live the best life I can because I only get one. If I want to look and *feel* younger, that's okay. Men don't have to worry about it because society says they look 'distinguished' when they age. But fuck that. Society can eat a bag of dicks."

"Oh, yummy. A bag of dicks. Just what I want to think about while I'm eating," YoYo joked.

A howl erupted in the kitchen that sounded like music to Emma's ears. It was like they were all home again in this warm place, united on a quest. Each of them secure with their place in the world, together.

Buttery sunbeams poured into the room through the open window, saturating them in the morning light. It bounced off their hair and made the lines in the corners of their sleepy eyes look extra warm and ethereal. Emma looked around the table at her friends, trying to decide the best time to deliver her sad news. She knew it wouldn't be easy to do but was nonetheless quite surprised by just *how* difficult it was to bring to her lips. To break the mood. To be that serious. To introduce the uninvited guest to the party. Endearingly, she looked at them one at a time, catching glimpses across the table or over the rims of coffee-stained mugs, and she could still quite plainly see the silly, wild, and rebellious teens that each of them used to be—peeking out at her from behind heavy eyelids and chunky readers.

Emma pushed Susan playfully in the ribs in agreement with her latest sentiment. "Girl, who cares what anyone—especially men—think about what we do. We're doing this for *ourselves* and *all womankind*, past, present, and future. Like you said—no guilt is necessary. The thing that *I* can't help but wonder about is what our mothers went through back in the day."

"Holy crap. That's a good point. I was always so wrapped up in *me* at that time, I never even considered what my mom might have been going through," Rachel said while stirring the honey in her teacup. "Honestly, I never even thought about menopause or the fact that my mom might be in it. Teenagers are so selfish, so self-absorbed. I barely remember what she was even like at that time in my life—at least not on a day-to-day basis, ya know?"

"Damn," said Susan with a faraway look in her eyes, "that's so true. I remember certain events, and of course, some holidays. Oh, and a few family vacations spring to mind where I can picture my mother and remember how she acted. But mostly I just remember being annoyed by her twenty-four seven, and that she seemed to yell at me for just about everything I did."

"That's exactly what I mean," Emma continued. "Now that I'm entrenched in this menopausal mania myself, I try to think back to when my mom would have been going through the change herself. She's so old-school, she still won't talk about it with me—even now. At that time, though, since I was the center of my own universe like all teenagers are, I thought her cranky times or moodiness were a result of my continuous, unwanted shenanigans. I also worried for a very long time that she silently blamed me for Rick and everything that happened."

"Your mom would never blame you for that, Ma," Yolanda said, and everyone else immediately nodded in agreement. Rachel placed her hand over Emma's. It felt unusually hot from her cup of tea. "Now that we're in it ourselves, we know what she was probably going through, and that it had nothing to do with us. And what happened to Rick had nothing to do with us, either. Except that it brought us all even closer together."

Emma tried to fight back giant droplets of tears until they finally won the battle and rolled rapidly down her cheeks. She swiped at them and shook her head as if she was physically telling the tears, "Nope. Not today." She shook the image of Labor Day out of her mind. "Well," —she sniffled— "if *we* think no one talks about the big M *now*, imagine what it was like for our mothers back in the 80s?"

"Like Susan, I can only remember certain holidays and celebrations, and I have no idea what my mom really felt when I was young," Heather said. To lighten the mood and lift Emma's spirits, she decided to tell a story from her sister's sixth birthday party, which suddenly seemed a terribly long time ago. "Here's a memory for the record books that I have from back in the day, when my sister Nancy turned six and my whole family was crammed around the dining room table to sing Happy Birthday to her.

"So, you know, all the usual adults were there. Aunts, uncles, cousins, and grandparents. My mom made this grand entrance into the room with my sister's cake. She held the cake up in front of her like Simba's presentation ceremony in the *Lion King*, or something. The candles were all burning brightly, and Nancy was super excited. So, my mom set the cake down in front of Nancy on the fancy plastic floral tablecloth that was, of course, littered with open Lite Beer cans, and a round, brown ashtray that looked like it was made from old beer bottles. The thing was overflowing with cigarette butts."

"Hilarious." Susan deadpanned. "I'm pretty sure those ashtrays came with every home in the seventies, and what children's party was complete without them?"

"Exactly." Heather almost spit out her coffee when a wave of laughter escaped her lips. "Anyway, we all finished singing to Nancy, who was sitting next to our grandpa, who was telling one of his loud, elaborate stories even as she blew out her candles. He didn't care that he was talking over the big moment—the whole reason everyone was even gathered around the table in the first place. Nancy had to lean her chin over the giant ashtray to reach the cake, and in doing so, she got way too close to the flames, and her hair caught on fire."

Heather acted out the scene by leaning over the platter of crumbs and picked-over scones, and purposely dipped the tip of her long ponytail into Susan's coffee cup.

"Stop it. You're killing me," Susan squealed as she held her stomach in mock pain. "Why don't I remember this story? What happened to Nancy's hair?"

"Well, my grandpa, in true form, didn't miss a beat with the story he was telling, even though his granddaughter's head was literally ablaze. He just banged her in the head with his hand to put out the fire as he continued his conversation without pausing to take a breath."

Emma and the girls exploded in glee, and tears were shed by all of them, this time from the sheer hilariousness of the picture they held in their minds of Zipper's grandpa nonchalantly patting out a fire on her sister's head at her own birthday party. The volume in the room got louder and louder, so Heather simply spoke over it as she continued between snorts, trying to catch her breath.

"I'm talking sizable flames too. It wasn't just a little sizzle on the ends of her pigtails. And not one adult at the table thought anything of this situation. The little round cake with white frosting and fat blue flowers—along with a little hair ash—was cut and served after the last flame went out on both Nancy's head *and* the candles." She let out a deep sigh as she caught her breath. "Those were the days."

Yolanda also held her stomach. "I can totally picture the whole scene, and I'm dead." She collected herself and wiped her brow with the back of her hand. "Man, shit really was different back then. It was a different time. It's a wonder any of us survived into our teens, let alone adulthood."

"It *was* a different time," Emma agreed. "In those days they had 'beauty secrets,' and couldn't admit in public they had dyed their hair."

"But not giving a crap when your kid's head was on fire was apparently socially acceptable," Susan joked.

Determined to share and maybe hash out her feelings about this, Emma continued to elaborate. "At our birthday parties, or holiday gatherings, when the adults sat around smoking and drinking and the kids ran in and out of the house like wild animals, I wonder if the moms ever got together and talked about beauty treatments or anti-aging strategies like we do. I truly don't think they did, or at least I don't recall overhearing it. And now I can't help but think there just might be something *to* that. I mean, can you imagine taking away the laser focus on staying young forever? It has permeated our normal lives; it would be kind of freeing for it to go away. I'm not saying they were happier or better moms for it, seeing as how they *did* let us roll around loose in the back of station wagons. And we all know "Mother's Little Helper" wasn't a fairytale made up by the Rolling Stones. But it does make me wonder if they were, silently and internally, boiling over?"

Nodding in agreement, YoYo added, "Right? Did they whisper their true thoughts and feelings about what they were going through during menopause to their best friend on the phone that was attached to the wall? With a neighbor listening in on the party line?"

"If they did, they would have had to pull its four hundred-foot cord into another room or closet for privacy, and then watch it whip and twist around like those crazy water wiggle sprinklers as they went to hang up the receiver," Heather said with a tiny snort.

Emma peered into her now empty coffee cup and pushed on. "It's like things like looks and trying to defy the aging process just did not make the list of important things to do, like, say, organizing carpool rides and considering giving that crazy new exercise class called aerobics a try? Or was it just not a thing yet because of the lack of products and procedures at that time? Just like we didn't have iPhones, the technology, and all the things that *our* kids grew up with, our moms just didn't have access to everything the Kardashians have made commonplace for people today. There just wasn't the same relentless marketing, or Amazon, where you can buy shit twenty-four seven."

"They must have *felt* the same feelings, though, right? It just wasn't articulated the way it is now, I guess. I wonder if that made them feel liberated from the pressure to remain youthful-looking. Or was it *more* suffocating, like being a prisoner in their own minds because they couldn't let their real thoughts about it be known? *We* didn't *invent* vanity," RaRa added. "I just think they weren't talking about the newest innovations in skincare and anti-aging tools because those things didn't exist. But I'm sure their feelings did."

"But that's what I mean," Emma said. "Did the absence of those things mean they didn't care about it? Didn't think about it? Oh my gosh, do y'all remember Noxema and that Sea Breeze stuff? The commercials said the 'breath of fresh air sting' you got from Sea Breeze was how you knew it was working."

"I remember the burn! The alcohol content in Sea Breeze was probably ten times stronger than my parent's evening martinis. I used to love that stuff!" Susan said with a wistful smile.

"I don't know what our moms went through internally when it came to all this, but what I *do* know is I now want a martini. And, truthfully, I bet ya if *I* had access to all the esthetic procedures of today's world when I was young, I would have pumped my lips so full of filler they would have looked like balloons in the Macy's Thanksgiving Day Parade," Heather interjected.

"Hair of the dog, Zipper. That's so you," Susan said without skipping a beat. "I'm kind of glad we didn't have all that cosmetic stuff—or social media, for that matter—back when we were younger. And I have to say, I took great pride in my ability to eavesdrop on the adults back then, and I truly don't remember the moms talking about their beauty routines, or how they felt about their looks in general–except for the topics of weight and dieting. Being on a diet was a way of life for all the adult women I knew, as evidenced by an abundance of Tab in most every home I entered during the 80s. Along with those weird "diet aide" chocolate and caramel squares that were supposed to suppress the appetite. For any woman on a quest to get and stay svelte, discovering a candy that made you thin was like some kind of miracle."

Yolanda perked up and practically squealed, "Yes! My mom had those chocolates. She tried to hide them from us, but I found them and almost barfed when I tried one. They were kind of bitter, as I recall. Baker's chocolate tasted better; I think."

RaRa giggled. "I just remember the Aqua Net clouds that could choke a horse. Oh my God, and when I was eight years old, my mom took me to the beauty parlor with her. It was in the basement of that woman from our church. Do y'all remember the little white house with the picket fence down near Townes Street? The one with the big wishing well in the front yard? I can still smell that weird combination of perm solution, hair spray, and cigarettes."

"Yummy," said YoYo with a smile.

"I can also picture the neat row of church ladies sitting under giant hood dryers, looking at magazines, smoking, and gossiping loudly over all the noise. She had a little white poodle that traipsed around looking like it just got a fresh blowout, as well. It's funny how everyone smoked, especially in a basement with no open windows or ventilation, and yet, at the same time, they would do whatever 'exercise' was the newest craze."

"Some of us still smoke, sweetie," Heather said with a wink. "But I remember that house. I used to throw pennies in that wishing well and secretly worried about falling into it. I would lean way over the edge and try to see beyond the point where darkness swallowed the penny and listened for something to happen when it finally hit the bottom. Sometimes it freaked me out because I imagined monsters or ogres were living down there. And this was years before Stephen King even wrote *It*. I had no idea there was a beauty parlor in that house. Now that I think about it, I have no idea where my mom got her hair done, but the hairspray and perm solution she used makes me think of the utter *lack* of beauty products she had in comparison to the arsenal *I* use daily. I mean, I know I'm a product whore, but the few things my mom used in her beauty regimen all fit quite neatly into our medicine cabinet and that weird plastic space-saving shelf that she wedged against the wall above our toilet. The orange and avocado green crocheted toilet paper holder took up more room in our bathroom than my mom's beauty products.

"While I, on the other hand, have accumulated a vast wasteland of anti-aging products that densely populate my vanity, the top of my dresser, and the medicine cabinet in the bathroom. They are lined up in rows like soldiers waiting to go to battle against fine lines and wrinkles. The war on sun damage from laying out with tin foil and baby oil requires a front-line formation, field army, and reserves. I buy new products before the others are used up and keep them all. It's both an arsenal and a graveyard of the not-quite-good-enough, but highly expensive potions and oils in an array of fancy packaging. No one touches my product graveyard but me. I mean, who is going to throw this shit out? It means more to me than it should, and I just might be obsessed with trying new ones."

Waves of nostalgia continued to wash over them all. Heather continued to ponder the slim pickings her mom had in terms of beauty products, and the fact that anything she *did* have was fair game to everyone in the house. "In the shower, I was supposed to use the Suave Shampoo, but usually used my mom's Wella Balsam or Finesse. Nothing was sacred or belonged to her alone," she said. "Oil Of Olay and Ponds Cold Cream were her tried and true products of choice. When I discovered her Ponds Cold Cream could remove the thick spider leg clumps of Maybelline Great Lash Mascara from my lashes, that shit became mine as well."

A brief lull in the conversation stood out to Emma as a sign that she should break the news to her friends and stop prolonging the inevitable. She knew her hesitation in delivering the news had more to do with wanting to shield them from the pain that *she* had been dealing with. Of going from not knowing to having this colossally life-altering information suddenly thrust upon you. Far better just to talk about cosmetics forever. In her mind, the initial delivery, or receipt, was the absolute worst part. Once the words were *spoken* and acceptance finally began to permeate her sadness, sludge, and seeing red, the focus became about how she would choose to deal with it. It was about accepting what she couldn't change and trying to train all her energy on the things she could. Like that damn Catholic prayer, which she had to admit contained some serious wisdom, whatever she thought about the Church. She knew she was about to do to her friends, what her doctor did to her with a simple shuffling of some papers as she described the inoperable glioblastoma.

On the opposite side of the desk, Emma recalled quite clearly how the initial blow of the news felt like she was a bird, and the doctor's flick of the wrist was what she did to throw a blanket over the cage. One minute she was a happy little bird, flitting around from perch to perch on a sunny day, and the next minute—*whoosh.* Instantaneously, her world stopped, and she had no concept of time. What was once light was suddenly dark. Like an eclipse. The blanket of cancer had control of everything. She had felt suffocated by the blanket at first. But eventually the air returned to her lungs.

Her emotions were a white-water river, and she was thrown into them without a raft. Drowning often felt like a very real possibility and she felt guilty for being the one responsible for putting her friends in the same position—again.

At first, her words created a deafening silence. It felt like there was less air to breathe than before in her once airy kitchen, and a wave of shock cursed the room like someone had slapped the devil.

Then came the flood of questions. She was ready for that now that the hardest part was over. Holding back those heavy words from her best friends was like trying to keep millions of gallons of water behind a crumbling dam—or hauling a man out of Lake Michigan. Now that the news was out there, she could inform them that the tendrils the tumor had formed were winding around areas that couldn't be operated on without doing severe damage. She explained how she found out about the tumor, and that her symptoms of confusion, memory loss, irritability, and speech difficulties made her think the diagnosis would simply be menopause. A biopsy proved her wrong in that regard, but she *did* have the distinct pleasure and good fortune of also entering menopause at the same time.

The barrage of kindness, support, and love from her friends overtook her in the best of ways, and she answered their questions until they went from a flood to a trickle. It was perfect timing to spring the news after they talked so long about the things their mothers didn't have, and that testing this elixir is quite important, and not at all frivolous or judgmental—if those things were still a concern.

She couldn't lie to them. Of course, she wanted—and truly hoped—they would all do this with her, but she also let them know that if there were still trepidations, and anyone wanted to bail, she would understand.

"I think we all got pretty caught up in everything last night, but I hope that y'all stay with me on this. Caroline said she would come home and do it with me, but she doesn't quite fit the age requirement," Emma said with an endearing smile as she thought of her daughter. "Besides, I don't want her to put her life on hold for me. I know all too well what it's like to do that for someone, and although it's coming from a beautiful place, I want her to keep living her life while I live out the rest of mine."

Tears mingled together as they huddled in a group hug.

"I'm not saying any of this to make you feel obligated in any way. I mean, of course. But the mere thought of embarking on this adventure with y'all has already begun to quell the waves that have been drowning me. Ya know? And I just can't imagine being in *another* drowning situation without every single one of you."

Slick with tears, each of them met Emma's gaze, and let her know they agreed to be part of the testing with her, and it was their honor to do something so meaningful together once again. And this time, no one was going to die.

Chapter 6

The next two months flew by at warp speed, but Ma and the girls worked their magic and, together, made sure their trip to Taos was perfectly planned. After the long day of travel and dealing with airports and too many people, they were simply giddy to finally see the house they had picked online in real life, to be in the Land of Enchantment, and to have had such an unusually short time in between their last get together—not to mention the true motivating factor for why they were there in the first place. Nestled among huge willow trees in an expansive, private park-like setting, the adobe house emanated powerful "off the grid vibes" and Emma thought it was a boho lover's wet dream. "I feel like this is my mothership," she exclaimed as the tires of their rental car made a most satisfying crunch on the stone and gravel driveway. It was music to her ears.

Gallery worthy sculptures surrounded the expansive, secluded property, and created a secret garden-like wall. Each unique piece of art echoed the color palette of the desert landscape itself, with luscious shades of warm tan, dusty rose, rusty red, and muted orange. Some leaned ever so slightly in either direction, yet each seemed to stand with pride and conviction in an unwavering commitment to their guardian duties. A few of the less abstract pieces had faces with eyes that gleamed with a hint of mischief. Their watchful stares appeared to be trained on the mountains and nearby nature trails and radiated a barely discernable glow that must have been absorbed by the light of the moon and the sun.

"Some of those statues are beautiful, and others are kind of creepy," RaRa said from the backseat as Ma parked the car off to the side of the house. A cream-colored crochet hammock hung invitingly from two trees next to the back door. The women piled out of the car like an excited group of kids on a school field trip to the zoo.

"I love everything about this place, and we haven't even gone inside yet," YoYo said as she completed a 360-degree turn. With a big, brilliant smile and almost childlike wonder, she slowly took in the panoramic view. "I must admit…y'all were right about dry heat being different from the heat in Miami. I could get used to the lack of humidity, and I *know* my hair will appreciate it too."

"Let's unload our stuff. I can't wait to see inside," Emma exclaimed as she popped open the back hatch of the SUV and pulled out pieces of luggage and a couple bags of groceries containing snacks and beverages.

"Hell yeah." Heather agreed. "It will be dark soon, and I was hoping we could fire up that stone pit." She already had a huge duffel bag slung across her chest and picked up three of the grocery bags from the driveway. "We have precious cargo here," she said endearingly, patting a brown paper bag containing some of their drinks like it was the big, diapered butt of a baby. "We made it this far", she joked. "Let's get these babies inside and ready for a night in the desert."

It took a few trips for all of them to unload the car, but not one of them minded the effort. Each time they stepped over the camel-colored doormat (complete with an intricate mountain scene design) and into the open layout of the five-bedroom house, it never failed to take their breath away. They were almost giddy as they took in the tranquil, southwestern, bohemian surroundings that included distressed wood ceiling beams, white walls, and a cactus and fiddle fig plant placed perfectly on either end of another crocheted hammock that hung in the living room.

A few handmade dream catchers hung in the hallways leading to the downstairs bathroom and the kitchen. They could almost see their own dreams in the center of each intricately woven mandala. Large windows let in a warm, serene, natural light that made Emma sigh out loud. She made her way to the kitchen, where Heather was putting away the few bags of snacks, adult bevies, and other essentials.

"Can you believe this place?" she said to Emma from halfway inside the high-tech fridge made to look vintage as she leaned in to arrange cans, bottles, and jars of various drinks, olives, mustards, and marmalades.

Emma stood at the kitchen sink and stared out the giant window just above it. She thought about how tranquil it will be to sip her morning coffee while being greeted by the sun as it crests over the Sangria De Cristo Mountains.

She turned around and immediately felt bad for not helping Heather unload the groceries. She picked up the empty brown bags and folded them neatly. With a quick scan around the spacious kitchen, she spotted a small pantry door, walked over, and tucked them away inside on a clean, white shelf.

"Did you see the swinging egg chairs in the living room? I could die—but I think I'm already in heaven." she said.

"I know. The furniture, the cream cushions and blankets, and the fluffy white throw rugs are making *my* heart leap…so I can just *imagine* how you feel." Heather said sweetly.

Emma shut the cabinet door, wiped her hands on her jeans, and nodded in agreement. "Yeah, the color scheme is gorgeous, but we probably need to protect it by taking our shoes off every time we come inside. We don't want to get desert dust and dirt on the beautiful rugs and couches."

"For sure. From now on, we'll do that. For now…let's go upstairs. I'll race you."

They took off running toward the terracotta and Spanish tiled staircase. Heather bound up the stairs two at a time, but Emma stopped in her tracks as a hallway with another tall cactus caught her eye. She followed it into an amazing sunroom that was decked out with little twinkle lights hung around large picture windows. She stepped inside the room and marveled at the Moroccan poufs in shades of jade, orange and purple, and how the low, mango wood coffee and side tables (complete with a carved, lattice design) mingled perfectly with giant potted plants and a geode that stood almost as tall as her. Turkish lanterns and lamps hung from the ceiling and sat majestically on wooden stumps. Eclectic and tasteful art—that she assumed was done by local artists—hung on the walls and seemed to add to the palpable energy of the ethereal, vast, and practically psychedelic desert. There were colors that only made sense in this arid landscape. Aside from the paintings, the best part of the room was the angled obelisk orange-colored chiminea.

Emma, breathless, felt like she had just stumbled into the most wonderful opium den in the world. Wondering if she should move to Taos, Emma was startled out of her daydream when she heard the rest of the girls calling her from upstairs.

"Coming," she yelled back, but felt a magnetic pull created by the beauty and character of the room kept her from wanting to leave it.

Upstairs, her friends were gathered in one of the larger bedrooms.

"We figured you'd want to be part of the room selection process," YoYo said as Emma walked into the room. Heather was sprawled out sideways on the bed, playing with a big bag of Gummy Bears, looking way too excited and proud to possess.

"Oh, yeah, and Zipper managed to get a whole batch of weed gummies on the plane without getting caught."

"That's right. No sniffer dogs in the airport, and they look like regular old Gummy Bears. It was worth the risk. We can eat them tonight around the fire pit."

Emma just shook her head and smiled. It already felt like summer camp and she was the only responsible adult. She tucked her hair behind her ears while scanning the rest of the room.

"Wow. Look at all this space. Is that a pullout couch?" she asked as she picked up a couple of cream throw pillows and tried to remove one of the puffy cushions.

"No. We tried it already. But we found an air mattress in the closet that looks like it's high quality," said Susan. "We were thinking Heather and I could share a room, and y'all can divvy up the rest of them. Someone must share, so it might as well be us. The doctor is going to need his own room, right?"

"I'm not entirely sure, but I think Dr. Wallace is going to stay someplace close by on his own, so none of us will need to share after all," Emma answered.

****

The air was heady with a clean, earthy scent punctuated by herbal and floral notes that are distinctly unique to the desert and its intoxicating magic. Emma leaned back in her Adirondack chair, tilted her head back, and closed her eyes, inhaling the enchanting aroma and made a mental note to create a reed diffuser with a signature scent that she would name Taos. She opened her eyes to take in the magic of the Milky Way as it danced like a seductive ghost, weaving its way through icy white stars in an inky black sky. A sudden flurry of desert nightlife became a nocturnal chorus of rustling shrubs, chirps, and calls from invisible owls and other creatures as they began to forage and frolic. A subtle breeze created a loud crackle and pop in the firepit–but it was the eruption of not-so-subtle and uncontrollable laughter that brought her attention back to her friends—their faces reflecting a beautiful orange glow from the flames. *Maybe I should call the signature scent Crackling Flames and Cackling Dames.*

Susan and Heather were sitting on the edge of their seats, trying to catch their breath in between uncontrollable cackling fits. "This Is The Day" by the band The The was playing on a small speaker that

YoYo set up on the patio to crank some playlists. Sleazin was bent over, holding her stomach with both hands, while Zipper placed her hand over her eyes like she was trying to get a grip on herself but couldn't.

"Why is this song so long?" Zipper said in between contagious guffaws, rendering it almost impossible to understand what she said.

"If you're going to ingest too many edibles, a secluded Airbnb in Taos, NM is probably the place to do it. But damn, how many of them did you eat?" YoYo said in between her own fits of merriment.

"Mine haven't kicked in yet," RaRa said like a kid who didn't get what she wanted for Christmas.

"Seriously, this song has been playing for about an hour," Zipper squeaked out between gut-busting chortles. She straightened the already straight bill of her baseball cap and added, "I need to ask y'all something important. Why do other women look ethereal and sexy with loose hair hanging out of their baseball hat, but when I do it, I look like Mike Myers in *Wayne's World*?"

Rachel burst into giggles. "I think you look beautiful. Maybe more like Garth than Wayne, foxy lady."

"Very funny, Rapunzel. You stole my line," Susan interjected. "I was gonna say the same thing."

"This is so great. I'm glad we decided to come a few days before Dr. Wallace to settle in and get all the wiggles out before we start what we're here to do." RaRa got up from her chair and stood a little closer to the fire. She put her hands out, allowing the warmth to permeate her skin. "I think they might be kicking in," she said with another bout of giggles.

Zipper and Sleazin slid back in their chairs and let out a simultaneous, loud sigh like an exclamation point, punctuating their happiness.

"When will the good doctor arrive?" Susan asked as she brushed away the lingering tears on her cheeks from cracking up way too hard at nothing in particular.

"He will be here tomorrow by dinner time, I believe. After he settles in and meets everyone. I was thinking we can discuss plans, or he can answer any questions over dinner, and then we'll start the trial the next morning."

"I'm glad we got here before him as well. It's amazing to be here with all of you," Emma said. "It's so tranquil and beautiful. Well, it *was* until *we* got here."

All her best friends are here for her today. Surely, they feel as liberated as she does. She reminds herself that nobody ever says how they *really* feel, but these are her friends. The closest thing to actual sisters. There is no safer place to be herself and she takes a minute to acknowledge what a treasure it is to have such a special bond with these women. It's rare and she knows how lucky she is, even if they don't see each other very often. She knows that her tribe of warriors can and will withstand anything life tries to chuck at their heads if they have each other.

Out loud Emma says, "Right now, this whole thing reminds me of being on the merry-go-round as a little kid and trying to reach the brass ring. Some of the creatures remained still as they spun around, but I only chose the horses that also moved up and down because it made it more challenging to reach the ring of gold as you passed it. Each time I whirred past it, I would lean as far as I could without falling off the horse and felt a special thrill of apprehension and fear in the challenge of getting the ring. I never knew if I could do it, but when I did, it was the most amazing feeling of accomplishment and pride as I threw it into the basket with the others and waved excitedly at my dad—hoping he saw what I managed to do. Upon passing it, whether I grabbed it or not, I would mentally reset and start the process all over again, and the thrill was just as strong as if it were the first time every time around. Every time you got it, a bell clanked to announce your victory to the world.

"It was like chasing something beautiful that wasn't guaranteed, but the thrill of the unknown and the sheer possibility made it worth leaning way off the side of the giant horse and getting yelled at to stay seated. There was a magic in it, yet it was so basic and simple. This feels like the same thing to me. We're chasing something that has no guarantee, but I feel so alive right now that it's worth the risk. I'm happy to lean all the way off this sucker and grab the brass ring so I can hear that triumphant bell ring, or just whir past and try again the next time around."

She paused for a moment and silently considered what she just tried to articulate. Most people don't think the way she does, and they often can't relate to what she tries to convey, which is why she rarely shares her silly sentiments. None of the others said anything, so Emma shook her head to clear her thoughts like an Etch A Sketch and quickly dug into the bag she brought outside filled with wine, glasses, and snacks. "You girls are going to love this wine. It will simply transport your beautiful little palates along a silk road of discovery, which I thought would be the perfect way for us to toast this endeavor. It's an adventure, or I suppose an E-venture, and I am so appreciative of each of you for taking part in it. Let's get some of this exuberant ruby red in all our glasses, shall we?"

"For sure. Hey, maybe we'll get lucky in town and get transported to a hottie's hacienda," Heather chimed in.

"Girls…we have to take this seriously." Emma let the words slip from her lips before she thought better of it. In hearing this, all of them were instantly beside themselves once again until tears rolled down their cheeks and their abs felt like they were doing a challenging core workout.

Susan managed to squeak out, "Okay, Mrs. Garrett. I'll make sure Blair, Jo, and Tootie behave."

The hoots echoed around them, merging with the ones made by actual owls.

"No, I know. We're here to have fun too. I think I'm just nervous. Gimme one of those gummies," said Ma.

"Oh, shit. Ma's gonna eat a gummy," YoYo said enthusiastically.

"Why not? I might as well since this is TITS," Ma said. "I really feel like this is my chance to do something wild and crazy for once, and to do it for me, myself, and I." She popped the gummy into her mouth with extra flair to emphasize her point.

RaRa walked over to the grass and got down on her knees. "Watch me do a headstand," she said with a wobbly voice. "Does anyone want to walk the stone labyrinth with me tomorrow?" She got into a crow pose.

YoYo laughed and said, "Okay, Yoga Meister. Let's see it. If you can do a headstand for at least thirty seconds, I'll walk the labyrinth with you."

"That's Yoga *Master*. And thanks for the compliment." Rachel said with a sassy smirk. It took her two times to do it, but RaRa did a perfect headstand complete with an added show of dropping her legs out to her sides in a wide Y position, and then scissoring them back and forth for a full minute until she fell over in the grass laughing her head off. She laid on her back and stared up at the sky with wide eyes. "Isn't it beautiful out here in the desert? And *you're* gonna love the labyrinth, YoYo." she said in a joking manner that also emphasized the fact she had just won their bet.

"It really is. And I'm sure I will," YoYo agreed as she shook her head in an affectionate way. "The sky and the air are so different here. It's fucking magical. Oh, damn, I guess my gummies have kicked in, as well. You never see stars like this back home." She rubbed her forehead with the palm of her hand. "But for real, I've been meaning to tell you and Susan what an amazing job you both did in finding this place. I love how it's far away enough from town to feel like we're here alone, but close enough in case we need something. Or to go out and cause trouble. Right, Ma?"

"Yes, thank you both. I can't believe you managed to find something so perfect and charming, and on such short notice. It's great to be far enough from downtown Taos to remain as inconspicuous as possible if things get a little crazy."

"Oh, it was our pleasure, right, RaRa?" Susan looked over at RaRa, who was still flat on her back on the ground but had raised an arm over her head and giving a big thumbs-up to the group. "Between my real estate connections at work and Rachel's huge network of Southwestern outdoorsy types, we really couldn't lose," Susan said with a wink. She threw a thumbs-up back in Rachel's direction, which Rachel didn't see because she had her eyes closed. But the feeling of unspoken appreciation was understood by everyone just the same.

"Well, here's to both of you," Emma said as she lifted her almost empty glass. "We appreciate your efforts. And here's to this amazing space, and to all of you for being here with me. I'm just in heaven. Let's play a little game while I wait for my buzz to kick in, or for y'all to come down a little. We can go around the circle and do a little campfire confessions session."

"Campfire confessions. Sounds like a reality show," Susan said matter-of-factly.

"Oh. My. God. We should have made this *whole thing* a reality show. How awesome would that have been?" Heather piped in, her eyes wide and filled with excitement.

Susan pointed at Heather and announced, "Your eyes look like one of those black and white Kit-Cat clocks. You know, the ones with the wagging tail and bug eyes that move back and forth from the 1950s?" They both looked at each other and chuckled.

"Don't forget about its irresistible, contagious grin," Heather retorted without skipping a beat.

"Not awesome at all if it goes tits up," RaRa said from her spot on the ground, completely ignoring the conversation about the kitschy, yet hugely popular, dapper feline kitchen clock. "I think we're pioneering enough shit for now. We can start the Reality TV show after this is over." She let out a throaty giggle. "Tits up. I made a funny." She added, more to herself than to the rest of them.

"Hey, a reality show isn't a horrible idea," Emma answered. "And things won't go tits up."

Zipper finished the remainder of her White Claw by tipping her head way back to get every last drop. Once the can was truly empty, she said, "While we're here, I intend to do things besides just sit around and wait for something good, bad, or indifferent to happen. This is an artist town with incredible wineries, galleries, shops, and bars. Maybe I'll get to try the hand of a sexy rancher."

Susan added, "Gives new meaning to the term ranch hand, I guess."

"You still have that invisible lasso, Wonder Woman?" YoYo said to Zipper, smirking.

A rumbling of giggles percolated from deep in Heather's belly. She wrapped her blanket around her shoulders a little tighter, tipped her hat at YoYo, and with a hugely exaggerated, open-mouthed wink she said, "You know it, Cowgirl. I've hogtied a good number of cow pokes with it too."

"Of course, you said pokes," YoYo prodded with a big, toothy grin.

"I couldn't resist. And I'm gonna get some practice with my lasso right now, by reigning us back in for Emma's Confessional Campfire."

"Aww. That's Campfire Confessions, but thanks." Emma said with a demure wave of her hand.

"Giddyup!" Heather squealed in her enthusiastic yet sarcastic way. "What exactly are we confessing? But wait—wasn't that what the kiki thing was for?"

Emma felt a comfortable fuzziness envelope her mind like a cashmere wrap, and she noticed she was a little dry in the mouth as well. She paused to gather her thoughts about the difference between having the kiki at her house and coming together at the Airbnb a night before Dr. Wallace joined them. She took a long sip from her glass of Pinot Noir and said, "The kiki was like a way to vent our feelings mixed with a stroll down memory lane and just getting everything out on the table. I needed to get a lot off my chest and had these huge things to share with y'all. But now that we're all here, I think we should all go around the circle, reach down deep into our heart of hearts, and give voice to *why* we want to test this crazy elixir. I mean, something great could happen, something bad could happen, or *nothing* could happen. So, I guess I want to know the real motivations behind each of us wanting to try it, and why are we willing to test it when he should probably be doing legit clinical studies and not doling it out to us in the desert like drugs on a playground."

"Are you trying to talk us out of this now that we're here?" RaRa said as she rolled over onto her stomach. She propped up her head with bent elbows, her chin gracefully resting in the cradle of her hands. She looked like a little kid on the floor in front of the TV, watching cartoons on a Saturday morning.

"Oh my gosh, no!" exclaimed Ma. "Not at all. I just want to know the real reasons why each of us is here. Plus, I'm a lightweight and I think I'm already starting to feel high as hell. Talking about it will make me feel better. Less paranoid, maybe? Think about it, y'all, if you could dive back twenty years, which body of water would you choose? A lake? A stream? A river?

A dream, ice cream, an orgasmic scream? An ocean, pool, or pond? A notion, creek, or womb? A bath or a tomb?"

"That's freakin' hilarious. I love this so much," Susan said with a flick of her hair. "I love seeing you let loose a little, Ma. It's awesome."

YoYo hooted, "Whoa, Nelly. How many edibles did you eat?"

Ma smiled and threw Susan a kiss through the crisp night air. "Do you wanna go first?" she asked her.

"Sure." Susan reached up and caught the kiss in mid-air and planted it firmly on her jutted out butt. "We are going to say what we want out of this, assuming it will rewind the clock, right? And no judgments?" she asked somewhat tentatively.

"Exactly," Ma said. "No judgments whatsoever, and as blatantly honest as you can be."

"Well then, I want to be seen and adored before I become the invisible woman," said Susan pertly.

"Me next, me next," Zipper said while jumping up and down so her boobs would bounce in shared excitement. "I want to have as many hot men as I can handle. I don't care if it's shallow. It's an exhilarating drug that makes me feel powerful, and I know the day will come when I will no longer experience and know that rush. Every woman has a last fuckable day, right? Well, I think it should fuck off for as long as possible, so I want to push that day out as far as it can go."

"Well, I just want Bobby Fisk to eat my ass," Emma barely squeaked out in between laughing fits. They all howled under the moon like coyotes. Primal animal sounds of unabashed joy echoed around them. "Y'all, I'm half kidding. I would love for him to want me back just for one minute so I could squash him like a bug. But mostly I want to help people with this study. Maybe even people with cancer." She turned to Yolanda and, because she was having a difficult time gauging the volume of her voice, whispered, "How 'bout you, YoYo?"

Yolanda leaned her head back in thought, and said, "Well, first of all, I may never recover from hearing Ma say the words 'eat my ass,' and second, I want to run the hottest club in Miami. It would be a unique monstrosity of a venue that includes different types of entertainment on each of the building's levels. I'm talking dining, nightclub, fashion shows or concerts, and maybe even a sex club with a dominatrix dungeon, all in one that would make the original Studio 54 look like a library in a monastery."

With a giggle, "Rachel flipped over onto her back in the warm spot of Earth she seemed to be melting into and said, "I just want world peace. Or maybe whirled peas? I can't decide."

Chapter 7

The morning was blue and breezy when Dr. Wallace rang the doorbell right on time–not one minute late and not one minute early. *How do people do that?* Ma wondered. She overcame an adolescence of tardiness by being ten minutes early to everything–and still felt she couldn't get the knack of timing. They had already finished their scones and Greek yogurt and were refilling their coffee in the kitchen for an hour, RaRa and Heather confessing they'd barely slept from nervous excitement and anxiety. They froze in place while the chimes died down before all looking to Ma to answer the door.

Dr. Walter Wallace had come, as promised, to dinner the night before to discuss the game plan. The first day they would have just one dose in the morning, and if they tolerated that well, they would ramp up to twice a day for the remaining four days they were "on-site" as he said. "And you'll then take a maintenance dose every day at bedtime when you return to your respective homes, and we will check in once per week initially, then once per month thereafter," His terse formal manner had softened by a warm soothing voice. "Be certain to have a light breakfast at least a half hour before," he had said, "so that if you're sensitive to any of the ingredients they are less likely to upset your stomach. I'll come by at nine tomorrow morning."

With all of them standing around the kitchen counter, Dr. Wallace shook a black glass jar over an open palm and several bright goldenrod-colored capsules tumbled into his hand. Emma had handed each of the women a bottle of Fiji water, and the doctor placed two pills in each of five little plastic cups and set one cup in front of each of them.

"Let's get this party started." RaRa said a little too loudly, her nerves shaking like a cheerleader's pom-poms right after a touchdown.

Emma took her cup between her thumb and forefinger and raised it ceremoniously. "Here's to loving ourselves."

"And living life to the fullest," Susan added, as they all raised their cups.

"And friendship," said Heather.

"All right. Let's do this already," exclaimed Rachel, tossing the pills back, picking up her water, and gulping half the bottle in mere seconds. They all quickly followed suit, diving in before they had time for second thoughts.

"Now, while we wait and I monitor you all in case of any reactions, there are some preliminary forms for you to fill out. Since this research may help others, we need to document as much as possible how you react and what changes take place. This first form is the longest and will establish a baseline for how you're feeling right now. Then, I ask that you complete a short form each day while you're here, and then once per week for the next six months," said Dr. Wallace as he pulled five clipboards from his bag on the bar stool. "This will probably take forty to fifty minutes. And remember, in order to maximize the effectiveness of the treatments, nothing to eat for sixty minutes–so, not until ten-fifteen."

They each drifted to chairs and couches and outside hammocks to complete their surveys. The questions probed how they felt about themselves, from hair and skin to emotional state and mental acuity. Dr. Wallace broke the silence to announce that everything was extremely confidential. "And your thoroughness and honesty are crucial and much appreciated. This really is very important."

Emma asked him if it would be okay for them to have tea, then took a moment to put on the kettle and arrange cups along with the assortment of herbal tea that came with the house. They enjoyed sharing about themselves during the break; the silence interrupted occasionally with giggles at some questions requested in the questionnaire.

Emma was the last to turn in her questionnaire, and the doctor broke the silence asking how they felt. "I expect it to take at least fourteen days–if not twice that to start seeing any effects, but I do want you to make a note of anything at all that seems out of the ordinary, whether nausea–however slight, change in energy–whether more tired or less, or any other reaction. And if you feel anything that worries you–anything at all—please don't hesitate to call. I'm just down the road and could be here in minutes."

They each reported that they felt just fine, though Rachel said she thought she might be having a bit of nausea. "Try some ginger tea and see if that takes care of it. If not, please call me, and I can prescribe something stronger," responded Dr. Wallace. "Besides drinking extra water and going easy on the alcohol, feel free to go about your day as you normally would, well, as much as you can, given you're not in your normal environments. I'll be back this evening at five to check in again, and if everyone is feeling well, we'll do the second dose tomorrow morning at nine," he said as he saw himself out.

"Well, girls, I'm feeling fantastic and want to explore the town. Maybe there are some desert hotties wandering around," said YoYo.

"And I'm certain one of these hippie coffee shops will have ginger tea for RaRa," said Emma. "Maybe a crunchy granola lesbian coffee shop, even."

"I know what the doctor said, but I'm on vacation, and I want some Baileys in my latte," said Heather. "Do you think granola crunchy lesbian hippie coffee shops serve alcohol in Taos?" She snorted.

"Let's head to the Old Towne Plaza–I think that's the name–and we can probably find something for everyone," said Emma. "I did a little research before we came."

"Of course you did, Ma," replied Susan. "Always looking out for us."

"I'm just thrilled to be here with each of you. We don't know what the future holds–or how long it will last, but I just know that I want to spend as much of it as I can with the friends I love most. Thank you all," said Emma, growing emotional that they were all doing this together and trying to hide the apprehension she felt about her cancer diagnosis–and the wild hope that this treatment might have some impact on the prognosis.

RaRa was standing next to Emma and put her arms around her. "No need to thank us. We bonded on our first trip together, and I'm sure this won't be our last."

"All right, you two. If we don't break this up, y'all are gonna have to get a room," joked Yolanda. "How much time do you babes need to get ready to go?"

"How about we leave in twenty minutes?" said Emma. "We'll get coffee, browse some galleries, get some lunch, and still have time to dip in the hot tub before the good doctor makes his evening house call."

Before long, they all piled in the car and backed out of the drive.

"Guys, look at that woman," Susan said, pointing out the passenger side window. "That woman on the beach cruiser looks just like Fozzy Bear. WockaWocka." Everyone turned to get a look and saw a woman with bright orange hair and big, round eyes riding happily down the street with an open-mouthed smile like a Muppet.

"Oh my god, stop. She really does."

"Hey, she must live here. I know if I did, I would be sporting that WockaWocka bliss twenty-four seven too," said Susan. "I wonder if that's the key to looking young as you age."

"What? Having orange hair?" joked YoYo. "Or riding a bike?"

"Ha. Ha," said Susan dryly. "But I'm being serious. I guess what I mean is that I feel like living in the city takes a toll. All that hustle and bustle. Well, sometimes all that activity keeps you feeling youthful, too, I suppose. But all that driving and stress and just being so damn busy all the time. And all those gray days. And pollution and grime. Sometimes I feel like it coats my soul with soot. You know? Weighs me down. But then I see the stars out here at night, and…and…I guess I just feel…lighter—"

"I think I know what you mean," said Rachel. "Ever since Ma propositioned us," —she winked— "I've been thinking a lot about what makes us feel older and trying to sort out how much is external and how much is internal. Like, what can we control? For example, I know that getting enough sleep and exercise helps me feel better, more energetic. As does eating good food. I mean, that seems obvious. But I've also been wondering whether, like, dying my hair makes me feel younger or whether that illusion is holding me back. As much as I've thought about this, you'd think I could explain it." She let out a soft sigh.

"I'm pretty sure that if I didn't dye my hair," said Heather, "I'd look ten, maybe twenty years older than all the other women my age. And I'm not ready for that. I know I'm not going to look twenty-five again, but I'm not ready to look like a grandma."

"But maybe this magic elixir *will* make us look twenty-five again," said Emma. "Who knows?"

"But I think that's what I'm pondering," continued Rachel. "I'm gonna try to make this make sense. It's like, if I dye my hair, am I turning my back on all the wisdom I've gained with the years?"

"I sure don't feel like I'm wise enough to be gray-haired." Susan said with a faraway stare.

Rachel looked at her friend with loving and empathetic eyes. "Maybe wise isn't the right word, but by trying to look younger, am I somehow not getting all I can out of today? By trying to turn back the clock on my looks, would I be, like, diminishing all the experiences that have made me who I am? I mean, I've been through some shit–we all have–and isn't that a kind of beautiful thing, too? Ugh. I'm not making sense."

"Maybe some edibles will help," joked Susan. "Make the thoughts flow free." She flapped her hands like a bird flying.

"I must sound like I'm high already." Rachel said as she shook her head in short, brisk movements.

"I think you might be onto something," said Emma as she pulled into a parking space. "I've been thinking a lot since," —she paused to choose the right word— "the diagnosis, about how much time we have left, all of us…" She opened her car door, grateful to have an excuse to end that train of thought. "But we can talk about that more later. I'm ready for a latte."

After coffee, ginger tea, gallery hopping, and lunch, they had some hot tub time before getting cleaned up and dressed for their check-in with the doctor. The doorbell rang at exactly five o'clock, and Emma escorted Dr. Wallace through the living room into the kitchen where they were waiting, perched on bar stools, or standing around the white marble island, pouring each other more Merlot. "None of the ingredients should be affected by alcohol consumption. However, for those of you unaccustomed to the dryness of Taos, do be cognizant of the dehydrating effects of alcohol and increase your water intake accordingly. I am interested to see the effect of the formulation on hot flashes, which I'm sure you've noticed, can be exacerbated by wine consumption."

"Oh my god!" interrupted Susan. "I never made that connection. Wine. How disappointing. As if menopause could be less fun than it already is, I should be avoiding wine."

"I'm sorry, my dear. Alcohol consumption also can contribute to cognition and memory issues. And of course, one should drink extra water to compensate for the dehydrating effects of the alcohol. Women have less dehydrogenase than men to begin with, and during menopause, they lose water in their cartilage and tendons, which all contribute to menopausal women not metabolizing alcohol, as well. Of course, skin dryness and weight gain are issues, as well. Two or three drinks per week may help relieve stress, but more than that can be a problem. And red wine especially is linked to hot flashes."

"I, for one," responded YoYo, "am not about to trade my Shiraz for a Chardonnay. I'll just shine a little brighter," she said adamantly, "and wear less clothing while I do it."

"While heavy alcohol consumption is not recommended," replied the doctor, "in the interest of science, it would be helpful if you maintain your usual habits, including, for example, alcohol intake, as well as coffee usage, sleep, exercise practices, skincare regimens, and the like. All that to say, for the situation at hand, if you drink no more or less than usual, that would be optimal for noticing the effects of this trial. Having used some of the various individual ingredients myself, I expect that you will start to see the benefits to some degree in as little as fourteen days. However, the full effect could take up to six months to exhibit, depending, of course, on individual metabolisms, body compositions, and hormone levels. That being said, how are you all feeling after the first dose?"

Rachel reported that her nausea had vanished by lunchtime. They all laughed when Susan said she was encouraged because she hadn't yet sprouted a third arm or a second head. "As useful as that could be," —she paused for effect— "especially in the bedroom. I mean, consider the full possibilities for ménage à trois."

"Well," said the doctor, "I can assure you that no one will grow additional body parts. However, we are hopeful that this formulation will reverse the waning libido that typically accompanies menopause along with the concomitant dryness that many women experience."

"Yeah, there are parts of me that are used to being in the desert, if you know what I mean," said Heather. "And increased hydration has not been shown by research to increase lubrication."

They all twittered, out of commiseration and nervousness, feeling a little shy about discussing such intimate details with a doctor they had just met. "On that note," said Heather, "would you like a glass of wine, Dr. Wallace?"

He demurred, saying he was meeting a college friend for cocktails at six and would be on his way if they had no further questions or concerns. "I'll see you at nine o'clock sharp tomorrow. I can see myself out."

"I know we're here for a serious experiment, and all, but that one needs to loosen up a bit. Maybe we should invite him to use the hot tub," said Heather after he left. "I have officially decided we were wrong when we said he looks like the guy who stole Woody from the garage sale in Toy Story. That must have been a bad picture of him. Now that I've seen him in person, I think he looks more like a youngish Stanley Tucci—with a goatee. He's kinda cute."

"I thought you were looking for a ranch hand," replied Emma.

"Well, maybe I'll grow two vaginas and I can have both at once. Double the pleasure."

"Maybe *that's* what was going on in those gum commercials," exclaimed Susan. "Some adman's fantasy gets a slot on prime-time TV."

"Ha. You said 'slot.'" Zipper snorted.

"Well," interrupted Emma, "are y'all ready to go find our ranch hand? I mean, actually, I made reservations for us in town for seven o'clock. And apparently, they're famous for their margaritas. But it doesn't sound like a rancher kind of place. I didn't realize that was on the agenda." "This is more like a professor type of place. Or doctor. Something a little fancy for our first night out."

RaRa collected all the corks that littered the kitchen island and threw them into the large, antique gold ceramic bowl that served as a centerpiece, catchall, and piece of art all at once. Its graceful, organic edges were perfectly imperfect, like the flower petals that most likely inspired its design. "I'm up for anything, really. I want to do what we're supposed to for this thing to be legit, and to get the best possible results, but enjoying Taos is high on my list too," she said.

"Girl, with all this talk about alcohol, edibles, and vaginas, I'm pretty sure that having fun on this trip won't be an issue," YoYo said with a wink at RaRa that made her blush. "Whatever itinerary Ma has mapped out for us is fine with me," YoYo added as she packed up the box of Rosemary Triscuits and put them in the designated snack cupboard.

"Fancy stuff tonight followed by down and dirty later on sounds great to me," added Susan.

"I'm in. I already know what I'm gonna wear,"

Heather squealed as she turned on her heel, and dashed from the room. "If any of you hoes think you're getting in the shower before me, you got another thing coming." she yelled in between cackles as she bounded up the stairs two at a time.

Ma raised her eyebrows and shrugged. The brightest smile crept across her face as she confirmed, "Margaritas it is, then."

****

The following morning, the doctor appeared again promptly at nine o'clock. Emma had picked up a tin of ginger tea, and Rachel was sipping on it when Dr. Wallace handed out the third dose. "I'll stay for a little bit again today, making sure there are no immediate issues. Same form as yesterday. You'll be asked the same set of questions daily for the remainder of your time on site. Since these are subjective, please keep in mind that your first instinct is your best answer."

Once he collected the forms, reminded them to wait at least a minimum of an hour to eat, and said that he'd be back at five o'clock for their first evening dose, he saw himself out. The routine and attention to detail was already beginning to make Emma feel like they were in the movie "*Groundhog Day*". In this scenario, however, that was probably a very good thing.

While the previous day had been lazy and taken up mainly with the hot tub and lounging in hammocks, Emma had arranged for them to visit the Earthships north of Taos before needing to be back at the house at five o'clock. After dressing for their outing and getting breakfast at the house, they took the minivan to the coffee shop they had found the first day. Susan was looking for their Fozzie friend on the bike again and didn't see her. But they did see a striking woman at the coffee shop in flowing sage-colored pants, a cream tunic, and silver and turquoise jewelry. And a man who sat on a bench outside a pottery studio with two giant Irish Wolf Hounds that flanked him like matching bookends. Dusty smears of clay and creativity covered his clothing, which he wore like a badge of honor.

Back in the car, Susan remarked that she looked so youthful even though she had long silver hair. "How is that possible?" she said. "I've been dying my hair for so long; I don't even know what its original color is anymore. And I'm pretty sure I'd look like a great-grandmother if I didn't dye it."

"She looked like an Eileen Fisher model. Or maybe it was Eileen Fisher herself," said Emma. "But I'm sure I'd look fifty years older if I let my hair go."

"I don't know," said Rachel. "I'm considering transitioning to my natural color. Whatever that is. I mean, I know I was a redhead as a girl, and my hairdresser said that gingers don't really go gray–it's more like we just lose pigment and fade to a lighter red. But I've been dyeing it for so long, I don't even know anymore."

"So, what you're saying is that if you stop dyeing your hair, you'll look less like Nicole Kidman and more like a blond Rapunzel. Well, y'all, if I stop dyeing my hair, I'll look like an old hag, and the only dark hair I'll have will be the whiskers growing out of warts on my chin." Heather snort giggled.

"Y'all remember, like ten or fifteen years ago, when there was this attempt to reclaim the word 'crone'?" asked Emma. "I know it was supposed to be an insulting term for an old woman, but it also meant that she was magical or supernatural. At the time, I was still young enough to think that it was really cool, that older women maybe should be revered as having special wisdom and some sort of special power."

"Ha," added Susan, "maybe all the drying up of the libido leaves more energy for other things. Maybe that's the special power. We become sexless but super focused. God knows I could use a little help in the focus department. If I'm being honest, I know that I waste way too much time thinking about men, sex, and putting the brakes on that bullet train to irrelevance."

"Amen, sister," exclaimed Heather in unadulterated agreement.

"I don't know about all that," said Emma. "I mean, after Bobby left–like really left–and he had been leaving for years–I started feeling sexual again. For the first time in a long time. While he had been off, revving his engine with some young thing, our sex life had stalled, and I actually didn't miss it that much. I was so focused on growing my business that it felt comfortable to not have to worry about sex all the time. I could just do my own thing."

"Yeah, I read somewhere that with menopause, women lose their susceptibility to society's beauty standards," said Rachel. "Interesting, right?"

"You mean that menopause is an excuse for women to let themselves go?" quipped Heather.

"I guess you could see it that way," said Rachel. "But I think of it more like, well, as older women, we don't just automatically assume there's one right way to look. Or that beauty is the be all and end all."

"'Older women,'" retorted Yolanda. "I'm not so sure I like the sound of that. At least, I don't want it to apply to me."

"Yeah, but it's not as bad as 'elderly'." Susan said as she playfully clapped her hands together.

"Yikes. 'Elderly'." said Heather. "That's for great grandmas."

"But really, by now, we've had so many experiences," said Emma, "that we realize looks don't matter that much, right? All that effort I put into looking my best, and Bobby still left. I'm glad I put so much into my part of the business, at least. That's a more faithful friend than my looks–or that loser."

"Oh, honey," soothed YoYo, "I love your attitude. He is definitely a loser for not being able to keep a badass woman like you."

"Aw. Thank you. You're so sweet," replied Emma. "But, as y'all know, it really stung at first. Especially since he left me for a younger woman–how cliche, right? I was determined to not be part of his sorry little story. I was not going to play the part of Bitter Older Woman."

"Hells, yeah, Ma." said YoYo.

"You know, that's kind of what I mean when I say I'm thinking about not dyeing my hair," said Rachel. "Leaning into my age. Embracing it. Not thinking I have to compete with those younger women. I mean, I've earned my gray hair, lines, and wrinkles–and saggy boobs, for that matter. But it's not like it's a level playing field anymore."

"Saggy boobs. That's no joke. They're like those balloons you find weeks after the party, deflated, and withered, under the couch covered in dust." They all joined in, laughing along with Ma.

"Yeah. That's why I don't regret my boob job,"

said Heather. "I wasn't feeling so great about my body, and then I had decent boobs again–and *voila.* Sexy mama. But I didn't think of it as a way to look younger. I just wanted to be happy in my own skin."

"Decent boobs?" said YoYo. "You mean beautiful. And I've studied a lot of boobs."

"I don't think I'm dyeing my hair because I'm trying to look younger. I just like the way it looks and makes me feel when I get some fresh color, but I'm definitely not excited about looking older. And I also don't regret getting this beautiful pair of Gummy Bears." explained Susan as she cupped her boobs and pushed them up and down like a juggler.

"Girl, those are some spectacular mounds. Yummy Gummies. Not to take away from that view right there, but holy crap, this scenery is otherworldly," remarked Yolanda. "Coming from Florida, it's like a different planet here."

"Speaking of mounds; do you see those little mounds up there?" asked Emma. "I think those might be the Earthships."

"Little mounds? You must be referring to YoYo's titties. No, I see something. But what are Earthships? Something like spaceships?" joked Heather.

Susan added in a silly voice, "Maybe they are Motherships. Ma, isn't the store, Anthroplogie, your Mothership?"

Yolanda's cackle resounded through the air between them as she exclaimed, "Ya'll are hilarious. We're talking about quality over quantity over here. And I never get any complaints about *any* of my mounds, if ya know what I'm sayin'."

"There was an article about them in *Architectural*

Digest a while back, and I didn't want to miss a chance to see them in person since we'd be close," explained Emma with a smile, purposefully ignoring the goofy banter.

"Well, it looks like Mars," said Yo. "And it's almost hot enough. So, they *are* spaceships. Isn't Area 51 nearby, too?"

"That's Roswell. But same idea," replied Emma. "I came across it when I was looking for things to do in New Mexico. And Mars is cool, so to speak, not hot."

"Okay, professor. So, Ma, what's up with these spaceships we're going to see?" said YoYo.

"The Earthships are houses built using recycled materials, and they're meant to be fully sustainable. But the real attraction for me is that they're gorgeous. They have curves instead of sharp corners, and the natural colors and shapes are really soothing." "I don't actually know much more about them, but I thought y'all might enjoy seeing them, too."

As they drove up to the Visitor Center, they were struck by the whimsical character of the buildings–nothing like conventional square and rectangular houses. While they had the adobe characteristic of the Southwest, they also possessed curving walls, round arches, large banks of glass walls, and even miniature minarets topped with domes. Some walls seemed almost like stained glass. They each grabbed their waters and headed out into the dry air.

As they approached the building, they were struck by how the low houses blended into the landscape, merging with the honey-colored sand and sagebrush of the surrounding desert. As they entered the Visitor Center, they noticed what looked like stained glass was hundreds if not thousands of glass bottles on their sides, with the bottoms showing through the exterior walls, catching the bright sunlight. The displays inside explained the building principles and processes. Walls were made of rammed earth–dirt harvested from the surrounding land and pounded into discarded tires, then mudded over in smooth adobe; they boasted of helping to deal with the human-created trash problem by repurposing items as building materials that would otherwise end up in landfills. It wouldn't solve the issue, but it was something.

In addition, the houses were mostly self-sufficient. Because of their building style, they needed neither air-conditioning nor heating, and the little electricity they used to power lights could be generated by solar panels on the south-facing roofs. Even the rainwater and gray water–water from showering and doing dishes and other non-sewage water–was collected and reused. Most of the buildings had greenhouses that grew enough vegetables and fruit for a family.

But Emma was most in awe of the design. Besides the southwest vibe, the Earthship made interesting use of color and shapes–not anything like the gray and moss that were currently in vogue in traditional houses. The palette blended with the surrounding desert: terra-cotta, sagebrush, ochre, and burnt orange, with occasional pops of cyan and blue bringing the rooms to life. They read about the enormous amount of trash generated by the average American way of life and how the Earthships helped keep some of it out of landfills and reduced the need for so much packaging.

There were other visitors–mostly hippies in jeans and flip-flops–so they didn't speak much while inside the Visitor Center. But Emma nudged YoYo and Rachel, pointing discretely down the hall at a white-haired man who had just came in. “That’s Michael something or other–the guy who started this whole Earthship thing,” she whispered. They turned to look at the shaggy guy with wild, shoulder-length hair flying out from under his straw hat and gray beard stubble above the blue bandana he wore around his neck.

“Maybe that’s Heather’s ranch hand,” joked Yolanda.

“I bet he has strong hands,” purred Rachel. “But I think Heather might have had in mind someone a little, um, less experienced.”

“Do you mean ‘younger’?” asked Emma. “Because this guy seems youthful–despite his hair and the lines around his face. He certainly looks strong. Vitality is a word that comes to mind.”

“Hey. What are y’all whispering about?” said Susan, sauntering over to join them.

“We’ll tell you in the car–I don’t want to be too obvious.” Emma winked.

As they closed the car doors, they shared their sighting with Heather, and she said she had seen him, too. “He certainly had some sex appeal even though there’s a twenty-year age difference,” she said, “and not in the direction I usually go.”

“Why is that?” said Susan. “Why can guys be seen as sexier as they get older but women who want to be sexy are seen as trying too hard? Like Robert Redford, right? Did y’all see that Marvel movie with him? He was damn sexy even if he was a bad guy. But women that age? Society says they have no sex appeal.”

“Except maybe Jamie Lee Curtis,” Yolanda said.

"That woman still has it going on. But I know what you mean–even though I think it's harder for straight women—and maybe white women as well. Let's face it, we all know the old saying 'black don't crack' is true, and I think the queer community has navigated the aging thing a little differently. Maybe it's because lots of gay women don't really fit the gender stereotypes, so there's a little more awareness of the arbitrariness of the so-called beauty standards of mainstream culture. I'm also not sure I can fully buy into the notion that in order to matter—according to our youth-obsessed culture—you have to be young and hot, or whatever. Maybe when we get older, we have less collagen, and our skin doesn't constantly glow—no matter what color we are—but part of me wants to reject all of that. To get older also means you have gained experience and beauty in so many other ways. I think every year I travel around the sun, I'm a lot closer to being who I was really meant to be. But I can't lie. I do want to remain hot and sexy in my own ways as well…so maybe don't listen to my ramblings."

"Easy for you to say, Yo," replied Heather. "You've always been gorgeous. And you don't even work at it. And it's not fair that 'black don't crack!' I am legitimately jealous, but not a hater," she added with a wink."

"Well, thank you?" said YoYo. "But I've had my share of struggles with self-image. I feel like it got a little easier in my thirties and forties, but now, I don't quite feel at home in my body. It feels like it's changing. Foreign."

"I know I have said this before, but I really can't help but wonder if guys struggle with the aging thing like we do," said Susan.

"Maybe we should invite the doctor to the hot tub and uncover some of his, um, thoughts on the topic," joked Heather.

"Wow, Zip…you keep bringing him up. I thought you were looking for a rough and rugged ranch hand," said YoYo, "not a genteel doctor."

"Who says I can't want both?" Maybe me and Susan can share him and then share some insight." You know, see what revelations come up."

"How did I get roped—or hog-tied—into your lustful scenario?" Susan asked through a burst of laughter, almost spitting out a mouthful of water.

"Well, tomorrow, I thought we'd go visit the Georgia O'Keeffe museum and home after our morning dose and then check out the local rancher scene after our evening dose," said Emma. "How's that sound?"

"Isn't she the one who painted all the flowers that look like labia and vulvas?" Rachel asked.

"Yup. That's her," said Emma. "And she lived part-time in Santa Fe, in Abiquiu, and summered at the Ghost Ranch outside of Taos."

"I think I read somewhere that she insisted her flowers were just flowers–nothing sexual," said Rachel.

"I guess we'll see tomorrow. I, for one, wouldn't mind looking at a bunch of labia and vulvas." Yolanda let out a hearty giggle.

"Of course not." said Heather. "You can analyze the paintings for us. So, what's on the agenda for the rest of today?"

"Well, we'll get back to the house in time to lounge a bit and clean up before WW comes at five," said Emma. "After that, what do y'all want to do?"

"I don't know," said Susan. "I'm fine with anything. WW for Walter Wallace? I like it. Or, if Zipper had it her way, WW would stand for Wet Weiner."

A burst of chuckles exploded throughout the minivan until RaRa shrugged sheepishly and said, "I don't want to be a party pooper, but I'm still feeling a little tired, y'all. There were some old DVDs in the cabinet in the living room, and that feels about my speed right now. You know, sometimes it takes getting away to realize how tired and stressed you were."

"I know what you mean, Ra. Are you up for dinner?" asked Emma.

"Oh, sure. Maybe we'll even find Heather's loverboy."

"Well, there was this great place I wanted us to try if everyone is cool with it. And then let's see how we feel," said Emma.

"Honestly, I know I'm talking a big game about a ranch hand, but really, I'm just happy to get time with you all and some relaxation. That hot tub is simply delish. And the hammocks. And the sun. Does a body good," said Heather. "But if we stumbled upon a hot, young thing and he was up for it, that would be okay, too."

"Well, someone's libido is not affected by menopause." Yo whistled. "You go, girl."

"Honestly, it kind of is," said Zipper. "But I refuse to give in. I keep fightin' for my right…"

And they all joined in singing, "…to party."

Chapter 8

The chimes rang at exactly five o'clock, and as Emma walked Dr. Wallace to the kitchen, they made small talk. She reported that they all had been feeling fine–maybe just a bit tired. "But maybe that's just me–you know, the cancer," she said, "or the dry air. But we're ready for you and our evening dose."

Again, the doctor shook the citron-colored capsules into plastic cups and each of the women downed them with the glasses of water Emma had set out. They all reported no ill effects so far, other than maybe being a bit tired. "That is more likely from the desert air and elevation–we are at around seven thousand feet, and most of us live closer to sea level, so you should be drinking water even before you think you need it. I recommend carrying water with you everywhere. I'm sure you have all noticed that most locals–and the tourists for that matter–seem to all have water bottles on their persons."

"I completely understand the importance of hydration, and that more time in the hot tub won't exactly help us in that department," joked Heather. "But we all know we're gonna do it anyway, and I hope you know that you're welcome to join us anytime you would like."

Dr. Wallace tilted his head in a way that expressed serious contemplation in his own subdued way, and quietly thanked her for the invitation and then—almost as an afterthought—added that he would take her up on it. “Maybe tomorrow,” he muttered as he turned toward the door to leave.

“Well, that wasn’t awkward at all,” Susan said. “I guess hydration is the key to everything around here. Seems simple and obvious enough, but it’s also easy to forget. I don’t feel sweaty here…so I forget to drink unless it’s coffee or alcohol. So, I guess, it’s not as easy as one would think.”

“Perhaps WW isn’t as easy as one would have thought either,” Susan quipped as she playfully pretended to elbow Heather in the ribs.

“Speaking of hydration, did y’all read that display about plastic recycling?” asked Rachel. “Or, I should say, plastic *not* recycling?”

“Yeah. I did, and I, for one, felt super self-conscious about carrying around my Fiji bottle. And I kinda wish I hadn’t bought two cases of water bottles, which, of course, themselves come wrapped in plastic. But I almost bought four cases, so at least there’s that,” said Emma with a shrug.

“Hold on. What’s this? I didn’t see it,” said Susan.

“Well, you know how the Earthships are all about reusing building materials,” said Rachel, “so there was a display about what happens to all the stuff we throw out. Which, come to think about it, means all those shampoo and conditioner bottles don’t recycle either. So, I have to choose between having long, luscious hair and saving the planet. Shit.”

“But I put all my plastic bottles and takeout containers and everything in the recycle bin,” said Susan, “so what’s the dillio?”

"Well, apparently," said Emma, "even though the plastic is advertised as being recyclable, like ninety-five percent of it ends up in landfills. Or worse–the ocean."

"Holy hell." said Susan. "No way. Like, everything comes in plastic. Everything at the grocery store. All of my beauty products. Here I was thinking I'm taking care of myself by taking a water bottle everywhere, and you're saying I'm destroying the planet?"

"Well, you're not single-handedly 'destroying the planet,'" said Ma. "But it is kinda depressing, right?"

"Yeah, it's a total bummer. That'd dampen the libido if menopause didn't already," said Heather. "Nothing sexy about oceans full of trash."

"Yeah, I Googled it while I was standing there, and it's legit. I didn't want to believe it," said Rachel.

"I switched to a reusable water bottle a couple of years ago," said Yo. "One of my dates was, like, super '*green.*' She got me a nice Yeti insulated bottle. And while that relationship didn't last, the bottle did." She laughed. "And I may have, well, put that nice firm bottle *in position*, if you know what I mean, on a long car drive now and again to break up the monotony."

"What?" exclaimed Susan. "Seriously? Why did I not know about this? You, um, rub one out while driving? Can't other people in their cars see?"

"Well, I'm being discreet." Yolanda laughed. "When I forget my pocket vibrator, I put the bottle between my legs and squeeze. It's not like I do it at stoplights. Hold on–I'm not the only one, right?"

"Hell no.," said Heather. "There was this one time, though, that was kind of embarrassing when I was on the highway and, like, no one was around and I'm going, you know, to '*town*' using a tin of mints I had in the console for something to bump up against, and then suddenly there's all this traffic. I had the sunroof open, and a semi pulled up next to me. I'm pretty sure he could see in. I changed lanes and got out of sight as quickly as I could. And then," —she laughed— "finished off with extreme enthusiasm, of course."

Susan looked at her friend, blinked her eyes, and deadpanned, "That gives new meaning to the slogan, "Curiously Strong Mints." And then doubled over in laughter with the rest of them.

Emma shook her head and playfully rolled her eyes. "What on Earth, y'all. Seriously. You have an orgasm while driving, the next thing you know you're getting an unscheduled ride to the ER—and that's if you're lucky. And on that note—" "look at the time. We need to leave in about a half hour for our dinner reservation." She got up and walked away, fanning herself off with her hand and feigned light-headedness with the other. As she made her way to her room to freshen up before dinner, she endearingly called over her shoulder, "Only y'all can turn a conversation about environmental consciousness into one about conscious masturbation out in the environment."

They could barely hear her over the loud snorts of laughter.

****

As the doctor left the next morning after their first dose of the day, he said he might be interested in checking out the hot tub later. As the resident Julie McCoy-Cruise Director—from the old show "The Love Boat", Emma relayed that they were going sightseeing for a while but then would be back in time for their evening dose at five, but he could come back after dinner to take a dip.

"Y'all. I've been thinking about *Benjamin Button* ever since we watched it last night," said Rachel as they were getting in the car. "It seems like an interesting coincidence that of all the movies in the world, *that* was one of the few choices in the movie library. I mean, considering what we're doing here—and it totally reminded me of that last line from *Gatsby*, you know, 'So we beat on, boats against the current, borne back ceaselessly into the past' "Don't you remember? Mrs. Teddrich made us memorize it."

"OMG! I haven't thought of that in years." said Susan. "Though I did see that movie when it came out. *Benjamin Button* was weird. I mean Daisy having sex with him when he was younger–and older."

"But I see what you mean about that quote. Benjamin Button was literally being born back into the past," said Emma. "Oh my god. Is that what we're doing taking this TITS elixir? Are we trying to live in the past?"

"I don't think so," said Heather. "I think we're just trying to make the most out of the present."

"If anything," said Susan, "I think that the possibility that this treatment will help alleviate menopause symptoms is all about just being our best selves. It's not trying to turn back the clock; it's about claiming our current power. You know, having the energy to put all our experience to good use. Continuing to create and evolve." She paused. "And to ride this bitch until the wheels fall off," she added half-kiddingly.

****

The Georgia O'Keeffe Museum had her paintings

as well as photographs of her taken by her husband and others. They were struck by how self-possessed and ageless she seemed–even in pictures of her later in life.

"And her flower paintings are so goddam sensual," said Yo to Emma. "They just pull you in and wrap you up in their voluptuousness. You can practically feel the velvety softness of the flowers."

"Damn, that's poetic." replied Emma. "Didn't she have some women lovers, in addition to being married?"

"I actually don't know that much about her. I mean, I'm familiar with her Calla Lily, of course. I probably paid a little more attention to Frida Khalo. But I wonder what that would have been like–to be one of her lovers. I mean, she looks so serious."

"I can't believe she lived to almost 100." said Emma. "I wonder what her secret was."

"I bet it was her diet," Yo said, and then whispered, "like eating pussy."

"You're too much." Emma gushed and blushed at the same time. "But if that's the secret, I think I could get behind that."

"Did y'all see this display?" said Rachel, walking up and guiding them over to the photo by the window. "I love this quote of hers: 'I've been absolutely terrified every moment of my life, and I've never let it keep me from a single thing that I wanted to do.' Damn. Right? I don't admit that to many people, but I can relate."

"You?" said Emma. "You seem so calm and centered, Miss Yogapants," she joked affectionately.

"Well, thank you, I guess? But how I really feel is insecure and scared most of the time. There's so much bad stuff that can happen. That sooner or later will happen. Of course, I keep going, you know. It's like the Buddhists say, that trying to avoid difficulty is what causes suffering."

"Hey. Have you ever heard of the Buddhist mortality meditation? Or something like that," asked Emma. "I came across it when I was researching cancer support groups online."

"The idea that contemplating death helps you appreciate being alive?" said Rachel. "Is that what you mean?"

"Yeah. Something like that. I've been thinking about that a lot lately. And while life seems more precious—and precarious—now than ever, I want to try this anti-aging treatment because I'm just not ready. I mean, I know no one gets out of here alive, but I still feel like I have a lot to do. And there's Caroline, of course. She's too young to lose a mother. I haven't even told her yet. I wanted to wait until I started this treatment and had some idea of my prognosis. So, if this might turn things around, that would make it easier to break the news."

Susan and Heather walked up, and Heather pointed to a nearby painting, "How does she make some leaves look so sexual? Right?"

Emma shrugged and shook her head slowly, glad to change the subject. "Speaking of which, you still want to try to find some local talent? Or are you after the doctor now?"

"Can't it be both?" Heather asked and then stuck her tongue out between her front teeth. "The hot tub is big enough for a party. Or at least a threesome. And company."

****

The ambiance of the bar boasted an uncanny combination of being clean and updated, but with just enough old-fashioned charm–like it hadn't been renovated since the Reagan Era. Somehow, it just worked. They were having a late dinner after they did their five o'clock dose and spent an uneventful hour or so in the hot tub with the doctor.

"Did you see this? These burgers are from cows less than thirty miles away. Talk about farm to table." said Susan.

"Wow. That's cool. But I'm too busy people-watching," said Heather. "It looks like it might be a good place for some plaid shirts, cowboy boots, and laaaarge belt buckles."

"Ra, they also have a house-made green-chili, bean, and quinoa veggie burger. I bet that's good, too," said Ma.

As they finished their meals, the barstools started filling up and the jukebox cranked out country tunes. They'd had enough margaritas by then to join the bouncing and swaying bodies on the dance floor.

"Hey, where'd Heather get to?" Susan asked Ma. "I look up and suddenly she's missing."

"She went to get beer. Said she was getting hot."

"Sounds like a good idea," Susan replied. "I could use a cold one. Want anything, Ma?"

"Thanks, but honestly, I'm happy to be the designated driver tonight, like old times."

Yo leaned over and nodded toward the bar, and Emma turned to look. "Looks like Heather's charms work just as well in Taos as they did in high school."

"Maybe she'll get her ranch hand after all." Ma giggled.

"Where are all the cowgirls?" Yo swayed her hands as though swinging a lasso. "That's what I want to know."

After a second beer, Heather came back over. "He has to head out tonight, but he gave me his number in case I'm free tomorrow." She let out a boisterous whoop. "Name's Javier. What a hottie."

"Yeah. He looked pretty cute from over here," said Ma. "And it looked like you two were more than hitting it off."

"Um, yeah. And he's a good kisser. Yum."

Sleazin' and Ra came back from the bathroom. "How y'all holding up?" asked Ra. "I gotta admit I'm running out of gas."

"Ha. That bean burger will change that." shouted Susan over the music.

"Hilarious." Rachel scanned the room, her gaze landing on three women playing darts.

"This place is hoppin'. But I haven't seen any hot cowgirls walk in." Yo winked. "I'm okay with heading out."

"What about them, Yo?" Rachel asked as she nodded in the direction of a jean skirt-clad trio standing near the dartboard.

"Heather is pretty wasted, y'all. She's making out in public, which is her tell," Emma said while absentmindedly straightening up the empty glasses and peeling beer labels off bottles.

"I'm fine," Heather yelled while brandishing a fresh beer in the air, waving it back and forth to the beat of "Achy Breaky Heart."

"Damn. I haven't heard this song in sooooo long," exclaimed Susan. She instinctively belted out the lyrics in perfect harmony with Billy Ray Cyrus as he crooned from the jukebox.

"I'm suddenly in the mood to play darts," Yolanda said, and walked away.

Heather trotted right behind her and yelled, "Me too." And then tripped on a line dancer's swinging boot and went flying forward through the air. She landed hard on her stomach, with her long legs stretched out behind her like a frog. Time seemed to stop for a split second as everyone who saw it caught their breath and froze, waiting to see if she was okay. Zipper was on the ground amongst bar sludge and peanut shells, but the Cheshire Cat grin she boasted never left her face. Her beer remained firmly in her grip, held up over her head proudly like the Statue of Liberty's torch, without spilling a single drop. She might as well have been laying on a massage table in a high-end spa as opposed to a boot-scootin' bar in New Mexico. It didn't faze her in the least, and without skipping a beat, she popped back up and caught up with Yolanda, who was already shooting darts with her new friends.

Emma, who was watching the whole thing in mock horror from their table, finally exhaled, looked at Rachel, and exclaimed, "This is like herding cats. If the cancer doesn't kill me…." she trailed off with a huge smile. These were her girls, and she was happy.

****

They came down for their morning dose barely in time, still sleepy and recovering from their late night. As Dr. Wallace left, he said he might come by again for the hot tub after their evening dose. "If that's okay?"

"Of course." said Emma. "We'd be happy to have you."

"Just bring the margaritas," Heather said.

They all shot her a look, but were on the same page.

"Hair of the dog and all that, right?" She looked at Dr. Wallace and told him earnestly. "Don't worry, I'm properly hydrating. You should definitely come over for a soak."

"I just might," he said as he walked toward the door. He seemed to stop for a moment after a loud noise that sounded like a shoe, or a book being dropped on the ground came from upstairs. His hand lingered on the doorknob, but the look on his face indicated that whatever the noise was it wasn't his business, so he opened the door and left in his usual polite manner.

The second the door shut, they all burst out laughing, since everyone knew the three denim mamas were still upstairs and probably getting ready to leave after spending the night with YoYo.

They all simultaneously glued their eyes on Yolanda, who looked like the cat that ate the proverbial canary.

"I don't know much about darts," Susan said, "but I believe someone hit a bullseye last night."

"She hit something, that's for sure." Heather went over to Yolanda and playfully pinched her cheek. "Why, Miss YoYo, you are plumb heated. If I didn't know better, I would say that you're blushing."

Yolanda flashed her megawatt model smile. "Nah, just a little dehydrated. Hand me some water and hide me before they come down."

"How about keeping this party going with some mimosas and lounging for our second-to-last day?" said Emma. "After our house guests depart, that is."

"Alcohol in the morning?" asked Yo. "Really, Ma. What is this world coming to?"

"I just feel like celebrating y'all's company. And lounging in a hammock."

"You make the best, so I'm in. What's your secret ingredient?" Susan looked over at Emma.

"If I tell you, it won't be a secret." Emma winked. "But it's just a pinch of fresh-grated ginger."

"I thought you were going to say the secret ingredient is love." Susan chuckled. "And lounging sounds perfect. We're all going to head back to the real world way too soon. Let's enjoy this while we can."

"I agree," Heather said, rubbing her temples. "I know why I have a bit of a headache this morning, but is anyone feeling anything at all that they think is related to our TITS elixir?"

They all shook their heads.

"Nope," Susan said.

"Not at all," agreed RaRa.

"That's probably a good thing," said Ma as she flitted about the kitchen, gathering the ingredients for her perfect Mimosas. "No news is good news, so to speak. At least for now, right?" she asked hypothetically, with a cheery smile.

By the time Dr. Wallace arrived with their second dose of the day, most of them had napped, showered, and taken care of their laundry in the well-appointed laundry room off the kitchen. It came with Eco-friendly lavender soap sheets, which they'd heard of but never used. A clothesline was strung up along the wall with a sign that said how quickly clothes can dry naturally in the desert, so Rachel and Susan tried that.

After they all swallowed their little pills the color

of dandelions, they invited the doctor to come back for dinner and stay for margaritas.

"And the hot tub," added Heather.

After he left, while they were sharing the work of putting together a taco and burrito bar, Heather ducked out to take a call. She stuck her head back in to ask, "Y'all okay with me inviting my 'ranch hand' Javier over for margaritas later?"

They glanced around at each other and gave her the thumbs-up.

****

They cleared the plates and started the dishwasher while YoYo fired up the blender, and Heather finally figured out how to play her playlist over the whole-house sound system. The sunset lit the western sky on fire, silhouetting pinon, juniper, and willow in the foreground and turning Taos Mountain golden in the distance. The patio over the hot tub was strung with chili pepper lights, which somehow worked with the fine-art statuary. The doctor was on his third round of margaritas in his blue Speedo when Heather got out of the hot tub to check the front door. She had an uncanny ability to detect the arrival of a hot man.

While the hot tub fit four comfortably, more than that would be a crowd, so Emma, Susan, and YoYo said they'd check the margarita supply–to discreetly make room for their newest guest and his primary host.

When the three of them reached the kitchen, Susan couldn't hold back her giggles any longer. "Jesus, y'all, is it just me, or does the good doctor have an inordinate amount of back hair?"

Emma chortled so hard she slapped her knee and then held her stomach as if trying to maintain or resurrect some sense of dignity and said, "All I'm going to say is… that tiny banana hammock he's sporting certainly isn't distracting enough to pull attention away from it."

Susan said, "I'm pretty sure if I held onto a single strand of that hair, and he walked away from me, his entire back would unravel like a poorly knit sweater."

"Oh my gosh. Stop." Emma playfully punched her friend's shoulder, which caused her to spill Tequila on the countertop.

"What? It really looks like he's wearing a sweater. Sorry, I couldn't help myself."""

"Susan." Ma scolded half-heartedly. "Shhh. He's gonna hear y'all." She barely enunciated struggling to control herself.

The timing was perfect because Heather blew into the kitchen like a hurricane.

"Do y'all remember the old *Saturday Night Live* skit that Eddie Murphy did that was called James Brown's Celebrity Hot Tub Party?" she said as she whipped open the fridge and grabbed a couple of beers. She held a bottle to her lips like a microphone and mimicked Eddie Murphy's impersonation of James Brown singing. "" She didn't wait for a reply and went on to wave her hand in front of her crotch as if to fan it off and said, "I know I have complained about being dry, but that Javier is so sexy he's making my frog burp." With that, she turned on her heel and quickly left the room, leaving her friends in hysterics and spluttering, "Ribbit. Ribbit. Ribbit."

When Heather returned outside with Javier's drink, Dr. Wallace was leaning toward him, asking him whether he rode horses. Javier was clearly distracted by

Heather's return and stood to help her get into the dark, swirling water. By this time, the steps into the hot tub and the surrounding deck were all slippery from so many comings and goings, so whether Heather fell into him by accident or on purpose, it wasn't clear.

"Hey, y'all," said Rachel, walking through the sliding door into the kitchen. "Are there plastic glasses somewhere in here? It's getting kind of slick out there."

"Already ready for ya," said Emma, pointing to the tray where Yolanda was pouring drinks into plastic glasses with saguaro-shaped stems. "Aren't those fun?" "Somehow, since they're in this gorgeous house, they manage to not be tacky. They would look ridiculous in Greenville."

"This is what I love about travel," said Yo. "It opens the mind. And the legs."

"Ha," said Ma. "I think it might be gummies opening your mind right now."

"Hmmm," said Yo. "You wouldn't be wrong."

"I wouldn't mind some," said Rachel. "I don't know why, but the doctor being here is making me anxious. And this whole experiment. It's getting too real."

"Why? Are you starting to feel something?" asked Emma.

"No. It's not that. It's just kind of the whole idea of it. But maybe I'm just tired."

Just then, there was the sound of metal scraping along the deck and Heather yelling, "Watch out!"

Rachel hurried to the door in time to see the sound was coming from Dr. Wallace, who was holding onto a chair as it slid away from him, and then he went down. "I'm okay. I'm okay." he exclaimed before he hit the ground. As Rachel rushed out the door and over to him, followed by Emma and Yolanda, she was having flashbacks of that day on the boat when they were trying to hold on to Rick while he was dying. She walked quickly but deliberately, mindful of the slippery surface.

The doctor was lying stretched out on his stomach when she reached him, and as she gingerly reached out to shake his shoulder, she was trembling, suddenly chilled and feeling like she was in a black hole closing around her. "No. No. No." she shouted.

By that time, Javier was also there, and as he rolled the doctor onto his back, the doctor was shouting, "I'm okay. I'm okay." Slowly, he sat up. "I think maybe I should call it a night. Those margaritas mixed with the hot tub sure do pack a wallop, especially in the desert," he slurred, uncharacteristically casual. "I should know better."

"Since you're so close, we can run you home," said Emma, with a nod in Yolanda's direction. "And not to worry, I'll come back and get you tomorrow, first thing, in plenty of time for the morning dose."

"Thank you so much," he said. "Lemme jus get my shirr on."

Yolanda and Javier each took an elbow and led the doctor to the car where Yolanda sat in the back with him, and Emma drove. Susan and Heather went inside with Rachel. "I can't believe it. I come to the desert," Rachel said in a panic, "because no one fucking drowns in the desert, and here our *doctor* fucking slips and almost passes out. I just don't know about all this."

"Here," said Susan, handing RaRa a freshly poured glass, "have some ice water. Everything is okay. That wasn't our fault then, and this isn't our fault now. Rick was an adult and an extremely experienced diver. It was just a freak accident. Dr. Wallace is an adult and just let loose a little too much. But he's okay. We all go a little overboard sometimes."

As Susan handed Rachel tissues, Rachel said, "Really? You had to say 'overboard'? I know, girl. I know you're right in theory, but it's just so hard to see."

"It's all right, doll. You can be upset," Susan said as she wrapped a blanket and her arms around Rachel. "I'm ready to call it a night. How 'bout you? I'll walk you up?"

Rachel nodded and gently laid her head on her friend's shoulder as they slowly made their way up the staircase.

When Emma and Yolanda returned, it was clear that the party in the hot tub was now private, so they hollered their goodnights to Heather and turned out all but the light over the stove in the kitchen.

****

The next morning, Emma picked up Dr. Wallace, as promised, and they drove back to the house together in an awkward but cordial silence. Clouds of red dust kicked up as they pulled into the driveway, and it even tried to follow them inside as they entered the house, but Emma quickly shut the door behind them. She could hear some muffled conversations and giggles as they made their way deeper inside, and practically ran into Heather, who was finally coming downstairs.

"Looks like someone had a good time last night," Yo joked.

"My 'ranch hand' was quite handy, if you must know." Heather laughed as the doctor walked in and they all hushed.

"Good morning. How is everyone feeling this morning? Any side effects from the treatment?" he said as he shook the pills into paper cups. "As usual, here are the forms, so once you've taken today's dose, you can fill out the questionnaire. I can collect them when I return at five," he said as he started walking toward the door. "Have a great day, ladies. And be sure to hydrate." He made little eye contact with them, and blew out of the room as briskly as he came in.

"That was weird," said Susan. "Did he say anything to you, Ma?"

"Nope. When I picked him up, he just made small talk about Taos and complimented us on last night's dinner, and the rest of the time we drove without saying a word."

"Well, I guess that's a good sign," said Heather. "He must have recovered?"

"Seems like it," said Susan. "He's most likely just really embarrassed. It wasn't that big of a deal to me, but it wasn't super professional either. I doubt the FDA would approve of his patient interactions."

"Are you kidding me? That was a disaster," exclaimed Rachel. "I could hardly sleep last night. I just kept having visions of being on a lake of desert sand and the doctor lying on the floor of a wrecked boat, twitching."

"Oh my god, Ra. I'm so sorry," said Emma.

"It's not your fault. It was just," —she paused— "intense. I mean, I haven't thought of that day much in a while, but when I saw him lying there in a pool of water, it just all came flooding back."

"I know," said Susan. "It was upsetting. So much

so that I almost kept myself from pointing out that you said 'flooding' just now."

"Susan. You're terrible. But please stay true to yourself because I do find you hilarious. Honestly, though, I think the whole incident was just a good reminder about how precious life is," said Yolanda.

"For sure," said Emma. "And you never know what will happen, so you should take life by the balls. I'm just grateful that we can all grab those balls together. I don't know what I'd do without you."

"Ah, Ma. Of course. We don't know what we'd do without you, either," said YoYo. "But can we skip the balls analogy? They're so nasty and uninspiring," she said with a giant grin. "Let's get back to TITS. I like them much better than a pair of gnarly-ass testicles." She lifted a mug of black coffee from the table and held it in the air. "Here's to us and to TITS *being* tits and to it *doing* its shit," she managed to say as she laughed, and hoped to lighten everyone's mood.

"Seriously. You all make my life and my current situation so much better. I don't mean to get mushy, again, but I honestly don't think you will ever know how much I love and appreciate y'all. You are rare gems, and I just want to say thanks again to each of you for coming out here for this. It means the world to me," said Emma.

She too lifted her coffee cup, and the rest followed suit. A slight clink of mugs and a few sniffles seemed to be the only sounds in the whole house.

"But okay," she said after she cleared her throat and brushed away a rogue tear with the back of her hand. "If it's okay with everyone, I thought we'd take one last trip to our favorite coffee shop and maybe see our WockaWocka friend. But no hurry. Y'all are lookin' a little, um, rough. Especially some of y'all," she said, winking at Heather.

"Rough, but, um, well-ridden," she retorted. "How about we just go for an early lunch?"

They all agreed to be ready at eleven and went to clean up or lounge.

Rachel found Emma in a hammock. "Hey there, Ma. I am so grateful for this time with y'all. Thank you for arranging and coordinating everything. It has been the best trip I've taken in a long time."

"Of course. I wouldn't have it any other way."

"I feel really bad about this, but…" She paused for a moment. "I'm having second thoughts about this treatment."

Emma sat up and turned to face her friend. "Oh no, hon. I thought the nausea was gone after the first day."

"Yeah. It's not that. It's just…" She stared off at the mountains and willows.

"I would completely understand if it were, but I hope it's not because of what happened last night with WW. He just overindulged when he probably shouldn't have. Whatever it is, you have the right to your feelings, but you know we all want you to remain part of this crazy thing we're doing," said Emma slowly. "But no matter what you're about to tell me, just know that I'll understand, and I'll always love you."

"Oh, I know. It's just that, even though I've been thinking about this nonstop for the past two days, I don't know how to say it. This just doesn't feel right for me. I mean, I wanted to do it, and I was excited about it–even though I was also nervous. But once we got here and it got real, I dunno."

"It's okay."" You really don't have to explain. I'm just grateful you came."

"I know. But I can't help feeling like I'm letting you down. Not being supportive. You know. Of your *situation*. Your *condition*."

"Oh that," she said as she casually swatted the air in front of her face as if an invisible fly buzzed annoyingly between them." You're being super supportive. Y'all are truly the best. This has been the best week *I've* had in years."

"I mean, I knew you'd be understanding, but thank you." She paused and reached for Emma's hand. "It just doesn't feel right. Like I'm not being true to myself. And the accident last night just put it all in perspective. Life is precious. We all found that out that day on the lake, if we didn't know before. And I think I *want* to age. Doing this experiment–for *me*–feels like I'm trying to cheat. All that we've seen and done here has honestly just helped me see that I want to lean into myself as I am now."

"Honey, I love that about you. I love that you think about things like you do. That's what makes us such an incredible tribe. We're all so similar and yet *so* different at the same time. We complement each other, lend our strengths where another might be weak, and we *always* keep things interesting."

"Thank you, Ma. But I don't want to make a big deal about it. And I certainly don't want to rain on y'all's parade. I'm not leaving or anything, but I'm not going to keep taking the capsules. I still want to be connected to TITS, though, and I'm excited to see how this all works out for y'all."

"Me too," said Emma. "I'm super hopeful. I don't

know why, or if I'm being naive, but I'm truly eager to see what happens next."

Chapter 9

Three Months After Taos

Summer in Greenville always felt like a magical time for Emma. Everything seemed more alive during those long days and warm nights, especially on Main Street, where the city often blocked off large sections for incredible live music, events, or festivals. All her favorite restaurants offered alfresco dining, and every street corner hummed harmoniously with unique and talented musicians. The aroma of delicious delicacies danced together upon light evening breezes and their mingling aroma was always enough to make her mouth water.

Blueberry season began in May and maintained its magnificence until it was inevitably forced to give way to peach season in July, which, to Emma, was like a shot of heaven with a sunshine chaser. Her happy heart buzzed louder than the bees, and she was inspired by the color and scent of the moonflowers and lavender that abound in large fields all around Greenville during the summer. But the enchantment of these warmer months hit differently this year. While they still included sundresses, swimming holes, and snow cones, there was also a sudden surge of heat and youthfulness that overtook her entire being on that humid but breezy July evening.

Emma flipped the sign on the door to "Closed" and locked up the shop after a particularly busy day of helping both locals and tourists discover new scents and home decor when she felt something within her…shift. If she hadn't been so closely in tune with every little twinge in her body for the past three months since returning to her normal life after Taos, she would have thought it was gas or maybe a hot flash. "No," she told herself out loud in the now quiet, dimly lit shop, "this is different."

Emma was pretty sure what had happened, but she didn't want to get too excited about it until she was positive.

How could it be anything else? She knew darn well that Heather, Susan, and Yolanda had *all* experienced an esthetic and internal energy change that was no less than miraculous within the first four weeks after their time in New Mexico.

Her body seemed to be a little more resistant or stubborn since she hadn't felt or looked one bit different from when they were in Taos, while her friends all *looked* and *felt* like they were thirty years old. She wouldn't have believed it if she hadn't seen them on the Zoom calls and heard what they had been up to since their extraordinary and otherworldly transformation. She read and reread their text messages on an almost daily basis with the latest incredible stories of how the elixir really *was* TITS after all.

Seeing and *feeling* the hands of time reversed so profoundly was hard proof, yet they each remained in a state of shock and disbelief that WW's crazy concoction actually worked, and that it also brought them closer to their dreams faster than they ever would have thought possible. Their shiny new exteriors combined with boundless, youthful energy catapulted each of them ahead in the pursuit of their individual goals.

The clock had quite literally been turned back, and thankfully, there wasn't one single negative side effect to speak of, other than having to explain to people how they did it. Susan said she told people she switched to a plant-based diet, quit smoking, and bumped up her fitness routines. She said they looked at her funny, because there's no way that would be enough to shave more than twenty years from her looks, but it was enough to appease them. "I mean, what else are they going to say?"

She said the bulk of the questions and bewilderment came from co-workers and colleagues, so she decided this was the perfect time to take all the vacation days she had been squirreling away, as well as a leave of absence, and pursue the stand-up comedy dream she had been holding so close to her heart. Her confidence had sky-rocketed, as did her name and the demand to see her act.

Heather had been basking in the afterglow of the miraculous, if not witchy, spell, and proudly told anyone who asked her how she achieved her new look that she simply increased her daily number of orgasms. When that wasn't enough to keep further, prying questions at bay, she would go into a detailed explanation regarding the scientific proof that having the Big O helps people stay healthy and younger looking due to increased blood flow to the skin and, of course, the boatloads of DHEA, an anti-aging steroid hormone, that keeps you looking and feeling like a teenager again. According to Zip, this had been enough to subdue even the most inquisitive and incredulous individuals. Her husband barely looked at her anymore, anyway, so she wasn't sure if he even noticed the difference.

Yolanda said she didn't explain herself to too many people when she was grilled about her secret to staying so youthful—and asked if she'd share the name of her plastic surgeon, and instead just shrugged it off in a show of modesty. She was more than happy with the new modeling gigs she had secured in such a short amount of time. In her industry, her biological age was considered prehistoric, but no one could argue the way she owned every runway she stepped foot on, and that her photos needed no filters. With the help of social media and a modeling agency in Milan, Yolanda had done more than make a comeback—she had taken the modeling scene by unfathomable force. Although she appeared more than twenty years younger, it was as clear as a glass of water that she was still considered "old" for the industry—a fact that ended up making her even *more* popular. She turned the modeling world upside down at a sizzling pace and took immense pleasure in debunking the well-established industry myth, which basically dictated that worthiness and success were only for the "young."

Each of them was fully aware that people most likely didn't believe their explanations for the way they looked and felt. Truly, they could barely believe it themselves, and they knew damn well that absolutely no amount of vitamins, exercise, clean eating, or orgasms would produce such extreme esthetic and physical changes. But they didn't care what other people thought or believed. It really didn't matter to them *how* people saw them; they knew the gift they had received was otherworldly, unexplainable, and would normally only occur in movies, books, and fantasy. At this point, what mattered was that they were euphoric with the results and were relieved and grateful there were no signs of negative side effects. It had been months, and they began to breathe sighs of relief that the only changes had been positive. Even Dr. Wallace agreed that they were in the clear, and if they hadn't experienced any ill effects yet, they most likely never would.

Emma knew this time it had to be *her* time, so she patted herself up and down like TSA at an airport security check, and silently took inventory of what her hands told her. The more she felt around, the harder her heart pounded. She stood still and noticed her necklace as it shuddered like oil on a hot griddle from the vibration in her chest. Her hands made their way up to her neck. *What the heck? Where is the little turkey waddle that made me chastise my neck on an almost daily basis?*

Slowly, albeit shakily, she cupped her cheeks simultaneously with both hands, her fingers pointing straight up on both sides of her face. A tiny gasp escaped her open mouth. With her hands firmly planted on what she knew was her face, she stood frozen because her face didn't feel like it belonged to her. She bit down nervously on her lower lip for what seemed like an eternity, afraid to make her way over to one of the antique mirrors that hung about the shop. Finally, she slowly and gingerly took a couple of baby steps forward with her hands glued to the supple skin of her cheeks. She gave an involuntary shudder as her blood pumped like an electrical current through her entire body. She felt like she could run back-to-back marathons—even backward—and they would be *easy*.

Emma tried to steady her breathing as she moved in the direction of a large 19th-century gilded mirror they had recently acquired from an estate in Rome. It hung at the perfect height for her to see her face, and her body too, if she stood on something. She didn't make it to the mirror, however, because on her way there she caught a glimpse of her reflection in the clean, shiny glass window of the shop's front entrance, and it revealed *everything*. She nervously peeked out of the window of the front door and looked up and down the street to be sure no one was there to see what had happened. Or maybe she hoped someone *had* witnessed what felt like an insane scenario, wanting a stranger's confirmation of what her own eyes and body had already told her was true. It was like that Cher song that came out the summer after Rick died. Then Emma had wanted to turn back time for very different reasons, but now suddenly it felt like she really had.

Emma promptly turned away from the door and swiftly made her way over to the Italian mirror for a second opinion. She got as close to the glass as physically possible and stared warily at the almost unrecognizable thirty-year-old reflection appearing and disappearing behind ghostly puffs of her own breath on the glass.

A lightning-fast shiver that she hadn't felt in ages rippled through her body like a shock wave accompanied by an equally brief flashback of the day they tried to save Rick's life on the boat. Suddenly, it didn't matter that she had both seen and accepted the fact that this crazy thing had already happened to the girls, and that she had been anxiously waiting for it to happen to her as well. Now that it finally had, it was quite evident that nothing in the world could have prepared her for the inconceivable way such a fantastical change in *herself* made her look and feel.

She wanted to scream. She wanted to cry. Instead, she broke into uncontrollable laughter.

Once the laughter subsided, and she batted away a few happy tears from her crease-free eyes, she scanned the shop for her phone and spotted it on the front counter. With excitement she hadn't felt in more than a decade, she practically floated over to the phone. She couldn't send the group text fast enough.

—Y'ALL! It happened!!—

Regardless of the different time zones, and their now even more exciting schedules, the responses came back almost immediately from everyone.

—Yeah, baby! Welcome to the club!— Heather responded (most likely from a bed where she lay waiting for her lover to be ready to go again.)

YoYo added, *—I'm so happy for you. You better go out and celebrate, girl. Get yourself a glass of wine on a rooftop bar and feel your sexy self.—*

—I'm about to go on stage for a show but wanted to send congratulatory hugs!— Susan texted. *—I know you are probably freaking out, but please embrace this, Ma! You deserve it.—*

Emma answered with *—Thanks, y'all! I can't explain all the feelings I'm having right now, but I'm thrilled that each of you is here for it. I'm gonna do what YoYo said and give my new look a test drive. LOL.*

I'll Facetime with WW—and Caroline—in the morning, to share the news. Love y'all. Have a great night.—

She set the phone down and burst into tears. This is what she wanted, but that didn't take away the fact that this whole thing was completely unbelievable, overwhelming, freaky, and a bit scary. She made sure the register was settled, and the rest of the lights were turned off before she left the comfort of the shop and stepped out into the street for the first time in this new state of being. Instinctively, and also in unyielding disbelief, she felt compelled to look at herself one more time before she walked out into the fragrant summer evening. She stood before another beautifully ornate mirror, not for purposes of vanity but instead to give herself a pep talk and hopefully become a little calmer and more collected.

Emma intently studied her reflection, her hand brushing her rosy cheeks and fingertips lingering on her lips. Thoughts of Caroline, her friends, and the years spent with Bobby flooded her brain. She stared into her own eyes as thoughts about how it felt when she was told she had a rare, aggressive form of cancer. She couldn't help but draw a direct line in her mind that contrasted how she looked and felt right now with how she had felt to learn about her illness. At the time, the pressing need to get her affairs in order when she first got the news had become a priority. Her hand dropped from her mouth and landed gently on her throat. She held both sides of her neck lightly between her fingers and her thumb while she took stock of herself, both inside and out.

Although scary to receive the news initially, it oddly became quite liberating in many ways as well.

She expected that was probably why she was so open to taking part in an experimental study that, at any other time in her life, she surely would have scoffed at. But it was like the prognosis had given her full permission to live for the now. The way *she* wanted to. She never admitted this to anyone else, but once the cancer news had settled in, she felt a certain amount of relief from the weight of expectations, and the inconsequential bullshit that sometimes seems to take over daily life.

She smoothed the non-existent creases of her jewel-green silk blouse around her chest and shoulders without breaking eye contact with the familiar stranger in the mirror. Her hands instinctively went to her hips as she thought about the fact that she hadn't always been as successful as she would have liked when it came to grabbing life by the horns and living the carpe diem out of it. But after the diagnosis, her perspective about what mattered changed. Once the words inoperable brain tumor rang in her ears, her life had abruptly changed. All of it. The good, the bad, the extraordinarily ugly, and the beautiful beyond words. How could she look at every day from here as anything but a bonus, an amazing new gift?

"It's time to celebrate life," she said loudly, and with a bright smile because she knew she meant it.

****

As she stepped into the clean, modern surroundings of Arbour, her absolute favorite and most frequented of all the bars and restaurants in Greenville, Emma felt like it was her first time there. She looked around the bustling, yet romantic restaurant, and it all appeared brighter. There was a lightness in the air (and in herself) that she couldn't quite put her finger on, but it felt crisp and clean like a white linen suit. Although she knew better, she could have sworn pure oxygen was being pumped directly into the atmosphere just for her, and she inhaled it deeply.

She had been in high heels all day, yet they felt like clouds on her feet, and she had an exceptionally unreal sensation of lightness. A vivacious vitality that oozed deliciously through her entire body. She scanned the indoor bar to see if she knew anybody, and saw a few familiar faces, but no one she knew. Emma wondered if she had been unconsciously—or consciously—looking for Bobby. This *was* a favorite destination for faculty and even some students from Furman—if they were using their parents' credit cards, as it was pretty pricey for college kids.

Clearing her mind of those ridiculous thoughts, she opened the door and took the stairs two at a time to the rooftop bar. She hadn't seen or heard from Bobby Fisk since he pulled out of the driveway, which by now, and with all that had happened, felt like another lifetime ago. No, she just wanted to breathe in the night air and enjoy the faint music of crickets mixed with a little live music as she sipped a big, beautiful red. Surprisingly, the spot in the place that was beautiful, historically most coveted, and vacant beckoned her to not only sit, but to unabashedly take up space under its black iron framework.

She happily made her way over to the impressive little structure covered in ivy and fat ropey leaves of a plant she didn't recognize. As she sat on the smooth, square couch of stone, she thought about how perfectly the designer pulled together the desired look for the space. It could have looked cold and uninviting were it not for their ridiculously huge, comfy cushions, the exact color of baby elephants, and puffy throw pillows in shades of fern green. And because it was surrounded on three sides by thick greenery in large, rectangular stone planters, it felt like a private cabana, yet it was situated perfectly for her to sit, and people watch without feeling too conspicuous in her new state. Two large trees (quite realistically made to look like they had grown straight out of the white tiled floor) flanked the romantic-looking structure like giant bookends. Their long branches drooped with octagonally shaped glass and metal lanterns. Fat, white pillar candles sat tall and proud inside each gently swaying lantern ready to cast their warm glow when the sun finally decided to clock out for the night.

She ordered a big, bold Cabernet, propped a pillow behind her back, and contentedly leaned back and took in her beautiful surroundings. She wanted to hug whoever designed the space and compliment them on their uncanny and successful execution of what she would consider English Garden charm meets New York City sleek. The waitress came back with her wine and placed it on one of the little round tables in front of her. Emma smiled at her and noticed the tops of the tables each had a small handle in the middle and had been constructed from beautiful black metal lids of gourmet cooking pots. Underneath the lids, each table had thin but sturdy brass-colored legs that came down on what looked like a tripod, which balanced them perfectly and also added a modern twist. She loved how the lush greenery mixed with slate, stone, and metal juxtaposed sturdiness and delicacy and lent itself perfectly to her own current feelings of vulnerability, strength, and vitality.

After a few gentle swirls of her wineglass, Emma tipped it toward her nose, closed her eyes, and took in its beautiful aroma. When she opened her eyes, she noticed a group of people had begun to file in two-by-two like the animals on Noah's ark. And then she remembered that everyone and every creature that didn't make it onto ark drowned—and she quickly pushed that thought from her mind before it soured her mood. They congregated near the bar in a fairly tight bunch, all smiles, elbows, and laughter. A young, attractive, and well-dressed couple broke away from the pack and approached the bar while the rest of the herd shouted out their drink orders. She scooted her butt to the edge of the seat cushion and turned her body in the direction of the couple to make it easier to both look at them and reach for her drink. Emma sat up straight and crossed her beautiful, smooth legs as she admired their fun and carefree demeanor, both balanced perfectly with an intensity that was clearly reserved only for one another.

The pair mesmerized her, and she thought for a moment that she actually *felt* the electricity they exuded in what felt like her own private little bungalow. In her mind, that kind of heat and energy could only be rivaled by the sun or stars in the sky. Perhaps they were stars. Emma enjoyed her creative and artistic side, which made her mind churn and allowed her the ability to look at things a little differently than most people. She took another long sip from her glass, closed her eyes, and playfully embellished them to be two movie stars from old Hollywood. That was the aura they exuded, and that was a time when glamor was real.

She opened her eyes and immediately looked at her glass to see if she had pounded her wine a little too quickly. The tiny pool of light red liquid at the bottom of her wineglass answered that question. She shook her head slightly and chuckled. Was she really romanticizing old-time, classic glamor while she simultaneously basked in her new, and let's not forget, intensely and highly desired youthful state of being? The complete irony of having these sentiments within her current situation was most definitely not lost on her.

****

Emma's laser-focused attention on the beautiful duo kept her so enthralled that she didn't notice the person standing just out of her peripheral vision and as close to her as he could before being considered creepy as dictated by social convention. The entire time she had been people watching, he couldn't take his eyes off her. He took note of her drink, and although she was a little older than the women he usually hit on, he ordered a house red for each of them as he mustered the courage to approach her. She seemed quite unlike the plethora of gorgeous co-eds he had been known to date. He didn't think it was the wine talking; he just thought that she was, hands down, the most exquisitely beautiful creature he had ever laid his eyes on. It seemed like he had been standing beside her for an eternity, although it was probably more like half a minute. As each second ticked by, his usual nerves of steel weakened. He was not accustomed to going unnoticed by women, especially if he paid them even the slightest bit of attention. Regardless, he found himself almost close enough to touch this exotic flower and still couldn't seem to divert her attention away from whatever it was that held it so firmly.

In an extremely unusual moment of insecurity, he felt like a silly schoolboy holding a flower he had plucked from his mom's garden for his pretty teacher instead of a worldly, confident man who wished to offer a glass of wine to a woman in a bar. In his mind, the stem of the glass at the end of his slightly outstretched arm began to look like the stem of a flower drooping pathetically over his tightly wound fist. Embarrassment made his neck tingle, along with a warm, gentle breeze as it caught and carried the sophisticated bouquet of the wine. By the time it reached his nose, however, the delicate aroma had transformed into a heavy waft of the earth and soil that clung messily from the dangling roots of his offering as he continued to go unnoticed by his teacher while she wrote assignments on the chalkboard behind her desk.

He had offered drinks, attention, and conversation quite successfully to tons of women, but this felt different somehow. This woman felt oddly familiar, comfortable, yet exciting and compelling all at once. He was completely drawn in by her, and the fact that she still hadn't noticed him and was slightly turned away made him even more intrigued. But enough was enough, so he cleared his throat to get her attention.

****

Emma's thoughts about the couple at the bar, as well as her own magical transformation and the possibilities it held for her, came to an abrupt halt. The impatient-sounding reverberation of someone's throat being cleared was like a record needle being dragged across spinning vinyl, and it jolted her back to whatever reality remained in her life.

As she turned toward the source of the sound, she had the sudden sensation she was moving in slow motion. He stood there holding out a glass of wine, awkwardly, and their eyes met. Just seconds before that, the air around her felt breezy and light. Now, as she looked at him trying to excavate his usual charms, the outdoors felt small and suffocating. The air was as heavy as a cement kite, and if there had been stars twinkling a few minutes ago, they had probably just burned themselves out.

For Emma, of course, recognition was immediate. However, the head tilt and confused expression on Bobby Fisk's face told her that his brain had yet to compute exactly who she was. He was working on it but needed a little help. She couldn't believe the sense of calm and confidence she felt—and exuded—as she lowered her chin and looked up at him with bedroom eyes and a sexy sideway smile. Acknowledgment flashed behind his eyes like lightning, and she watched as each individual finger weakened and peeled from the wineglass in his hand. He still hadn't spoken one single word and seemed almost frozen in place, even in the dense heat of the air. But the falling wineglass, somersaulting as it fell, and the resounding crash when it hit the floor, spoke volumes for him. Wine splashed around his feet, and time felt like it was suspended. But he didn't let go of her eyes. The connection had been made, and although his face registered confusion at first, it was quickly washed over with humiliation.

He stood before her with the gawkiness of a teenager. His insecurity was palpable, and most gratifying to her at that moment. This was not something Bobby was used to. Being awkward.

Looking bad. Not getting his way. Emma luxuriated in the moment like she was in a hot bubble bath after a cold run. She felt free and clean as she realized all the hurt and anger from his leaving was now falling away. She stood up from her comfy cushion to avoid being splashed by the droplets of red that rained down on Bobby's Italian loafers, picked up her handbag, and drew out enough money to pay for three bottles of Arbor's best wine. She set it down on the small table and inwardly argued with herself about what she should or shouldn't say before she walked away.

She decided there was nothing on earth—absolutely no words—that could make the moment feel any more satisfying. Before she reached the door, she glanced over her shoulder and saw Bobby Fisk as he remained in the mess of spilled wine and broken glass. His mouth hung open like he was trying to catch flies. It's not so much she was savoring his humiliation, but now no longer had the need to try to save him from himself. The feelings he was having were the consequences of his own behavior, his own arrogance, and self-absorption, and she no longer had to bend over backward to placate him or ease his discomfort.

Emma could barely contain herself as she reached the stairs. She felt like her legs were on autopilot as she flew down them two at a time. When she reached the street in front of the bar, she kept walking toward the shop. Her car was still parked there, but mostly, she wanted to put some distance from what had just happened. She hoped to God that Bobby couldn't see her from the roof and wished her mind and her fingers would slow down enough for her to get the group text sent to her girls. Emma wanted that moment and that look to be the one he remembered, and she had a feeling he always would.

Emma's fingers flew furiously as she sent the group text.

—*Girls. I'm freaking out.*

I was on the rooftop at Arbor and guess who tried to hit on me?

Bobby Fuckin' Fisk. Wish y'all could've seen it for yourselves.—

Rachel: —*AHHHHHHHH. NO WAY.*—

Yolanda: —*Did you tell him to–or get him to–eat your ass? LOL*—

Emma read the texts and laughed out loud. —*No. That's part of what was so amazing about it. Neither of us said one single word. His face did all the talking—and it was pathetic. Plus, along with his jaw, he dropped a full glass of wine he had bought for me. The glass shattered and wine spilled everywhere, but he didn't move a muscle. It was truly poetic.*—

Heather: —*Hold on. Back it up. He was hitting on you, and you crushed him like a bug without talking to him?*—

Emma: —*Yes. I had my back to him and didn't even know he was there at first. I was lost in my own world. People watching. He came up behind me with a glass of wine in each hand and, knowing him, had one of his pickup lines locked and loaded as well. Then he had the gall to clear his throat at me. When I turned around, he looked so awkward, sad, and foolish. Words would have ruined the whole thing. He was still standing there in the mess when I got up and walked out.*—

Yolanda: —*Damn, girl, that really is perfect poetic*

justice. I'm so happy for you. You kept it classy too. Not many people who feel vindicated with an ex can say that. This shit really is TITS.—

Emma: *—I know. I couldn't have planned it any better. It felt like a dream come true. I will be playing that scene back in my mind for a while.—*

Rachael: *—It was meant TO BE. I wish I could have seen his face. I'm thrilled for you, Ma.—*

Heather: *—You got that right. Speaking of TITS, I don't want to take away from Ma's amazing moment, especially with Sleazin' not responding—probably doing stand up. But I'm about to explode with our news too.—*

Emma: *—What news? Please share. There's nothing that could take away from this moment. It can only add to it. And truly, what just happened with Bobby was all I could have asked for, y'all. I honestly don't need anything else from this experiment. I'm over-the-top thrilled no matter what.—*

Yolanda: *—I don't think Sleazin' will care if we share the news. The ink on the contracts have barely dried, but I'm dying to tell Ma as well.—*

Heather: *—And now it's our turn to give her a proposition.—*

Rachael: *—We were going to spill the beans earlier...but Susan had a show. The finances and contracts have just been solidified, and, Ma, you just had your change...which was WAY more important at the time...so we put off the good news and our little proposition.—*

Emma: *—Contracts and propositions? You're killin' me. Just tell me, already.—*

Heather: *—It's huge and super exciting...two*

things that I would normally want to take charge of personally...but I'm going to let YoYo do the honors on this one. LOL.—

Yolanda: *—I can't believe what I'm about to say and couldn't be more excited about it. Ma, you might want to sit down. LOL Sleazin' and some folks from her company helped me find a 30,000 sq ft/ 4-level club space for sale in South Beach, and we have all pooled our expertise and resources to buy and run it.—*

Emma: *—No way. Oh my God. I don't know what to say. Shit...this is incredible, girls. I have so many questions. LOL What about Susan's job? Heather, what about your job and your hubby? And RaRa, your studio? Are y'all relocating? I'm getting in my car, turning on the AC and waiting for details. LOL—*

Yo: *—Can y'all FaceTime? This is getting too hard to type.—*

They all agreed and hopped on the video chat.

Heather: "YoYo had the initial dream, but it was only going to work if we all joined her. Ma, YOU made this possible by bringing us together again and getting us to try something outrageous and new. Without TITS, this wouldn't have happened, so we're naming the club TITS! This time, however, it will stand for Twist In Time Symposium.

"I'll be handing in my resignation at work next week. I believe Susan took a leave of absence but will most likely do the same. Also, hubby and I live separate lives and have an open marriage already, so when I move to Florida, it won't change a thing in that department. Ma, we want you to join us in the partnership, or at least to redesign the interior."

Rachel: "Yes, Ma. It wouldn't be TITS without

you. Please say you will join us.

"I'm sort of moving the studio to Florida. The club is going to be unlike any other. Each level will have its own flare. Night club, bistro, entertainment stages, and 'Sexy Wellness' that includes massage, yoga, reiki, and of course, there's a rooftop bar and pool. Imagine the best and sexiest performers, DJs, dancers, foodies, and wellness superfreaks. It will be like Studio 54 on steroids."

Emma: "This is incredible. I'm all about rooftop bars. LOL. But I can't take credit for your awesomeness. Y'all, I would love to be on the dream team, but I will be at the doctor tomorrow to go over treatment options. I need to stay here and take care of that. But would love to help with any and all design work if I can."

Yolanda: "We were all thinking about that, which is why we didn't tell you about the opportunity at first. With treatments and all, we didn't want to put any undue stress on you but didn't want to leave you out either. It was a weird place for us to be, but then again, we have all been in weirder places together. We just love you so much and want what's best for you, Ma. The invitation will remain open for you to join us, and you can always stay with me until you get settled, should you decide to move here. RaRa is moving in with me until she finds a place. The more the merrier."

Emma: "This is amazing. Tonight's news has all been so happy. I'm euphoric for all of us…don't go and make me cry now.

"Oh, my gosh. RaRa and YoYo as roomies. How fun is that?

"I love you girls too, and appreciate how you

thought of me and handled all of this. Don't think twice about it. I will be as much a part of the new TITS as I can from Greenville. Y'all are my heart, and I couldn't be happier for you. Twist In Time Symposium is an awesome name for so many reasons. It makes me think of bodies twisting in perfect time—dancing or otherwise. It's fresh too—like a twist of lemon or lime in a drink.

"Of course, it also makes me think of the way we have literally twisted time in the most incredible and unreal way. I know it will certainly be a club to experience a twisted time. I don't think I'll be able to sleep tonight with all that's happening. This will be the first time I won't be upset about having insomnia."

Yolanda: "Yes. Folks can get their freak on or their chill on—or a twist of both. Like a chocolate and vanilla twist soft ice cream. LOL.

"We knew you would get it right away. Thanks, Ma. We love ya like crazy. Get some rest, and good luck tomorrow."

Rachel: "Ma, you're truly the greatest. You really brought us all back together again in the most beautiful way possible. We can't say that enough. Please let us know everything the minute you get your treatments planned out. Hugs."

Emma: "Love y'all."

Heather: "Sleazin's gonna be pissed she missed all the excitement, but she's gonna love that you left Bobby dumbfounded and speechless, and that we shared our news with you about TITS. We'll all be waiting to hear about your treatment. Let us know ASAP. Love ya."

Emma: "Night, y'all. Thank you. Love you lots."

Emma set the phone down on the seat next to her and let out a long breath of air she hadn't realized she was holding deep in her lungs. It was like the entire night had been choreographed by angels, but she still couldn't help but feel anxious about her appointment with the oncologist. Moonlight poured over her as she gripped the steering wheel with both hands and locked eyes with herself in the rearview mirror. It made her look white as stone, feeling both delicate and severe all at once. "I'm not going to stress over what I can't control," she said to the ethereal reflection like she was her own personal life coach. Emma wiggled her butt back into the car seat, pressed her shoulders against the backrest, and lifted her chin as she continued her private pep talk with a loud, confident voice. "Your life finally feels like your own. Continue to be grateful for everyone and everything in it that makes it so beautiful and fulfilling." She closed the one-sided conversation with a determined-looking, tight-lipped smile and a quick nod of approval at herself. She would worry about tomorrow when it came, but for now, she decided to take off her shoes, crank up the radio, and open all the windows while she also left the AC on full blast. *Oh boy. Windows down and air conditioning on at the same time. That's really living life on the edge*. She laughed.

She wanted to literally feel everything on the drive home. The way it felt when she tapped the gas or brake pedal with the bare sole of her foot reminded her of long-ago summer nights when life eternally felt free, and possibilities were limitless. The simple act of driving barefoot brought her directly back to all the nights she served as the designated driver for Zip,

Sleazin, YoYo, and RaRa. She could almost smell the clash of Jovan Musk and Loves Baby Soft as they sang off-key much too loudly to Corey Hart's "Sunglasses at Night," and spilled Sun Country Wine Coolers in her backseat.

Bringing her attention back to the present moment, she noticed the spellbinding ambiance cast by the streetlights gleaming off the dashboard, and how it brushed across her cheeks in an alluring rhythm that seemed to keep time perfectly with the music on her radio. Most of all, she wanted to feel the hot, humid air as it poured in from outside, only to become immediately entangled with the chilly air from her car vents. Twisted extremes were a motif of sorts for the day, and perhaps for her life. She told herself she was "all in" and that she wanted to feel everything she possibly could—both good and bad—and be genuinely grateful for every shiny shard and tiny molecule of it. There was no time and no need for anything else.

As she pulled away from the curb, Shania Twain's "Man! I Feel Like a Woman!" began to play on the radio and she was positive it was a sign from above. She wiped away a few happy tears pooling in the corners of her brown eyes, pressed the gas pedal, and belted out the lyrics as loud as her voice would let her. At least for now, it felt like the universe was on her side.

****

The next morning, Emma made some extra strong black coffee and while she savored it from a mug Caroline had made for her in high school, she stared at nothing through the window above the sink. As she predicted, sleep hadn't come easily but she knew she must have slept a little because she remembered having a dream about being at a beach house with her parents. In the dream, the three of them huddled together in front of a small window frosted by silt blown in from the sea. An ominous feeling enveloped them as they watched massive waves swell and break repeatedly on the dark, tumultuous ocean just beyond the seawall. Each set of waves grew taller and taller and rapidly encroached on the tiny beach cottage. Grey and white clouds mixed with the white chop of the grey water, and a wave crescendo that looked like it had crested at more than twenty feet tall came crashing into their window, she woke with a start that made her sit straight up in bed.

Through her spotlessly clean and clear kitchen window, she caught sight of Boozy Becca as she came around the back corner of her house, yanking and dragging a twisted garden hose in what looked like a half-hearted attempt to water the lawn. She was wearing a red bikini top and cut-off shorts and seemed completely unaware that a lit cigarette dangled haphazardly from her lips. The arm that wasn't wrestling with the snake of a hose deftly balanced Chablis on her jutted left hip. Emma had never felt envy toward anyone in her life (especially not Boozy Becca), but something about witnessing that exact moment of her neighbor's life, at this exact moment of her own life, produced an alien emotion that couldn't be explained by any other way. She shook the feeling off, rubbed her eyes, and dumped the remains of her cup into the sink without bothering to put it into the dishwasher.

First there was the TITS experiment, then driving

with both windows down while the AC was on, and now leaving dishes in the sink? What could possibly be in store for me next with this newfound devil-may-care-attitude, she thought with a soft sarcastic chuckle. *The girls would be so proud of their Ma.*

Emma eased into the driver's seat, instinctively pulled her seat belt across her chest, and secured it with a loud click as if she was on autopilot. She pressed the button on the garage door opener, and as it yawned widely agape, she found herself deep in thought about the series of tests she went through last week in preparation for today's appointment. Her oncologist was of course blown away by her sudden transformation, and although the additional tests that had been scheduled were supposedly meant to indicate the best direction for a course of action, she couldn't help but wonder if they were also being done to see what could have caused such a drastic change in her chronological age. She had been wrestling with herself internally about what to do once she heard the treatment options. It was hard to imagine how she would feel, especially if it entailed aggressive chemotherapy. One doctor—whom she had seen as a fifth or sixth opinion—wanted to do surgery, but she could tell it mainly was because he was young and curious. He couldn't tell her the upside, and the risk of doing it seemed too great, and far outweighed the risks associated with not doing it.

The garage door glided upward slowly and smoothly until it came to a halt with a soft clunking noise that brought her thoughts back to the task at hand, which was simply to turn the key in the ignition and then drive the car out onto the road. The sudden blast of loud music from the radio made her jump and press her hand to her chest to calm her heart. She quickly turned it down with a snap of her wrist and laughed a little at the thought that last night's version of herself was clearly quite a bit different from who she was this morning.

Happy to delay the inevitable, Emma listened intently to the oddly gratifying sound of her tires as they slowly rolled in reverse over the gravel driveway. Each satisfying crunch resounded in her ears like a form of catharsis—just like when she munched on her favorite Cape Cod plain kettle chips. The already-blaring sun made her squint like a vampire in its light, but she chose to ignore it. When Emma finally reached the street and began to drive away, she glanced in the rearview mirror and was surprised to see Boozy Becca standing there, with Chablis still affixed to her hip, as she used her hand to make it look like the dog was waving goodbye.

Emma was so lost in thought; she barely remembered the rest of the drive to her appointment. One minute Chablis was waving a paw at her from the middle of the street, and the next she was parked in front of her doctor's office. Birds were singing from the branches of a small tree planted next to the main entry of the building. As she reached the large, glass double doors, she could also hear little wings flapping within its deep green foliage, and it made her think that no matter what a person is going through, life truly continues on.

She pulled the thick, silver door handle, stepped inside, and was immediately affronted with a blast of artificially arctic air. The sudden chill on her skin and its accompanying goosebumps brought her back to reality and reminded her that she left her cardigan at home again. *It's like a meat locker in here. I already feel like I need to defrost,* she thought as she briskly walked across the main lobby. The click, click, click of her slingbacks on the sterile, white linoleum produced loud echoes that engulfed her until she stopped in front of the elevator and hit the button for the third floor.

She was alone in the small elevator, but someone must have ridden in it only moments before because the overpowering aroma of cologne mixed with greasy food lingered heavily in the air. *Someone must have had breakfast at a greasy spoon, and it stuck to their clothes. I freaking hate that smell.*

The simultaneous sensations she felt as the elevator rose and her stomach dropped, made her think there was no way in hell she could endure chemotherapy.

You just need to hear them out. You just need to hear them out. She repeated that mantra until an extremely intrusive DING followed by a parting of the doors interrupted her thoughts and commanded her attention.

In the waiting room, a flustered-looking mom sat in the corner with an arsenal of toys, books, and snacks—presumably to pacify the toddler that was rolling around on the floor amongst crushed Cheerios and Goldfish Crackers. His little face was bright crimson, and his back was arched like he had no bones. The unnatural contortion that little kids are capable of reminded Emma of "The Exorcist." She saw the look in the young woman's eyes, and the sweat and snot that covered the little boy's face, and immediately felt worse for them than she did for herself. Empathy from one mother to another. She briefly wondered why they were there and who in their family was sick, but quickly pushed the thought from her mind.

She looked away from the unpleasant scene and stepped up to the sliding glass window. The other side of the glass buzzed like a hive as the busy nurses did their jobs. She put the pen down after signing in and was hit with that same smell from the elevator. She glanced around and saw an older gentleman seated next to a table strewn with too many magazines. His scruffy beard and unkempt hair were as white as the Styrofoam container on his lap that he gingerly held onto with both hands.

So that was you, Emma thought playfully, as if she had solved a crime of sorts. Just as she began to wonder what was in the container—*Bacon? Hashbrowns? Grits?*—and before she could even sit down, she was startled by the whoosh of the window when the nurse swiftly slid it open and called her back for her appointment.

Like a baby duck behind its mama, Emma followed the nurse down the seemingly endless corridor. She listened intently as the nurse turned her head and spoke to her over her shoulder in a curt yet kind manner.

"We won't be putting you in an exam room today," she said as they passed by the rooms where she had already been put through a plethora of tests.

"You'll be seen in the doctor's office."

Anxiety took hold of Emma's heart and squeezed. Something seemed odd and overwhelming about this appointment, aside from all the obvious reasons. She was escorted into the intimidating, yet tastefully decorated office, complete with diplomas adorning the walls and a potted eucalyptus tree in the corner by a window. The nurse gestured to the small, leather club chair positioned in front of a large cherry wood desk. It seemed that the nurse was purposely avoiding any eye contact as she took a step back and told Emma to have a seat.

"The doctor will be in shortly," she said then swiftly exited the room and pulled the door shut with a soft click.

Emma did what she was told, but felt like she was having an out-of-body experience and tried to steel herself for the worst news imaginable. *Why else would they put me in an office and not an exam room, like all my other visits?* She picked at a dry cuticle and tried to keep herself from nervously bouncing her knee.

Inhaling a deep breath and then letting it out slowly, an overwhelming tingling sensation coursed through her like the blood had been drained from her arms, and her hands were suddenly colder than her ex-husband's heart. She tucked both hands under her legs and chewed her bottom lip as she made a valiant effort to give herself a pep talk. *C'mon, Em. You literally just experienced the most unbelievable physical occurrence that has probably happened to anyone...ever. There's no way in hell that whatever news I'm about to get could even come close to that level of insane shock and surprise. Bring it, bitch. I'm ready.*

An hour later, Emma stepped out of the doctor's office, walked down the corridor in a daze, and straight into the wide-open mouth of the elevator that seemed to be waiting just for her. She pushed the button marked with an L and instinctively took a step backward as the elevator's sluggish silver doors shut obediently. She fixed her gaze on the warm white light that encircled her preferred floor like a halo and rubbed her arms absently as she took the first step needed to exit the building. Exit. Red. That was another set of colored lights altogether. It took every bit of strength in her being to focus on the red Exit sign that beckoned her with the promise of a way out of the building. *One thing at a time, Ma.* She heard the words in the voice of her mother. *Take one thing at a time, Sweets.*

She pushed the door open and stepped outside into the suffocatingly soupy air that pressed against her skin and weighed heavily on her chest like an X-ray apron. She looked at her phone for the third time since leaving her appointment and took notice of the stark contrast of the natural heat that surrounded her compared to the bone-chilling temperature she endured inside the building.

No matter how many times she looked, the clock on her phone continued to show that it was only an hour earlier that she had entered the building, yet, after absorbing the current prognosis from her doctor like a half-hardened sponge left in the sun, she could have sworn an eternity had passed. Dubious, and with a slight quiver in her stomach, she conceded that time had not sped up or stopped this time, but someone needed to clue her wobbly legs and pounding heart in on this fact. Her entire world had been turned on its ear once again and she wasn't sure she could handle any more voodoo magic or sorcery in her life—whether good or bad.

Even the weather seemed to be in on the conspiracy. When she arrived for her appointment, the deep blue skies and chirping birds were a veritable scene from a Disney movie. But a mere sixty minutes later, which somehow felt like a lifetime, she found herself surrounded by inky clouds and an impending storm. It was the quintessential night-and-day scenario. *Story of my life*, she thought with a shake of her head.

The little wooden bench—usually occupied by older folks waiting patiently for their rides to come get them or office staff enjoying a sunny break—sat empty on a neat rectangular plot of grass. Today it was all hers, and she felt like she needed it, so she plopped down with a bit of intentional over-exaggeration, truly taking a load off. Emma closed her eyes and took a few deep breaths before she attacked the task of making calls and sending texts to share the news.

With slightly shaky hands, she called Caroline first, but got no answer. *She's working. I'm not gonna leave a message like this. I'll try her again tonight.*

Emma dialed Dr. Wallace, YoYo, and then Susan but she reached each of their voicemails as well.

"Well, Holy Hell, I guess a group text it is, then," she said aloud without a care of who might notice she was talking to herself.

She had *never* expected to *say* or *type* these words, but they were the only ones in the world that mattered at that moment. To Emma, it didn't matter *how* they were conveyed, just that they were.

To: Caroline, Walter Wallace, RaRa, YoYo, Heather, Susan: *—Hey 'All. I know you're probably all at work and doing your thing, but I can't keep this news to myself for one more second. Get ready…it's even crazier than what the elixir did to our bodies and minds.*

I just came out of my appointment to talk about treatment options and set up a schedule, and my cancer is GONE. All scans, tests, cell counts, etc. show that the cancer and, more specifically, the tumor no longer exist in my body. An inoperable tumor. Vanished.

Y'all…this isn't a joke. TITS cured my cancer.---

Just as Emma hit send, the clouds broke above her head. She shoved her phone in her purse to protect it and then placed her purse under the bench. She leaned back, tilted her face toward the sky, and relished the cleansing and invigorating effect of every fat droplet as it washed over her like wine from the heavens, making her increasingly intoxicated by the promise of this new day.

Chapter 10

Susan opened her eyes, and as the sleek, sophisticated décor of the boutique hotel room slowly came into focus, so did her memory of where she was. Now that she had taken the comedy scene by storm and was either performing at TITS in Miami or out on tour, she'd become accustomed to forgetting where the hell she was when initially waking up. The back of some guy's head on the pillow next to her was generally a fuzzy first-thing view as well, but not this time. On this bright morning in San Francisco, she was alone and happy to be heading back to Miami in a few hours. She was still on cloud nine after her sold-out show in North Beach the night before, and going home to her friends, fans, and the incredible club they had created always made her very happy.

Although she had been taking the magical pills and monitoring their effects with nothing but good results for quite a while now, the way she started each new day remained the same no matter where she was or who was in her bed. It had been almost ten months, and nothing but amazing things had happened to any of them since they started the experiment. However, she still felt compelled to rip the covers off and hurry to the mirror like a kid on Christmas who rushed to the tree to see if Santa left everything she wanted. Or, maybe in her case, she was more concerned that the Grinch had taken everything *away* while she slept a little too soundly, blissfully ignorant, with a smile as sweet as sugar plumbs scrawled across her face.

It was a few short strides to the full-length mirror which, at least for another day, had not betrayed her. Joy and relief washed over her as she studied her reflection like it was a science project—because it basically was. In her rational mind, Susan knew exactly who the likeness was, yet it remained virtually impossible to not dissect every bit of the image and regard it as if it belonged to someone else.

This "other person" was like a beautiful unicorn who magically appeared before her every morning, but whose sighting elicited intense joy, as well as fear. Her rational mind told her often how ridiculous it was to be attached to something that didn't truly exist. And while she was immeasurably thrilled with the trajectory her life had taken since the elixir turned back the clock, the worry of losing such an inexplicable and unfathomable gift gnawed at her.

She gently ran her fingers over her breasts, her stomach, and her hips, reading her curves like braille. Susan took a step back from the mirror and wondered if the desire to be seen and adored had made her into some kind of attention whore. She hated the possibility that it had, but certainly wasn't ready to give any of it up either.

Is it so bad to want to be seen, adored, and touched? Sue me for not wanting to let go of sexual attention. Sue me for wanting it spoon-fed to me like thick, sweet honey until it drips slowly down my chin. She jutted her chin out defensively as she silently argued with her own ego.

As was often the case when she let the intense dichotomy of herself play out for much longer than it ever should, the urge to jam her hands into proverbial pots of golden liquid and devour it faster than a frenzied Pooh Bear continued to overtake her thoughts.

Shit, I've become worse than Zipper. A sly smile upturned her lips, and an immediate mental note to share this keen observation with her friend.

I've become a veritable vampire of lust that needs to feed and feed in order to feel alive, and it's not healthy. She continued to argue with herself for no real reason other than her latent feelings of guilt. *Nothing in excess ever is, but the day will come when the honey is dried up and the buzz in the hive is gone forever.*

She tilted her chin slightly upward. *I can still be a feminist and want to be desired at the same time. There are no rules, damn it.*

The rebel in her accepted all of these thoughts and emotions easily, but there was always a little piece of her that begged to differ. There was a little cartoon devil on one shoulder feeding her ego, while an angel sat on the other side and whispered rebuttals. "There simply *has* to be more to life than placing so much emphasis on aging, sexuality, sensuality, attention, and looks," the angel would say in a singsong voice.

But then, just like in the cartoons, the devil told the angel to shut up, or comically bopped it over the head and pushed it off its roost.

Still admiring herself, she momentarily considered masturbating but quickly chastised herself for becoming turned on so easily by her own body.

Sheesh. That's just weird, but then again, what about this isn't weird? A hearty laugh filled the air.

Instead of touching herself, she padded over to the cute area designated to make coffee or tea and popped out a French Roast from an intricately carved wooden box. She felt bad momentarily—what would Ra say about the waste of these little single-use coffee pods, but she needed her coffee, right? After pouring water into the plastic carafe in the back of the machine, she placed the pod in the filter and pushed the red button.

Susan found herself drawn in by the exotic-looking wooden box that housed the hotel's hot drink selections. She couldn't take her eyes off the gorgeous leaves and floral patterns that adorned the sides of the antique-looking box, and the dragon tail that wrapped around its lid. She jokingly made a mental note that it was actually quite nice to be enamored by something besides her own reflection for once. She hadn't become that narcissistic, had she?

Susan lightly ran her middle finger over a deeply etched cluster of leaves and then lifted and closed the lid of the box a few times like she had just unearthed a long-ago buried treasure. She wondered if it had been painted by hand as she admired the various shades of red and mustard yellow and how they melded perfectly with patina green. For all she knew the box had been purchased on clearance from TJ Maxx (or maybe in bulk from a Dollar Store) but at that moment, in her eyes, it was as mysterious, beautiful, and valuable as an artifact recovered by Indiana Jones.

The coffee maker began to crackle, sizzle, and drip as it dutifully created a hot cup of magic just for her while elaborate images of Pandora's Box brewed in her mind.

She thought about what temptation and curiosity

had done to Pandora, but laughed it off when she took her steaming, white porcelain cup of caffeinated perfection over to the window and looked down at Union Square from her hotel window. She had a great view of the statue of Nike, the goddess of Victory, where it stood triumphantly in the center of the square. *I like you better than Pandora, girl.* She held her cup in the air and tipped it slightly toward the statue with a conspiratorial click. *Cheers. And don't think I haven't noticed that you're both strong and beautiful.*

Wow. There seems to be some kind of Greek motif going on here. I kind of dig it. Maybe I should try to write it into an act. There's certainly something to all of this.

Susan sat bare-assed on the marble windowsill and did an online search for more information about the beautiful Greek Goddess. She read that Nike personified victory in all things and symbolized glory and fame as well as success in battle, and that the memorial statue she was looking at was dedicated to Admiral George Dewey in commemoration of his victory at the Battle of Manila Bay during the Spanish-American War and was also a tribute to sailors in the United States Navy. She set her phone aside for a moment and marveled at the statue's victorious, confident stance complete with a laurel wreath in one hand and a large trident in the other.

Maybe this crazy combo of Pandora and Nike is a sign that me and the girls messed with some dangerous shit but have somehow come out victorious? Kinda like selling our souls to the devil, but without the pitchforks and horns, she thought to herself as her hand subconsciously touched the top of her head to ensure she was indeed horn-free. Susan dropped her hand and sheepishly looked around the empty room as if she needed to be sure no one caught her checking herself for devil horns. *They say curiosity kills the cat, but that's not what this is.* She shook her head, popped up from her spot in the sun, and walked into the bedroom to pack her bag. Proud to have become adept at traveling light, Susan picked up from the floor and the lounge chair the few articles of clothing she had brought and thought about how they *had* taken a huge chance by experimenting with the TITS experiment—and that, in itself, involved danger or risk—but so much *good* had come of it instead.

In all the months that had gone by, the list of benefits kept getting longer and there were no negative side effects whatsoever for any of them. She shoved her black jeans, t-shirt, and a pair of running socks into her backpack and mentally listed all the positives to come out of giving the elixir a whirl that went above and beyond how they looked and felt.

First of all, she silently implored like a snotty teenager making her case to her mother with all the reasons why her curfew should be extended, *my comedy career has freakin' catapulted.*

Second of all, we never would have moved to Miami and gone into business together. If it weren't for TITS, there would be no TITS. she thought as she chuckled in both agreement with herself and admiration of her own witty observation.

She laid the clothes she planned to wear home on the bed next to her carry-on, and stepped into the bright white bathroom, perched herself delicately on the tub, and adjusted the fancy ceramic knobs marked H and C in a heavy black typewriter font, letting the water run until she figured out the right temperature for her shower.

Thirdly, she added to the list in her head because she was on a roll now, *the club is beyond thriving, and on a nightly basis we have more stars than freakin' Hollywood Boulevard itself.*

The tiny bathroom steamed up quickly, just the way she liked it. She stepped into the sparkling clean tub and pulled the shower curtain closed. As the water cascaded over her head, she closed her eyes and continued with her rant. She didn't fully understand why she felt the need to prove anything to herself—she just knew she needed to do it. Pandora be damned, she and the girls would remain victorious.

Fourthly, YoYo and RaRa moved in together, fell in love, and now I get to combine their names and call them YoRa, which I love. She giggled as she reached for the tiny travel-sized bottle of shampoo provided by the hotel. *It sounds like Yo-Ga. That's a good one. I crack myself up.*

While she worked up a good lather in her hair, she turned around to face the shower head and let the hot water hit her chest and stomach. *And last but certainly not least,* she announced to herself triumphantly, *the best and biggest thing to come of this is that Emma is now cancer free.*

Sudsy trails of shampoo slid down her back, and as was often the case (no matter where she was) Susan's thoughts flashed to when she first opened Ma's text and read that her cancer had completely vanished. Many months had passed since then, but it was another memory with her friends that will forever stay etched in her mind.

She was at the club running rehearsals and making last-minute adjustments to the agenda for that night's performances. Her blonde hair was pushed up into an ancient trucker's hat from Kid Rock's Cocky Tour, and she wore ripped black jeans and a sleeveless Ramones t-shirt. Intense heat from the stage lights was responsible for the little river that trickled and tickled its way into her cleavage. She reached down into her shirt and swiped at the sweat that had pooled between her boobs. After yanking her hand out, and wiping it on her jeans, she clapped her hands loudly and yelled, "Okay, everyone. Bryce is gonna get some coffee orders and we'll break for twenty when he comes back with them," she said as she gestured to one of the stagehands.

Almost an hour later, a sweat-slicked Bryce returned with two stacks of pulp fiber coffee carriers filled with four cups and balanced precariously on each of his forearms. He burst into the concert area by pushing the huge black doors open with his butt. Susan took one look at the sweaty, struggling guy and jumped up to relieve him of a couple of trays and to help him distribute the drinks. Although most of the white cups were stained with brown trails of spilled coffee, and they had basically all gone cold, she marveled at the fact that the leaning tower of lattes hadn't tumbled. Once all the drinks were handed out, everyone scattered like cockroaches.

Happy to have a moment to check her phone and get some much-needed caffeine into her system, Susan took a long drink through the little opening in the plastic lid and quickly realized her order had been messed up. She shook her head and rolled her eyes with a laugh, pulled her phone from her back pocket, and read Ma's momentous message. Her hand instinctively shot up to her face and covered her lips in what could have been an attempt to keep her heart from jumping straight up and out of her mouth. Susan's entire body shook with elation. The coffee cup tumbled out of her other hand, and she took off running in the direction of YoYo's office before it even hit the floor.

As she quickly made her way to YoYo's office, the little devil appeared on her shoulder for the briefest moment, and tried to cast doubt in her mind as he leaned in and whispered, "C'mon, the cure for cancer? That's impossible."

She had no intention of listening to the devil's bullshit and couldn't have been happier—or more relieved—when the tiny angel materialized and floated up toward her other ear, her long white robe rippling in a non-existent breeze while holding a miniature golden harp. She positioned herself as close to Susan's ear as possible, straightened her flimsy metal halo, and exclaimed, "That *same* pill made y'all look like a bunch of thirtysomethings, which was *also impossible,* so why the hell not?"

Not only did Susan recognize the angel's stellar point, but she also agreed with it wholeheartedly, and when she reached Yo's office and found the rest of the girls there, she quickly realized they agreed as well. Certainly, they were the last group of people on the planet who could ever doubt the Magic of the Universe, and they had also personally apparently proven that *nothing* is impossible.

Susan recalled the run through the club to find her

friends. She didn't bother to text any of them because she knew in her heart where they would be. The club had a completely different look and vibe during the day, and when all the lights were on, and no matter how many times she experienced it, the magnitude of everything that went into prepping to open the doors daily simply blew her away. There were so many people in the building getting ready for the night ahead that it almost looked like they were already open. Bartenders, cocktail waitresses, and DJs efficiently readied their areas and barely noticed Susan as she tore through and almost crashed into a barback, pushing a dolly full of clean glasses. She pushed past some backup dancers stretching in a circle, and the Cirque du Soleil-like performers in their sweats and tech fiber tanks, checking and double-checking their aerial swings and bird cages.

Sweaty and red-faced, she practically fell into YoYo's office, holding her phone out in front of her body in a valiant effort to let the message precede her. Yolanda, Rachel, and Heather turned and looked at her at the same time, cheeks slick with happy tears and broad smiles stretching across their faces like endless desert highways. With their arms outstretched in front of them like happy zombies, they walked toward her simultaneously and absorbed her into their blob of love. At that exact moment in time, no words were necessary, but their body language and unspoken communication screamed, "We know. Isn't it *incredible*?."

In between joyous hugs, Heather suggested they Facetime with Ma and celebrate with a toast before the club opened for the night.

"Yes, girl. *Yes*." Yolanda agreed.

In Susan's usual way, song lyrics popped into her head like the cork from a champagne bottle. In her best impersonation of Eve singing, "Let Me Blow Ya Mind." she recited, "Drop your glasses; shake your asses. Face screwed up like you having hot flashes."

RaRa laughed as she wiped her tear-stained cheek with the back of her hand and playfully asked, "What took you so long with the lyrics, my friend?" She squeezed Susan even harder. "I'll get Ma on Facetime. Let's hope she has some champagne just lying around the house for this very occasion."

Heather broke away from the group hug and ducked behind the black marble bar she had installed in her office. She pulled out a bottle of Ruinart from her subzero fridge that contained many bottles and an occasional to-go container of leftovers and said, "This *whole thing* continues to blow my mind, as does your creativity, Sleazin'. Thanks for that. While we wait for RaRa to reach Ma and give her a second to pop her own bubbly, let's prep our glasses and our asses, but fuck the hot flashes." she said with a hearty laugh as she popped the cork from the artsy, gold-and-white bottle.

In no time at all, they propped the phone on YoYo's desk and huddled in a tight, half circle around it, and the electricity surrounding them was palpable. Ma lit up the screen and sparkled like a star in the night sky. Susan remembered wondering which was more luminous—the shimmering liquid in her glass, or Emma's beautiful face.

Susan felt tipsy from excitement before she even took a sip, knowing she would never forget the energy of talking to Ma mingling perfectly with the Champagne's delicate perfume. She often replayed this entire scene in her mind on repeat. Effervescent bubbles bulleted through the liquid in her glass, stopping only to dance across the surface and then explode under her nose, bubbles tickling her senses. But she knew they weren't the true reason for the tears that escaped from her eyes.

Susan was the first to raise her glass, but the others quickly followed her lead.

"Shit, girls." Susan continued on her roll. "I remembered something my grandpa used to say to my dad all the time and I think it works in this crazy scenario. So, Gramps would light up a nonfiltered cigarette, take a deep draw from it, and say 'Son; never let a whiskey glass or a woman's ass ruin your life.' Of all the weird stories and expressions my grandpa spouted, that was probably the craziest. But my life is complete *because* of these glasses and *all* of your asses." They gently clinked their glasses as well as the screen on Rachel's phone where Emma held up her celebratory flute.

"I couldn't have said it better myself," they heard Ma say in between sips and sniffles as they all drank to friendship, their health, and the true miracle they have all had the good fortune to witness.

Susan stepped out of the shower onto the little white hand towel she threw on the floor so she wouldn't slip. There was a thick rectangular bathmat provided by the hotel, but those things always grossed her out, so she didn't use it. She had been so lost in thought while standing beneath the soothing stream of hot water that her fingers started to shrivel like raisins. She pulled a large fluffy bath towel from the neat stack piled on a shiny metal shelf. As she wrapped the thick, cozy towel around herself, she was also enveloped by a strong sense of gratitude for the slight distraction it provided from the barreling runaway train that too often was her brain. *Next stop. Walter Wallace.*

Thoughts of Emma's recovery always took a direct line to Dr. Wallace and how he handled the unusual and unprecedented circumstances. Ever the discerning professional, well, apart from his hot tub misadventure, he continued to monitor each of them, but immediately began studying Emma the most closely and told her to stop taking the pills for a month to see what would happen.

In the interest of this possibly fantastic discovery, Emma did as she was instructed, and when she was tested and scanned a few weeks later, the tumor was visible. Susan and the girls marveled at Ma's bravery, integrity, and commitment to the study, but they also worried about her health and safety, as well as their own. After a month without TITS, and a lot of confusion and dumbfounded reactions from her oncologist, WW asked her to start her regimen with the elixir one more time. Ma did as she was directed, and once again her cancer vanished.

They all marveled at the incredible effects the golden pills had on each of them, from the positive changes in their health to witnessing a real miracle. Ma's illness had taken a major turn for the better. Euphoria, gratitude, shock, and disbelief swept through each of them at the sight of Ma's improvement, leaving them in awe of the power of the pills. The initial desire to smooth out some fine lines and wrinkles and hopefully increase vim and vigor had literally morphed into an inconceivable medical discovery of gargantuan proportions.

Dr. Wallace was relentless. He put all of his time, efforts, and resources into his research of TITS, the girls, and Emma, but the time had come—much faster than any of them could have predicted—for WW to join forces with other doctors and scientists in order to conduct a more scientifically legitimate study of his concoction and what it could actually do.

Thoughts of time, how fast it went by, and how significantly things can change in such a short amount of it, momentarily returned Susan's thoughts to her flight home today. She told herself there was no need to rush, for once, and she planned to take advantage of that unusual luxury. After she finished getting dressed, she still had plenty of time to get something to eat and catch the hotel's shuttle to the airport. There would be no running through the airport like a madwoman.

The hotel's restaurant was surprisingly empty, so she took a seat on a beautiful lime green upholstered chair at a table by the window. The restaurant had a happy and quirky feel, induced by white tablecloths, wrought iron fixtures around the bar, funky glass chandeliers, and murals of mermaids and various other sea oddities—perfectly supporting her continued thoughts of Greek mythology and WW's efforts to legitimize his study.

A perky, blonde waitress in her early twenties handed her a menu and placed a tall glass of ice water in front of her. Susan accepted both with a smile, but instead of studying the menu, she stared out the window and contemplated the possible connection between WW's attempts to legitimize his study and all her thoughts surrounding Greek mythology—a topic she had never given a second thought to before.

In her mind, she rehashed the many phone conversations, texts, and emails she and the girls had after WW sold the rights to his elixir's proprietary recipe and the results of his findings for billions of dollars to the largest pharmaceutical company in North America, who, in turn, hired a team of researchers, doctors, and nurses as the principal investigators to conduct the multi-phased clinical trials required by the FDA. Although they were kept in the loop by WW every step of the way and were also kept on as the study's principal participants, there was a disconnect between understanding the necessity to sell to, and involve big pharma, and the trepidation that came along with it like a monkey on their back.

Her mind traveled directly to the multitude of conversations between the girls that always ended in the same old debate. Was the golden pill they were testing *the* golden ticket to scientific discovery in the form of a miracle medical cure, or was it a path paved in gold for a snake oil salesman? That's when it hit her like a lightning bolt from Zeus himself. The more she thought about it, the more glaringly clear it became that the seemingly odd presence of a Greek motif might have a greater importance than she had initially thought. She grabbed her phone and immediately searched the symbol for medicine in an effort to "fact check" her own epiphany. When the symbol popped up and the information said that the symbol for medicine was taken directly from Greek mythology, all she could think was *holy shit.* She put down her glass of Pinot Grigio and pushed away the seafood salad she had been picking on to concentrate on the connection she had made, feeling that this was significant in some way.

According to what she read, the historically correct symbol for the medical profession was two snakes winding around the winged staff of the Greek god, Hermes, and was meant to represent speed. As she dug further, she read about another school of thought, dictating a second commonly used symbol stemming from Aesculapius, the god of medicine, who was also the son of Apollo, the god of healing. This particular symbol differed in that it was a staff made of a rough-hewn branch meant to represent plants and growth entwined by only one snake.

Shit, shit, shit! Susan's mind ricocheted like a pinball between the golden pills they had been taking, Nike's golden sandals and wings, and her powers of speed, the golden wings and speed associated with Hermes, the healing power of plants, and the fact that one or more snakes were tightly wrapped around the symbols for medicine. Susan didn't believe in coincidences, and although she knew she had been given a sign of some sort, the meaning of it was, she thought, chuckling at her cleverness, all Greek to her.

She paid her check and walked to the hotel lobby to wait for the airport shuttle service to pick her up. In the meantime, she wondered if the snakes—single or multiple—represented false hope (after all, trusting one hadn't exactly done Eve much good—rather than eternal life in paradise with a hot guy, it had only brought her pain and death) and if so, could they be overpowered by the golden wings and exceptional speed of the gods and goddesses who prevailed in battles of all kinds, including cancer? Or *maybe* it was meant to be interpreted as an answer to their recurring debate about WW and how he profited from the sale of the golden pills. That *both* science *and* nature must entwine in the most perfect and perhaps mystical ways for speedy wings of wellness and healing to be granted from the universe. She decided the latter idea was probably the correlation she had been searching for and didn't realize the shuttle bus driver had been standing in front of her until he tapped her on the shoulder and asked if she was waiting for a ride to the airport.

She jumped up and apologized for being so oblivious as she attempted to shake off the thoughts of Emma, WW, her own fate, and how this could all be connected in some strange way to Greek mythology. As she climbed in the back of the van, the driver informed her that he had one more stop to make to pick up another traveler headed to the airport. Within ten minutes, the shuttle pulled up in front of a row of apartments she figured were Airbnbs. They looked really nice from the outside and wondered what they looked like inside when the one in the center with the red door swung open. At first, all she noticed was a large backpack being pushed through the doorway. The person wearing it looked like a tall guy, but he stepped backward through the door to pull it shut and make sure it was locked. His head was lowered, so she couldn't really make out who her shuttle buddy was.

The driver stood at the curb and waited for the man to walk over. Back on the bus, he slid open the door with a forceful thud that rattled the door panels. The young man took off his backpack, bent over, and climbed in next to Susan, who quickly realized the resonation from the door panels weren't the only things getting rattled. He was probably the most beautiful man she had ever seen in her life, a Greek god who traveled through time to ride to the airport with her. She felt her stomach do a flip like it was on a trampoline, and *most* of the thoughts in her brain had evaporated. During the brief time it took for the driver to merge into traffic, and for the young man to get situated in his seat, Susan seized the opportunity to visually devour every inch of him, while making it appear as if she were looking out the passenger side window.

His khaki shorts and white tank top revealed a body that may as well have been chiseled from marble. It was so overwhelming, she literally wanted to tell him to just stop it already. (As if he could hit a switch and spontaneously stop being so incredibly sexy just by existing and sitting there.) It was too much. His skin. God, that beautiful, smooth, ebony skin was enough to make a Hell's Angel weep like a little girl, and his lips were two pillows of perfection. On his feet, he wore a pair of white Nike high tops with a gold swoosh. *No way. You've got to be kidding me.* She realized her mouth was now hanging open in surprise, so she quickly pressed her lips together.

He turned to her and put out his hand to introduce himself. "Hey there. I'm Daniel," he said with a smooth-as-silk British accent and a smile so bright and powerful it could knock you out and have you wondering what day it was when you finally came to.

She took his hand in hers, noting how strong it felt, shook it briefly—but didn't want to let go of it—and replied, "Hi, Daniel. Nice to meet you. I'm Susan. Where are you from?"

Holy crap on toast. Is this what the sign was alluding to with all that Greek shit?

"From London. I graduated from medical school recently and took a bit of an extended holiday in the States before going back home for a two-year Foundation Program. I've always wanted to travel around California. How about you?"

Christ on a cracker. That smile sends an electrical charge straight to my clit that would make Zeus's thunderbolt seem weak.

"Oh, I live in Miami, Florida now, but I'm originally from South Carolina. I lived in New Jersey for a long time as well. Wow, London. I've never been there but have always wanted to go," she said, hoping she didn't seem too nervous or distracted.

That freaking accent. This must be the Greek fucking god with golden wings like Hermes or Nike that he'll use to fly swiftly to victory in my vagina. Shit, maybe that medical symbol really does have two snakes: one for scientific medicine and the other for sexual healing. I knew it was a sign.

"Oh, you should. It's really quite nice—well, parts of it are. South Carolina. I've never been to the East Coast," he said as he turned his body in her direction. "Were you traveling for work or for fun?"

Susan turned toward him as well, and with knees almost touching, their polite small talk quickly turned into playful banter. She took great pleasure in the fact that he wasn't looking through her or at his phone but was taking her in like a beautiful sunset. His big brown eyes and intense gaze made her feel the furthest thing from invisible, and if she had to guess what a hit of heroin rushing through her veins actually felt like, this would be it. She felt the high, and only hated herself the tiniest bit for loving being truly seen by this incredibly sexy man.

Susan realized they were almost at the airport and wondered where all the heavy California traffic was when you needed it.

Inside the airport, they said their goodbyes and began to walk their separate ways. She almost let him get away, realizing having sex in an airport was both crazy and dangerous, but then reminded herself they had the gods on their side. There was also something about being on the elixir that made her feel invincible. Besides all that, plain old lust just took over any semblance of rationality and, therefore, it seemed like the perfect idea to catch up to him, tap him on the shoulder, and see if he would do her in a bathroom stall.

She jogged up behind him and placed her hand lightly on his shoulder. He turned around quickly and gave her a look that told her he was relieved she didn't let him go. His face conveyed a beautiful longing, as if he had already missed her. She got straight to the point, but before she could even finish her proposition, he interrupted her in hasty agreement.

Daniel gently took Susan by the hand, and they walked together in silence toward the nearest restroom, appearing like any couple traveling together. This provided an extra thrill for Susan.

On the way to the restroom, Susan took in the delicious smell of buttery pretzels. Random flight announcements and a baby's cry echoed off the polished floor as they walked past a large wooden door that appeared to be a utility closet of some kind. Noticing it at the same exact time, they immediately turned to look at each other and locked eyes. Ding, ding, ding, we have a winner! They backed up a few steps and gave the metal door handle a try. As luck would have it, the door was unlocked.

The space was much more private than a bathroom stall would have been in a crowded airport, so it was perfect. The only glitch was that it housed a large air ventilation system that sat smack in the middle of the closet, with limited space on either side of the shiny metal vent. They shoved their bags into the space on the right side of the vent, swiftly stepped into the area on the left side, and swung the door shut behind them as fast as possible, both of them hoping to god they had gone unnoticed.

Inside, the closet was as stifling as a desert. Like preteens playing Seven Minutes in Heaven at a classmate's basement birthday party, they were suddenly crammed face to face in complete darkness, sandwiched between a concrete wall on one side and the galvanized steel air duct on the other. Their breath mingled feverishly in the minuscule space between their longing mouths.

"It's dark as fuck in here," he whispered huskily as he wrapped his arms around her and squeezed her firm ass.

With a hushed giggle—and an anguished throbbing between her legs—she placed her hands on his chest and pushed back ever so slightly. "Well, we need to be quick and quiet, but luckily, the one thing we *don't* need, is to see."

Susan took hold of his shorts and pulled them down swiftly. With nimble fingers, she found his balls first. She kissed his neck while cupping and fondling the perfect package under his now throbbing dick. Fingertips graced his taint. And then again. Daniel moaned a little as he bit her shoulder and used the palm of his hand to press into her womanhood, feeling her desire through her pants. She began to feel dizzy, and her heart felt like a jackhammer in her chest. For what felt to her like an excruciatingly long second, he seemed to disappear into the darkness, until she found him with her imploring lips.

He became bigger and harder inside her mouth with every lick of her wet, warm tongue. It was the place where the ocean and earth met and caressed.

His quickened, heavy breathing turned her on beyond belief. He placed his hands gently on the top of her head and whispered huskily, "I'm gonna come."

She quickly stood up and kissed his mouth hungrily, happy to taste the tiny drop that had formed on his tip as it melted between their tongues. Susan yanked her leggings down and told him to fuck her like a dog. Like a well-choreographed dance move, he flipped her around and pushed into her. He wasn't wearing protection, and Susan thought that nothing about this was safe. The air around them felt electrically charged, like right before a thunderstorm. Hovering and waiting with a heavy thrum of danger, and she loved it.

Susan pressed into the vent to help her push back into him. The metal felt smooth and much cooler than the air under her palm, and she wanted to take as much of him in as she could. Daniel held her breasts and lightly pinched her nipples through her shirt as he plunged into her from behind. Susan bucked and heaved, and tried to stifle her own sounds of pleasure, but she couldn't keep the large duct from moaning under the weight of their bodies. As they pressed in and out, the vent whined, whooshed, and popped in a sensual rhythm. Susan hoped their metallic melody wouldn't draw the attention of the people passing by on the other side of the door.

Their bodies clicked together, then repelled like magnets. They were both sweating in the sauna-like heat, but neither one cared. Dust was their confetti. They both sucked dry air in greedily and blew it out with an unyielding force, mouths open, teeth bared like animals. Even in the dusty surroundings and rising temps of the cramped space, everything that mattered stayed wet, and her body shook with the intense pleasure created by their slippery skin. Time wasn't on their side, making them more eager.

"I want to feel you blow up inside of me while I come on your dick," Susan said, deep and throaty.

That was all he needed to hear. Daniel lifted, heaved, and pushed deeply until they both came in long, trembling convulsions. After the explosion, he leaned into her briefly and breathlessly whispered, "Who *are* you?" and they both laughed. In as much haste as was physically possible in such tight quarters, they pulled up their pants, grabbed their bags, and practically rolled out the door like a couple of bowling balls in an overstuffed junk closet before slamming it shut behind them.

Susan felt amazing, but also very strange. Her legs were a bit wobbly, and she felt like the Earth had literally moved or shifted on its axis. Something didn't feel quite right, but she chalked it up to sucking in all that dust combined with the adrenaline dump associated with having mind-blowing sex in a freaking airport utility closet. She squatted to pick up her bag from the floor and glanced around to ensure no one had caught them. There were probably more security cameras in the average airport than anywhere but the Pentagon and the White House. People were going about their business as usual, and no one was even looking in their direction. The coast seemed to be clear, so she took a couple of steps away from the door to create some space from the scene of the crime while she waited for Daniel to pick up his bag as well.

He swung it onto his shoulder and just before they went their separate ways, she looked at him and jokingly said, “Friend me on Facebook?” She thought for sure he would laugh since neither of them bothered to share any personal details other than their first names and the cities in which they lived.

Instead of amusement, the look on his face registered shock and confusion. She could swear she recognized something in his eyes that resembled horror as well. *What the hell? Is he scared of me?* For a couple of seconds, Daniel stood completely frozen like he had just looked Medusa in the eyes, and then, without a word, turned on his heels and practically took off running in the opposite direction.

Susan hadn’t moved a muscle, standing there dumbfounded, and feeling like she needed to nap for about a year, when she saw the airport version of Paul Blart flying toward her on his Segway.

Oh shit! Someone did hear us and called security. Now I’m really gonna be fucked in every way possible.

She let her backpack drop from her shoulder in a self-defeating manner and tried to steel herself for what she imagined was about to happen. She was positive a world of hurt that entailed a good deal of embarrassment, a fine, and possibly jail time was coming her way. *What will they do to me? I mean, have I even done anything illegal? I'm a consenting adult, and it's not a crime to fuck. It wasn't like we did it in public for all to see. Will they put me in an underground holding cell? Is there such a thing here? Is there a horrendous cavity search in my very near future?*

She amazed herself with the staggering number of questions firing through her brain before the security officer even reached her. But as he neared, he simply slowed down a little bit, looked her over briefly, flashed a look in the general direction of the utility closet, and then took off again.

How the hell did he not know I was the one in the closet? I'm sweaty, disheveled, and probably look guilty as hell to boot. He didn't even ask me if I saw anything suspicious or call for backup. Something is seriously wrong. She rushed to the restroom and looked in the mirror.

At first glance, Susan simply couldn't accept the fact that she was looking at herself. She grimaced under the harsh fluorescent lights as she stood before the glass and waited for the smeared colors and faint details to finally bring her real features into focus.

No, no, NO! That's not me. She grabbed ahold of the sloppy sink with both hands and leaned in toward the reflection. The woman looking back at her reminded her of the witch in the story "Snow White." Or maybe a cadaver. She tried to stifle a scream, but it escaped her wrinkled lips as a long, high-pitched whimper. Overcome by a horrible sensation, she felt as though hung upside down for so long that all of her blood had left her extremities and pooled in her head.

Dizzy and weak, she hoped that using the sink to prop herself up would be enough to keep her wobbly legs from collapsing.

People came and went, as they tend to do in busy airports. They moved about her like she wasn't there, slamming bathroom stall doors, flushing toilets, washing hands, using the air dryer, and checking their reflections while she stared at herself in both terror and sadness. The other shoe had finally dropped, which, to be honest, was a possibility she kept close in the back of her mind. She now looked more than ten years older—and much rougher—than she did when she first started taking the experimental elixir.

Her spirited plan to call Heather and tell her all about the earth-shattering sex she just had in an international airport shattered into a million little pieces and fell to the wayside.

Still rooted among errant paper towels, dirt, and the smell of sweaty, gassy travelers, she steadied herself, took out her phone, and pressed Heather's speed dial number.

Voicemail. Shit.

Overwhelmed, unable to look at herself any longer, she forced herself to leave the restroom. Susan walked slowly down long corridors in search of a somewhat private place to sit, even though finding privacy in an airport was like trying to obtain a condom in a convent. She took her time and finally came upon a section, which wasn't exactly deserted but had only a smattering of people charging their phones, enjoying Pinkberry, and lounging in comfortable-looking seats. Something about the terminal reminded her of the beautiful hotel she woke up in this morning—before her entire world crashed—and it almost distracted her enough to boost her mood. She plopped down into an empty seat with not too many people around while trying to keep her breathing calm, willing the fat, stingy tears that had welled up behind her eyes not to escape. The last thing she needed was for someone to call security or EMS to come help the haggard old woman having a coronary near the Gucci boutique in the beautifully modern surroundings of Terminal 2.

For what seemed like an eternity, she sat and stared idly at shiny reflections bouncing between beautiful lighting, marble floors, and sleek metal fixtures. It didn't matter if she missed her flight. She would sit there all night if she had to, and she wasn't going *anywhere* until she talked to the girls to see if they had changed as well—or at least let them know that she had.

She was about to call Emma when the group text feed began to blow up her phone. Her hands shook as she read the words from her friends. Susan slid her butt down into her chair like she was being swallowed by it, and fully immersed herself in the lengthy emotional text messages that pinged between them like bullets on metal. It was almost too great a challenge to keep up with the stories of how each of them changed, where they were when it happened, what they felt, and what they were going to do next as the texts poured in and overlapped with each other.

The extreme changes they had all recently experienced had them in varying stages of panic and freak-out mode, and while the places, times, and situations differed, of course, one of the major things they all had in common was that not one of them saw this coming. They were all in shock—and found it truly outrageous that so much time had passed with absolutely no side effects, leading them all to believe they were truly in the clear from ever having any. Even WW agreed they had very likely passed the point for any repercussions or illnesses to rear their ugly heads. Of course, there was always the possibility that in the long run, an illness or condition could arise from long-term use of TITS.

And to add insult to injury, they agreed that this shit wasn't just some run-of-the-mill negative side effects like the absurd list rattled off at warp speed at the end of a prescription drug commercial. ("Side-effects may cause drowsiness, itchy skin, suicidal thoughts, and anal leakage. Etc.") This freaking thing had shifted into reverse and had somehow kicked the aging process into overdrive. Not only did they no longer feel or look thirty years old, nor had they returned to their original fifty-four-year-old selves, they all seemed to be aging at triple the speed. It was insane, but they had simultaneously begun to shrivel up. They suddenly looked and felt like they were in their seventies or eighties, and it scared the crap out of all of them.

In between reading and responding to the barrage of messages coming and going from her phone, Susan let them all know she would be back in Miami ASAP, but that she missed her flight and was literally sitting in the airport in a complete daze. She told them they wouldn't believe what she was doing when her change occurred but was looking forward to telling them. She read that Heather had changed in the grocery store. Zipper explained it as a sudden pain or surge of some sort that shot through her solar plexus and caused her to drop a carton of eggs on the floor. She said that when she got down on her knees to pick up what she could of the runny mess, another customer rushed to her aide and called ma'am in a voice reserved for grannies. She said no one had called her ma'am in the longest time, and she certainly hadn't had *anyone* try to help her stand up from a kneeling position…ever…if we all caught her drift. All it took was a glimpse of herself reflected in the glass door of the dairy case and she knew that shit had just hit the fan.

Emma said she was struck with pressure in her stomach while at an appointment with WW, and had excused herself to use the restroom, believing she was about to be sick or had to poop. Unfortunately, she had grasped the reality that the experiment she'd proposed to her friends had suddenly changed. A monster dump would have been easier to process and breathe in than the knowledge that her experiment was the cause of these monstrously horrid changes in her best friends.

Yolanda had changed that afternoon while napping in bed with Ra, which she said had most likely made her experience a *little* less traumatic. Of course, she was freaking out and worried about her future on so many different levels, but Ra was there to soothe her. She held Yolanda close and reminded her of the real inner and outer beauty she had always felt she possessed and the love that Ra would have for her—no matter what. She also said she was grateful for the fact—and that all of them should be too—that Rachel was never one to say, "I told you so."

RaRa did her best to console them all and tried to remain the calming voice of reason. She wanted them all to know it would be fine, and no one was to blame for any of this. She tried to help with silver lining, positive words of support—like the fact that they had made it through traumatic times before and this would be just another setback they would experience together, but one that would probably reroute them to something even better in the future. There were no accidents and no rules when it came to their beautiful, badass tribe of women warriors.

Texts with a wide range of emotions, opinions, and concerns continued to flood the feed. Susan sat and read, as the world went on in the background like white noise—without her. The bustle and interesting people-watching of a big cosmopolitan airport melted away like Pinkberry left outside on a summer day in Greenville. Although she was still sitting there, shaken to the core, she was surprised by how comforting it was to have this communication with her girls. *Maybe I won't have to strangle RaRa after all*, she thought with a slightly sarcastic, but loving smirk.

Sitting up a little straighter, she took a deep, cleansing breath in Rachel's honor, and continued to take part in the text arsenal.

Emma: *—I'm so very sorry girls. I'm totally freaking out, but I want you to know we can fix this. I'm positive we can. WW and I have already contacted my oncologist to try and explain what's going on—as if that's possible. And he wants to see everyone in person to be checked, have blood taken, etc. He also wanted me to tell you to STOP taking the pills IMMEDIATELY. I mean, duh. As we have all determined already, the elixir has thrown our aging into overdrive, but if Y'ALL STOP ingesting them now, he hopes and believes YOU*

WILL ALL go back to normal. Or almost normal. Shoot. He thinks at the very worst, you will at least stay where you are right now chronologically.

WW will continue to check and monitor me here in Greenville—and he is a major part of the research team who is currently working on TITS, but he's going to fly out to see y'all in Miami ASAP. I have been texting with him about all of this as well, and he told me to let you know he will follow up with y'all right away to talk it through and plan his visit. So don't panic. We'll have better info soon.—

Yolanda: *—Wait. Hold up, Hon. What do you mean 'y'all might go back to normal'? Don't you mean 'WE' should ALL go back to normal?—*

Susan: *—I'm so afraid we'll never know what normal even means for us anymore. Like Ma had just alluded to, will normal be like before we started this thing? Will we revert back to our* middle-age *status, or will we have to accept the current state we're in as our new normal from here on out —*

Heather: *—Yeah, what YoRa said. I love that combo of their names. Sorry. Not the time. Susan has truly rubbed off on me in all the wrong ways. LOL. Also, Susan said buck. Shit, also not funny. Sorry. But for real, what's all this "Y'all" shit about, Ma? It's still a team effort for the most part, right?—*

Susan: *—Zipper, you're lucky I love you and I know that you—much like me—need to use humor in bad situations but fuck off. LOL. And I like that you said it's a team effort "for the most part" because I am here for y'all in every single way—but I want to officially announce that I'm no longer going to participate in any of the studies or clinical trials. No* *worries about my not taking the pills anymore. I'm done. Please don't be upset. I just can't do it anymore.—*

Heather: *—This blows, but I knew I could get you to laugh. I'm just trying to deal with it the best way I know how. But seriously, while we wait for Ma to respond about saying you vs us.... I agree with Susan and will also no longer be a principal participant in the trials. No hard feelings but I'm out as well.—*

Susan: *—Zip. This situation isn't the only thing that blows. I have a story for y'all...but clearly, it will have to be saved for another time. Emma. You're killing me, and clearly not telling us something. Spill it.—*

Emma: *—Girls, I completely understand if you pull out of the study. I have absolutely no hard feelings if that's the case for all of you. But here's the thing. I'm going to stay in it.*

This is the time for me to keep taking the supplement so WW and the research team can continue to work on it. They need to do tests, and extensive clinical trials WITH ME in order to keep all the positive results from the pills but completely rid them of their negative side effects.

Please think about it. This could be an actual cure for cancer if I stay in it, and it would do SO much good.—

Susan: *—Did WW talk you into this? Is he going to get more money by using you as his lab rat? I KNEW he was a SNAKE. I even had a premonition about it today in my hotel room.—*

Emma: *—No, no, no. WW actually didn't push me one way or the other. He simply presented the facts.*

Girls, please understand. At this stage in my life—

especially because the tumor has come and gone during the experiment—I need something to be my own, ya know? I need a legacy, an accomplishment that can only be achieved by me. After living in the shadows of Bobby and his family for so long. After what has felt like a lifetime of almosts, I want to see this through to the very end. NO ONE has pushed me in any direction.

I want to do it.—

Yolanda: *—No, Emma. I don't accept that. This isn't your responsibility. You deserve to live and not get blasted into old age just to help WW or science or ANYONE. I'm pulling out of the study as well. And although I seldom speak for others—that's Heather's department haha—I believe Ma should pull out too.—*

Susan: *—I agree with YoYo. I'm not happy with all the shit that's happening right now, and I'm scared out of my wits, but we all chose to do this knowing there would be risks. Now that we know what those risks are, you don't need to continue to put yourself in danger, Ma. None of us do. If WW made a killing on the sale of TITS, that's great for him, but we don't have an obligation to help him further his gains.—*

Emma: *—I love you all so much for being worried, and for always having my back, but I have made up my mind. Y'all need to stop the pills and continue with your amazingly beautiful lives.*

Oh, and y'all better take proper credit for your accomplishments, too. Sure, the sudden youthful appearance and energy may have been an initial catalyst for all the attention and success, but it certainly wasn't what kept it there. Believe that. RaRa is living proof of that since she wasn't even on the elixir.

I mean, it wasn't a placebo, obviously. But we

didn't need the pills to have achieved all that we did since the time we started taking them. The youth and vitality were fun and kicked our confidence and drive into high gear, but intelligence, courage, beauty, strength, and mad skills were things each of us already possessed. TITS didn't create any of those things; it just made us all recognize the fact that they were there and gave us the kick in the ass we needed to believe.

I think we can all agree that youth is beautiful and nice, but it's our wisdom, experience, talent, and female friendships that reign supreme. We traveled this road together and reached a beautiful destination. But I need to continue on solo.

I already spoke to Caroline about it, and she is at peace. I hope y'all—my best friends and my sisters—can be as well.—

Heather: *—Ma, you know we will always have your back no matter what, but this is seriously something we should all talk about in person, don't ya think?*

We love you and need to see you.

Come to Miami for a visit, and some sunshine and girl time. Please have Caroline join us as well if she can.—

Emma: *—I would love to come see y'all, and I'm taking you up on that.*

I can be there next week. But please know that I'm not changing my mind about this.—

Yolanda: *—Yes. You and Caroline. Both. Here. Next week. Done deal. But if this continues to age you at such an accelerated rate, who knows how long you will have. I'm not even joking, Ma. Even without the cancer. That isn't something I'm ready to deal with. None of us are.—*

RaRa: *—I agree with everyone on this, Ma, because I can't imagine life without you. My heart hurts so much just thinking about it. But if this is what you truly want, and you really believe that it's for the best, and what needs to be done for the greater good, I guess it's just like letting frogs go.—*

Emma: *—Ra, I can't believe you remembered that story. Thank you all. See y'all soon. And yeah, I'm letting frogs go.—*

Chapter 11

15 Months Later

It's a dark, rainy morning in Miami, and Yolanda and Rachel are up much earlier than either of them expected to be. They got home from the club at an ungodly hour as it was, and decompressing before they went to bed almost always posed a challenge for them. The alluring scent of RaRa's body wash filled the bathroom and spilled out into the rest of their apartment. Yolanda had stared up at the high ceiling and had every intention of staying in bed, until notes of bergamot, white sandalwood, citrus, rose, and dark almond created the familiar zesty and earthy scent she directly associated with her beautiful wife. The exotic scent stirred up a mental picture of RaRa with her face turned up toward the shower head as sudsy soap trails slid down her strong back until they disappeared into the voluptuous curve of her ass. No matter how tired or frazzled she felt, *that* particular combination was more than enough to pull her out of bed and pad down the short hallway to the bathroom. It had just begun to heat up, and she smiled at the tiny clouds of steam that had accumulated above the shower. She pulled her toothbrush from its stand on the white marble counter, squeezed a blob of toothpaste onto it, and leaned against the sink while she brushed her teeth.

"I hear you out there, sexy," Rachel chirped happily through the shower curtain. "I'm so sorry if I woke you, and that I tossed and turned all night. You should go back to bed, babe. Get some much-needed rest."

"It's okay, angel. I know both our minds are churning like crazy." Yolanda rinsed her mouth and then wiped the little white trail of toothpaste from her chin with a deep magenta Egyptian cotton hand towel. "I haven't been able to sleep either. Besides, I'd rather spend this time with you than in bed fighting with the Sand Man—and losing. Shit, with everything we've got going on right now, and that we've been through, it's a wonder we *ever* sleep. I think part of me worries that I'll wake up one day as a ninety-year-old woman."

"Ha." Rachel snorted sympathetically. "Well, that's not gonna happen. And even if it did, it wouldn't matter to me," Rachel said earnestly.

"I know," Yolanda answered. "But it would matter to me. What if, after quitting the pills, I had stayed in my seventies or eighties? Or if I had kept taking them—like Ma did—and they made me age at triple the speed of a normal human, as well? You and I would have had *a lot less* time to live out our lives together. Believe me, I'm truly grateful that me and the girls went back to our original selves after quitting the pills, and that luckily, we're no worse for wear. But it scares the hell out of me to think my life with you could have been—or still could be cut surprisingly short.

Yolanda peed, carefully closed the lid of the toilet, and had a seat. "Don't worry, I won't flush. I don't want you screaming in the shower unless it's because I'm in there with you." With both elbows resting on her knees, she let out a sigh and silently acknowledged the fact that she and Ra had some of their best and deepest conversations at their kitchen table, or through the deep turquoise shower curtain. "I truly don't know how I would have managed any of this without you. Especially losing Ma."

"Well, I would be a complete mess without you too," Rachel answered. "And you can't 'what if' any of this, babe, although I understand why you would. Even though I teach meditation, yoga, and breathing techniques, none of it has been enough to help me quiet my mind or to keep me from missing Ma. Having you, the girls, the club, and of course, opening the health and wellness center in Greenville to honor Ma is what keeps me sane."

Yolanda stood up, stretched, and then lifted her nightshirt, pulling it over her head, and shimmied out of her panties.

"The Center," YoYo said as a wistful and proud smile crept across her face. "I still have to pinch myself at times that it came to fruition. I mean, we all agreed on the idea, but the fact that WW bought the land outside of Greenville, hired the architects, and paid for every single bit of it, including construction, interior design, salaries, and additional startup capital.... Damn. It still feels like a complete dream to me."

"Well, he can certainly afford it. And Ma wasn't just a participant in his clinical trials, she was special to him too. Anyway, The Center is the reason I couldn't sleep last night. Here we have created this incredible space in Ma's honor; Zipper and Caroline have both moved back to freaking Greenville to run it; Caroline is going to keep—and live in Ma's house; the ribbon-cutting ceremony is only a few short months away, and we still haven't chosen a name worthy of it all. We can't just call it a 'Center for Women's Health, Wellness, and Creative Aging Med Spa.' There has to be a very special, very intentional overarching name."

Yolanda pulled the curtain open just enough to squeeze in without letting out too much heat. "I agree. And don't forget about the added stress that the signage still needs to be installed on the building, and the contractors set a deadline for next month to get it done in time. Jesus, coming up with the perfect name for The Center–that's worthy of the woman for whom it was constructed is a virtually impossible task." Then with her hands on Ra's wet hips, turning her around, she said, "Move over, I'm coming in to wash your back." And she stepped into the steam-filled space.

Rachel sighed and leaned her back into Yo's chest, relaxing and letting go of all that had been troubling her. Then, responding to Yo's hands on her hips, she turned into her partner, their wet legs sliding against each other. The second their eyes met they both lit up, as if their short time apart—separated by a mere curtain—made them miss each other terribly. Rachel leaned back to rinse the conditioner from her hair and said, "Well, that's *exactly* what I'm *dying* to tell you. While I tossed and turned last night, the perfect name came to me like an epiphany. I can't believe I didn't think of it sooner. It was like a message I received, special delivery, directly from Ma herself. I'm positive that once we share it with everyone, and tell them what it means, it'll be a done deal and we'll even have time left over for the sign guys," Rachel said with her eyes squeezed tightly shut to keep the conditioning treatment out.

After squeezing the excess water through her silky hair, she said, “It’s kind of a long story, but to really explain where the name came from, and why it’s so fucking perfect, I need to tell you about the time I went to Vermont with some of my yoga students.”

Then, changing subjects, Rachel took a step toward Yolanda so their nipples touched, and watched the water pool in the space where their breasts met—as they had done so many times before. “You know we never talk for very long when you’re in here with me,” she said, her voice husky and sultry.

Yolanda reached up and caressed Rachel’s rosy cheek with the back of her fingers. While holding her beautiful face, she smiled tenderly and said, “This is true.” Then with a playful giggle, she shimmied her shoulders slightly, so their breasts rubbed together. “Getting freaky in Vermont. I don’t think you’ve ever told me that one.”

“Very funny. I’m serious.” Rachel playfully reached around and slapped Yo on the ass in mock scolding.

Yolanda leaned in and lightly outlined Rachel’s full lips with the tip of her tongue and then nibbled her bottom lip followed by a tender kiss.

“Turn around and I’ll wash your back while you tell me about the perfect name for the center, and if something just *happens* to rudely interrupt your story, you can continue it over breakfast. I’ll cook.” She laughed and purred. “How does that sound?”

Rachel was already grinning and breathless with anticipation. “It seems like I suddenly don’t feel like talking anymore.” She kissed Yolanda’s neck and then licked it, and nibbling her earlobes as her hands slid down to Yo's waist and hips and then back up again until her fingertips lightly flicked and tugged Yolanda's now rock-hard nipples. Their mouths sought each other and met with lustful hunger, and they devoured each other's sweet, soft tongues and lips. Droplets of water dripped from the tendrils of Rachel's hair and Yolanda's breasts as they pushed into each other with a paradoxical fierce urgency and strained restraint; their breaths heavy and fast.

Yolanda gasped as Rachel rolled a nipple between her finger and thumb just before she broke their kiss to take it into her warm, wet mouth. She wrapped her eager lips around YoYo's buds, slowly sucking and licking and tugging the way Rachel knew could easily make her come. She stopped her ministrations to kiss Yo lightly on the nose. While this made YoYo pant with desire, Rachel teasingly asked if she should stop so Yo could rest from being up all night.

"You can keep my nipples up all night, you sexy mother fucker," YoYo said throatily in between a crescendo of approving moans. "You know, the way you play with my nips gets me off so hard. But I don't want to come yet, baby." She stepped back a little and deftly switched places with Rachel. Yolanda stood under the running water, turned Rachel around, and faced her against the large, white subway tiles of their shower. "I like to keep my promises," she said as she soaped up Rachel's back, and then brushed her tits up against her back before pushing into her so they could both enjoy the slippery sensation of their bodies moving together.

Yolanda used both hands to reach around from

behind and take hold of Rachel's pert, cone-shaped breasts, while RaRa arched her back and eagerly pressed her little round yoga ass against YoYo's bush. Yolanda let her soapy fingers rinse themselves off as they traveled slowly over the soft, smooth skin of Rachel's belly until they traveled over that trembling mound down to where Rachel's wet thighs met. She pressed into her swollen mons with her whole hand and then backed off and eased three fingers between slippery labia to create little circles around the clit—with the perfect amount of pressure and speed. Rachel moaned and bucked as she hit the steamy tiled wall with a closed fist, pushing her ass into Yolanda, looking for more.

"Fuck, I'm on the edge, baby," she managed to choke out in between gasps.

Yolanda increased the already fevered pace of the circular beat she was drumming on RaRa's clit while grinding her pussy against Ra's firm ass. She leaned in to kiss her neck and massage it with her tongue, nibbling and teasing her a bit before the fingers on her other hand plunged inside from behind. Yolanda pushed in and out of Rachel with slow, deep strokes while her other hand remained hummingbird fast as it flitted and flicked her clit.

"Yes, yes," Rachel begged. "Don't stop. I'm gonna come." She screamed as she gushed and shook, overcome with intense waves of pleasure.

She took a moment to catch her breath before turning around, her eyes filled with an intense fire like the tip of a burning cigarette.

"Now it's your turn."

Rachel licked the velvety skin of Yolanda's

clavicle and lightly traced her fingernails around her beautiful, large, brown areolas while using her knees to part Yolanda's legs as far as they would go. She kneeled, reached around, and took Yolanda's ass cheeks into her hands after giving them a few spanks. She parted them and knocked lightly on her back door with playful fingertips but pulled her forward forcefully so she could enter her from the front with her tongue. Rachel held onto Yo's ass and drew little circles around her sexy, puckering hole with her middle finger while she sucked and licked her pussy until her clit looked like it would explode.

In a fit of ecstasy, Yolanda tilted her head back and pinched her own nipples. Rachel continued to lap and kiss her while her fingers found their way into both holes. Her steady, rhythmic strokes became forceful and unforgiving as Yolanda begged, "Harder. Harder."

Rachel's fingers danced deep inside Yolanda's throbbing pussy and her tight ass. She knew Yolanda was about to go over the edge, and it turned her on so much it felt like an out-of-body experience. She was suddenly speaking in tongues all over her wife's lips. Rachel slowly pulled her fingers away from Yo's ass and let them find their way to the sopping-wet area between her own legs. With her face still buried in Yo's pussy, RaRa continued to drill into her with one hand while she used the other to rub herself with furious friction. No longer able to take it, YoYo grabbed Rachel's head and pressed into her face as she exclaimed, "Oh God. Fuck. Here it comes. Raaa-ahhh." Rachel answered Yolanda's primal call with her own muffled orgasmic scream. When she finally "came to," she was still kneeling between Yolanda's legs.

Completely spent and satisfied, her head rested on Yolanda's thigh while her arms snaked around her long legs, embracing them. Rachel stood up and kissed Yolanda gently. They tightly intertwined their bodies until they felt like one. Neither of them wanted to let go first. It felt too good. While planting sweet kisses on Yolanda's shoulder, Rachel said, "I love you."

Yolanda gently cupped and then squeezed Rachel's pink cherub ass and said, "I love you, too."

When they finished the actual washing, they stepped out of the shower, smiling from ear to ear as they stood in the steam-filled bathroom, water dripping on the floor. YoYo lovingly wrapped a beach towel around Rachel's body, gave her an extra hug, and then handed her one for her hair.

"Now that we've earned our breakfast, I'm ready to talk," Rachel said, wrapping her wavy long hair with the turquoise bath towel.

YoYo responded with a pat on Rachel's ass and a giggle. "See you in the kitchen."

RaRa stepped into the kitchen wearing baggy cotton shorts and a loose tank with no bra. The smell of coffee and toast filled the airy space and made her feel warm inside. Her Rapunzel-like hair was still damp, and although it was piled sky-high on top of her head, it wasn't nearly as high as she still felt from the afterglow of the shower. Yolanda was moving gracefully between the stove and the tiny butcher block island as she prepared tea for RaRa and French-pressed coffee for herself. RaRa leaned into her from behind and wrapped her arms around her. They squeezed each other while letting out contented sighs.

RaRa let go of Yolanda and went to the corner

hutch for the cutting board. She grabbed a clean, sharp knife from the dishwasher, and jokingly asked, “Now, *where* was I?”

Yolanda laughed heartily while she removed eggs, cheese, tomatoes, salsa, and cilantro from the Sub-Zero fridge and arranged them on the counter next to the stove. “I have *no* idea. I think you erased my mind while you were twisting my nips like Etch A Sketch dials.”

RaRa let out a loud squawk as she picked a large pomegranate from the fruit bowl. She carried everything over to the pedestal-based kitchen table and placed it gently onto the round gray and white marble top. A steaming cup of tea was waiting for her. She looked up at Yolanda and smiled at her with her eyes as she took a seat on the MCM dining chairs they had recently reupholstered together in a magenta-hued leather.

Although their kitchen was small, it was the heart of their home, and they moved around it with the ease and efficiency of an old couple doing a waltz. They knew the steps by heart, like second nature, and only bumped into each other when they intended to touch, hug, or grab each other’s butts. They had chosen it for its high ceilings and large windows, and for how much natural light poured in—even on rainy days. Vibrant jolts of jewel tones from art they had found on their honeymoon and the emerald-green backsplash stood out in an otherwise whitewashed room.

RaRa sliced the pomegranate down the middle and let it fall onto the cutting board in two juicy halves. She drew one leg up onto the chair and picked at the tart red fruit in between sips of tea. “No worries, babe. I believe

I can refresh your memory," she said flirtatiously while using the back of her hand to wipe pink juice from her lips.

"Cut that out, or we're gonna be back to where we started." Yolanda chuckled."

Rachel shook her head. "Oh no, we aren't. My Vermont story is way too important to stay untold for one more minute. I promise, once you hear it, you'll want to tell the others immediately, and we'll all be thrilled to have just the right name for the center. Plus, I'm starving. So, keep slicing, dicing, and cooking…and listen up," she said with a wink.

RaRa took a quick sip of tea, set the cup down, and excitedly dove into the story. It was the Fourth of July weekend about five years ago when she and three of her yoga students decided to attend a yoga and Reiki retreat in Vermont for something fun, different, and inspirational. They flew from Scottsdale to Boston Logan International and then hopped into their rental car for the roughly three-hour drive to Vermont. Rachel firmly believed that Ma brought this memory back to her last night as she fitfully tried to fall asleep. There was simply no other explanation, as she hadn't thought about it in years, and suddenly it had flooded her mind with uncanny detail and clarity.

She told Yolanda how it felt like yesterday when they pulled into the parking lot of a restaurant full of locals "my usual please" to grab a bite to eat when they reached Vermont. The diner looked like it was decorated for a movie set with red Formica tabletops trimmed in chrome and red-cushioned bar stools and pie displays on the counter. But unlike a movie set, this diner boasted decades of smokey, greasy smells produced by the kitchen and cheesy, mountain-themed décor. Everything bears and pine trees adorned the walls and shelves of the little restaurant. Next to the front entrance sat a huge statue of a bear carved out of wood and painted black. Above his head hung a giant wooden spoon and fork.

While they ate their iceberg lettuce salads, greasy burgers, and fries, Rachel received an unexpected notification from their hotel that their reservation for that night only had been canceled. When Rachel called to find out what the problem was, they offered profuse apologies for their mistake, and for the inconvenience, but they had confused her arrival date and had overbooked because of the holiday. The hotel's offer to stay the following night for free might have been a consolation if they had some idea where—besides the car—they could sleep for the current night.

She remembered trying to lighten the mood with some quick pep talks about living in the moment; being a yogi who goes with the flow; and that everything happens for a reason. None of them was happy about their situation as they walked out of the restaurant and piled back into the rental car, but they tried to make the best of it. A brief discussion ensued, and they all agreed to drive up the mountain to take in the sights and kill some time while they figured out what they were going to do. As they made the steep ascent into cloud-covered treetops, a mama moose with two babies in tow popped out of the woods and crossed the road right in front of them. Their speed at that point was basically a crawl, so it was easy to stop in time and watch them walk by. The surprise sighting elicited a jolt of palpable positive energy and awe that permeated the car. It happened so quickly that no one got their phones out in time to take a photo before the mama and her babies disappeared among green and brown brush, trees, and gray rocks on the other side. Forced to witness something so raw and beautiful with her eyes instead of through the lens of a camera made RaRa's stomach tickle from the thrill, the joy, and maybe a little altitude gains mixed in.

With no idea of where they would pull over, and no plans to do so, she continued to drive, gripping the steering wheel so tight that little white dots appeared on each of her knuckles. Completely out of nowhere, she felt overcome by an unexpected urge, a magnetic force, and a deep-seated need to pull into a tiny overlook with only two parking spots that had suddenly appeared on the other side of a particularly sharp, winding turn. RaRa almost drove right past it, but at the last minute, almost as if someone had grabbed the wheel and cranked it sharply to the left for her, she pulled into the only available parking spot.

Rachel turned off the ignition and opened the car door while her passengers sat for a moment in a slight state of shock and confusion, still bracing themselves from the abrupt turn. She stepped out of the car, the sound of gravel crunching beneath her feet. It was a sound she had always found deeply satisfying, and it made her happy. She looked down at the gray and black stones as she stepped back to shut the car door, making sure she didn't bump the red convertible with its top down in the space next to them. When she looked up, she was face to face with a woman who flashed a smile at Rachel that was warmer than the late afternoon sun.

The woman immediately greeted Rachel with a friendly hello and introduced herself as Pam. She jerked her head over her shoulder a few times, indicating the man standing next to the driver's side of the convertible, and happily conveyed that his name was Arthur, her husband of thirty-five years, and that today was their wedding anniversary. As outgoing and gregarious as Pam was, Arthur appeared to be equally quiet and demur. He seemed content to enjoy the view devoid of interaction with strangers, but you could just tell that after all those years with Pam, getting roped into idle chit-chat and unexpected conversations was something he was used to. He dug his hands in his pockets, gave RaRa a friendly nod, and turned his attention back to the stunning view from above the trees.

Rachel returned Pam's kind smile, wished her a happy anniversary, and had just introduced herself as the rest of the group came up behind her. They stretched, oohed and ahhed over the breathtaking scenery, and introduced themselves as well. Pam asked where they were all staying, eliciting a short bout of ironic chuckles to ripple through them. That was the question of the hour.

Worried that Pam might think they were laughing at her, RaRa explained the reason for their chuckles.

Pam's eyes widened, and her big smile somehow became even bigger as she proudly delivered the news that she and Arthur owned a B&B they had built on the land next to their home. She told the group that it had breathtaking views of the mountains, a swimming pool, a Zen Garden, and they were more than welcome to stay the night there, promising them a good rate. Excited and relieved by this incredible revelation, they asked Pam exactly what "a good rate" meant to her. She said she would charge them *exactly* half of whatever their nightly rate would have been at the inn. It was a done deal.

The second they were back in the rental car, and all the doors were closed, they all burst out laughing, happy and amazed at the way things had turned out. What were the odds that a couple with a vacant Bed and Breakfast seemed to be sitting there just waiting for them to show up in need of a place to stay?

When they arrived at Pam and Arthur's, and received the grand tour, they were blown away by how far it exceeded their expectations as well as how kind and accommodating the couple proved to be. The space they stayed in was basically a huge condo that could have easily slept six people and it was nothing short of magnificent. Floor-to-ceiling windows in the living room provided an astounding view of lavish lawns, trees, the Zen Garden with an impressively large statue of Buddha, an in-ground pool surrounded by a refined slate gray deck, and the mountains as a backdrop in varying shades of green as far as the eye could see. It was so beautiful it evoked feelings of spirituality that almost brought tears to Rachel's eyes. But as lovely and moving as all the scenery was, it was nothing compared to what she felt to be the best part about the entire place; the name Pam had chosen for it.

Anam Cara.

Rachel noticed the words carved into a wooden sign posted on the outside of the main building for every guest to see as they entered it. Rachel had always felt charmed by and strongly curious about the names people gave to their beach homes, cottages, ranches, or other properties, as well as the carved wooden signs that displayed these names proudly for all to see. They were a veritable statement to the world that the space was so unique, intriguing, and wonderful, it required its own special moniker—just like the nicknames for Rachel and her best friends. She immediately asked Pam what it meant and learned Anam Cara was Celtic for "Soul Friend." Pam went on to say that the Celts believed a soul friendship was sacred and precious because it was a friendship that made you feel like you were home.

Rachel felt haunted by the idea of Anam Cara the whole time they were in Vermont. When she returned to Arizona after the retreat, she looked it up online and learned a little more about it and what it meant. Every word she read about Anam Cara felt like a direct description of their sisterhood. An Anam Cara is the closest thing to having family members who know the real you and love you unconditionally. You can share your unadulterated truths with these people because they would never use it against you or pass judgment. They are friends that bring out and enhance the best in each other. A rare and special bond that absolutely nothing can break. Not even death. Friends like this are joined together forever, and there's no worry about letting them go, because you can't contain a soul in a shoebox. It will flow through you and float around you for as long as you live. Like a frog in a pond hopping among the lily pads, a soul is something wild and free, but it will exist and stay forever in a soul friend's heart.

Right now, she felt in her heart that last night, like a beacon, Ma had cast a light on these memories that were so bright they would no longer have to search because she had shown them the way.

When Rachel finished her story, she and Yolanda were holding hands across the kitchen table, tears in their eyes, and their plates pushed off to the side untouched. She said she had already sent an email to Pam to be sure it was okay to use the beautiful name of Anam Cara for the center. She was pretty sure Pam would love the idea, but felt it was best to ask. There was no other name in the universe that would capture the true essence of the sacred bond and every magical thing that comprised the group's soul friendship.

Anam Cara.

Chapter 12

It was noon on a not-so-typical Thursday. The sky was smeared in brushstrokes of inky black, slate gray, and midnight blue, and felt low enough to kiss the tops of trees. It was a dramatic and emotional pallet that promised rain but wasn't quite threatening enough to deter the large crowd that had gathered on the property about fifteen minutes outside of downtown Greenville.

On almost three and a half acres of land, Anam Cara, A Center for Women's Health, Wellness, & Creative Aging Med Spa sat in all its newly constructed glory waiting to be christened with a ribbon cutting ceremony by Caroline, Yolanda, Rachel, Heather, Susan, and WW.

With absolutely no corners cut by WW and the girls, the center was constructed with thoughtful architecture and a unique design that was clean and contemporary, but not the least bit sterile and cold. Spacious and open, with large windows instead of walls, Anam Cara had an elegance reminiscent of her home that would have brought happy tears to Ma's eyes.

Around the perimeter of the property, landscape designers had successfully installed moonflower, sunflower, and lavender fields, creating a soothing, secluded sanctuary perfect for mind, body, and soul health and rejuvenation, as well as personal reflection.

The girls were happy to add their input to an already robust landscape design with a list of all the things they deemed necessary for the outdoor amenities and charm to be complete. Included among their favorites were cedar-chipped walking trails, a gravel labyrinth, a frog pond, stone benches under drooping willow trees, and a white wooden gazebo big enough to hold yoga classes.

Things only got better on the structure's interior and the space was nothing if not inviting, bright, and airy. And because it was mostly glass walls, it allowed tons of light to pour in. It was no surprise during the planning process that Heather said Ma would have commented that they'd have to get a special window washing service for that much glass.

Organic lines and warm neutral colors dominated the inner space, making it feel quintessentially spa-like, and reception desks with waiting areas reminded you it was a medical space as well. Ma would have liked how the feathery black swirls in the white marble gave a warm feeling in the main entrance, some of the long hallways, and the waiting room.

Clean white linen sofas and MCM leather chairs contributed to the soothing ambiance. Accent pillows and flat weave rugs in muddy tones provided embellishments that complimented the natural surroundings. As an extra special touch, the girls had a system installed so that some of Emma's signature reed diffuser scents were pumped into certain areas of the building, making them simply giddy with their own special brand of ebullience.

Looking up at the sky and fidgeting like they had to pee, the normally calm, cool, confident, and accomplished group stood before the now quite substantial audience, feeling nervous, proud, and grateful to stand together in front of the magnificent thing they had created as they all prayed for the rain to hold off until later in the evening. The sky remained defiant but seemed to have acquiesced slightly in response to their repeated requests.

Heather looked at her friends with a smile that said, "This is it! Go time!" She gave them each a quick squeeze and promptly stepped up to the microphone at precisely noon. The oversized purple ribbon in front of her rippled in a sudden breeze. She enthusiastically thanked everyone for coming, and introduced herself as Heather Jordison, the CEO of Anam Cara, A Center for Women's Health, Wellness, & Creative Aging Med Spa. A round of applause that she hadn't expected spontaneously erupted and gave her a moment to wet her dry lips, smile, and take a deep, cleansing breath to help her maintain her composure. She expressed her immense gratitude to everyone in attendance, including the center's many employees, the Greenville Chamber of Commerce, and the incredible group of people standing with her and beside her on this momentous occasion. She gestured toward WW and thanked him earnestly for his financial backing and unwavering support that made the purchase of the lot, the building's construction, design, and operational expenses possible, as well as his continued contributions in the form of research and education that made their dream to honor their friend a reality.

She then turned slightly toward the girls, and with tears in her eyes, introduced each one individually and earnestly and full of emotion, saying that without each of them, the center would not exist, because they had collectively come up with the idea to erect a center in honor of their dearest friend, Emma, who was no longer physically with them, but would remain with them spiritually for all of eternity. It was Emma's friendship, who she was as a person, and what she brought out in others that made the name Anam Cara seem perfect.

A very special "last but not least" introduction of Caroline was made since she was not only Emma's daughter and a nurse practitioner, but she was also their Chief of Staff and the master ribbon-cutter for the event.

Heather briefly described the center's purpose and its goals, and let everyone know that she hoped they would stay for a tour after the ribbon cutting to witness the cutting-edge facility and all it had to offer. She explained how confident she and her colleagues were that this center would benefit Greenville and emphasized the hope and goal for it to draw people not only from around the area but also from around the country as well as the world. It was an incredible "one-stop shop," so to speak, for women's health in mind, body, and soul. For those who couldn't stay for the tour, she offered a brief description of the services provided in the space on each of the three floors. There was an actual rumbling of surprise, awe, and excitement that rippled through the audience while they learned there was a fitness and wellness center, offices for integrative health, functional medicine, women's reproductive health, a med spa, float Pods, Salt Cave, and a specialized department for medical research, development, and education.

Ever the pro at communication, Heather completed

the introductions, thank-yous, and basic descriptions in a way that was engaging, concise, and efficient. According to the agenda, it was time for the rest of the crew to step up and say a few words about the meaning of Anam Cara, the center, and their friendship with Emma. Everyone but Caroline and WW wanted to speak, but they all stood together as a united front.

Susan went first and opened with a lighthearted joke that they had spent countless hours in search of the perfect name for the center. She emphasized how incredibly challenging it was to find one that could even remotely live up to or properly honor the person who inspired the construction of such an amazing and empowering place for women and their vitality. A few Greek goddess names had come up, and were brought to the table, including the Greek Goddess, Nike—but alas, she quipped, that name was already taken. She paused happily as a wave of light laughter ensued. She continued her explanation with perfect timing, detailing why they chose the Celtic name, Anam Cara, for their business—meaning Soul Friend. "Emma had ignited a blazing fire within each of us and everyone whose lives she touched that is and always will be powerful, beautiful, and bright. Just like the light of her soul. She was a gift. A comet. An Anam Cara."

Susan stepped away from the mic so Yolanda could say what she felt in her heart. YoYo took Rachel's hand and stepped up to the microphone. She was choked up but managed to share her sentiments with a professional yet heartfelt delivery. She said that Emma could light up the darkest of days and heal your heart just by being who she was, and they all loved who they were when they were with her and because of her.

"In her beautifully unique way, she always brought us together, supported us at all times, and helped us navigate the roughest waters ever since we were in high school. She believed in our abilities and saw our true beauty even when we couldn't. Without Emma in our lives, our true potential may have never been uncovered as a result of her guiding light and support. She helped us learn how to trust ourselves and each other implicitly, to love unconditionally and openly, and to live with gratitude, grace, and humility."

Yolanda wiped the tears from her cheeks, let go of Rachel's hand, and stepped back to give her wife some space as she addressed the crowd. Rachel cleared her throat and looked out among the sea of faces, and immediately locked eyes with Pam. She smiled warmly and Pam returned the smile, nodding encouragingly. Rachel paused briefly and then told everyone in attendance that without Emma, none of the people standing before them would have trusted themselves enough to pursue their passions or been able to honestly express who they truly wanted to be. Emma was the ever-present force that made each of them feel comfortable enough to share the most intimate versions of themselves without any concern whatsoever of being judged—which is what an Anam Cara is all about. She said that having someone in your life like that is an amazing gift. Because of that, they would be eternally grateful and connected to her. She was the reason they had uncovered and recognized the unyielding possibilities within themselves, and had always epitomized the concept of an Anam Cara, making the center the perfect way to honor her.

She wiped her cheeks and tucked her hair behind

her ear as she explained that after receiving so many gifts from Emma over the years, it was an honor and a privilege for them to have the opportunity to repay her and celebrate her life with this amazing facility. Anam Cara will serve as her legacy to celebrate who she was, and everything she selflessly sacrificed to better the lives of others—especially her closest soul friends. She turned her body slightly, gestured behind her, and said, "This building will sing a song from our souls. It will help us let go of the heavy burden of loss but keep a tight hold on love." She took a deep breath and continued, "With that, I would like to direct your attention to her daughter Caroline, who will now cut the ribbon."

Susan had a custom-made pair of ribbon-cutting scissors specially made with gold, stainless steel blades and textured round handles shaped to resemble the grand, ornate wings of the goddess Nike. The thing weighed almost five pounds and was set on a small table next to the outrageously huge purple ribbon stretched between two pedestals. Caroline lifted them off the table, gripped the large, winged finger holes with both hands, and opened them up wide. She ceremoniously placed the ribbon between the two blades and held them there long enough for dramatic effect. It was so quiet you could hear a mouse fart. With powerful emphasis, she clamped the blades together, creating a loud noise like a clap that set off the final round of applause.

At the exact moment that the long, solid ribbon became two separate pieces falling away in opposite directions, the clouds magically parted as well. Bright, stunning beams of sunshine shone down like a laser and glinted off the golden wings that Caroline had yet to let go.

Anam Cara was born, memorializing the memory of their friend, Emma.

A word about the author…

Liz Ferro is an author, speaker, and the founder and CEO of Girls With Sole. Her other titles include Finish Line Feeling, Girls With Sole: A Girl Power Guide To Unleashing Your Inner Superhero, and Chameleon Girl. Her memoir, Finish Line Feeling, was awarded as a finalist for The Montaigne Medal from The Eric Hoffer Book Award.

As a child, Ferro experienced foster care and sexual abuse, but found solace in sports and fitness. The empowerment gained from sports led her to find the non-profit organization Girls With Sole, which has received extensive national attention for its innovative and award-winning program curriculum.

She has been featured on ESPN Sports Center, NBC TODAY Show, in SELF, Runner's World, Traditional Home, and Family Circle Magazine.

She is the recipient of the 2022 Toyota Everyday Hero Award from Toyota and ESPN W; 2018 Smartwomen Award for Progressive Organization; 2017 Community Changemaker Award from the Ohio Alliance To End Sexual Violence; 2016 Medical Mutual NEO Pillar Award and many more.

To date, Liz has completed 78 marathons, two 50K Ultras, five Ironman Triathlons, and countless other races of all kinds. She has completed a 26.2 marathon in all 50 States, as well as on the Great Wall of China, a Wildlife Preserve in South Africa, and Antartica. She also completed the iconic Escape From Alcatraz Triathlon in San Francisco, California.

Ferro graduated from Miami University in Oxford Ohio with a BA in Speech Communications. She is the mother of two children and lives in Ohio with her two rescue dogs and two rescue cats.

lizferro.com

Thank you for purchasing
this publication of The Wild Rose Press, Inc.

For questions or more information
contact us at
info@thewildrosepress.com.

The Wild Rose Press, Inc.
www.thewildrosepress.com

www.ingramcontent.com/pod-product-compliance
Lightning Source LLC
Chambersburg PA
CBHW070106030726
47506CB00002B/619

* 9 7 8 1 5 0 9 2 5 5 8 7 0 *